VIRAGO
MODERN CLASSICS
389

*Elaine Dundy*

Elaine Dundy was born and raised in New York. She worked as an actress in Paris and London, where she met her husband, Kenneth Tynan. After the birth of her first child, she turned to writing. Her first novel, *The Dud Avocado* (1958), based on the year she spent in Paris, was an immediate bestseller on both sides of the Atlantic. Two more novels and two plays followed. In 1964, divorced from Tynan, she returned to America where she wrote extensively for magazines before moving to Massachusetts where she directed and acted. She is the author of several biographies, including *Elvis and Gladys* (1985), and an autobiography, *Life Itself!* Elaine Dundy lives in Los Angeles.

By *Elaine Dundy*

*Novels*
The Dud Avocado
The Old Man and Me
The Injured Party

*Plays*
My Place
Death in the Country

*Biographies*
Finch, Bloody Finch
Elvis and Gladys
Ferriday, Louisiana

*Autobiography*
Life Itself!

# THE DUD
# AVOCADO

---

## Elaine Dundy

A *Virago* Book

Published by Virago Press 1993
Reprinted 1997, 2001 (three times), 2003

First published in Great Britain by Victor Gollancz Ltd 1958

Copyright © Elaine Dundy 1958

The moral right of the author has been asserted

A CIP catalogue record for this book is available
from the British Library

ISBN 1 85381 581 0

Printed and bound in Great Britain by
Clays Ltd, St Ives plc

Virago Press
An imprint of
Time Warner Books UK
Brettenham House
Lancaster Place
London WC2E 7EN

www.virago.co.uk

# PART ONE

"I want you to meet Miss Gorce, she's in the embalming game."
—JAMES THURBER (*Men, Women, and Dogs*)

# CHAPTER ONE

It was a hot, peaceful, optimistic sort of day in September. It was around eleven in the morning, I remember, and I was drifting down the Boulevard St. Michel, thoughts rising in my head like little puffs of smoke, when suddenly a voice bellowed into my ear: "Sally Jay Gorce! What the hell? Well, for Christ's sake, can this really be our own little Sally Jay Gorce?" I felt a hand ruffling my hair and I swung around, furious at being so rudely awakened.

Who should be standing there in front of me, in what I immediately spotted as the Left Bank uniform of the day, dark wool shirt and a pair of old Army suntans, but my old friend Larry Keevil. He was staring down at me with some alarm.

I said hello to him and added that he had frightened me, to cover any bad-tempered expression that might have been lingering on my face, but he just kept on staring dumbly at me.

"What *have* you been up to since . . . since . . . when the hell *was* it that I last saw you?" he asked finally.

Curiously enough I remembered exactly.

"It was just a week after I got here. The middle of June."

He kept on looking at me, or rather he kept on looking over me in that surprised way, and then he shook his head and said, "Christ, Gorce, can it only be three short months?" Then he grinned. "You've really flung yourself into this, haven't you?"

In a way it was exactly what I had been thinking, too, and I was on the point of saying, "Into what?", very innocently, you know, so that he could tell me how different I was, how much I'd changed and so forth, but all at once something stopped me. I knew I would have died rather than hear his reply.

So instead I said, "Ah well, don't we all?" which was my stock phrase when I couldn't think of anything else to say. There was a pause and then he asked me how I was and I said fine how was *he*, and he said fine, and I asked him what he was doing, and he said it would take too long to tell.

It was then we both noticed we were standing right across the street from the Café Dupont, the one near the Sorbonne.

"Shall we have a quick drink?" I heard him ask, needlessly, for I was already halfway across the street in that direction.

The café was very crowded and the only place we could find was on the very edge of the pavement. We just managed to squeeze under the shade of the shade of the awning. A waiter came and took our order. Larry leant back into the hum and buzz and brouhaha and smiled lazily. Suddenly, without quite knowing why, I found I was very glad to have run into him. And this was odd, because two Americans re-encountering each other after a certain time in a foreign land are supposed to clamber up their nearest lamp-posts and wait tremblingly for it all to blow over. Especially me. I'd made a vow when I got over here never to *speak* to anyone I'd ever known before. Yet here we were, two Americans who hadn't really seen each other for years; here was someone from 'home' who knew me *when*, of you like, and, instead of shambling back into the bushes like a startled rhino, I was absolutely thrilled at the whole idea.

"I like it here, don't you?" said Larry, indicating the café with a turn of his head.

I had to admit I'd never been there before.

He smiled quizzically. "You should come more often," he said. "It's practically the only non-tourist trap to survive on the Left Bank. It's *real*," he added.

Real, I thought . . . whatever that meant. I looked at the Sorbonne students surging around us, the tables fairly rocking under their pounding fists and thumping elbows. The whole vast panoramic carpet seemed to be woven out of old boots, checkered wool and wild, fuzzy hair. I don't suppose there is anything on earth to compare with a French student café in the late morning. You couldn't possibly reproduce the same numbers, noise, and intensity anywhere else without producing a riot as well. It really was the most colourful café I'd ever been in. As a matter of fact, the most *coloured* too; there was an especially large number of Singalese, Arab and African students, along with those from every other country.

I suppose Larry's 'reality' in this case was based on the café's internationality. But perhaps all cafés near a leading University have that authentic international atmosphere. At the table closest to us sat an ordinary-looking young girl with lank yellow hair and a grey-haired bespectacled middle-aged man. They had been conversing fiercely but quietly for some time now in a language I was not even able to *identify*.

All at once I knew that I liked this place, too.

Jammed in on all sides, with the goodish Tower of Babel working itself up to a frenzy around me, I felt safe and anonymous and, most of all, thankful we were going to be spared those devastating and shattering revelations one was always being treated to at the more English-speaking cafés like the Flore.

And, as I said, I was very glad to have run into Larry.

We talked a little about the various cafés and he explained carefully to me which were the tourist traps and which weren't. Glancing down at my Pernod, I discovered to my astonishment that I'd already finished it. Time was whizzing past.

I felt terribly excited.

"White smoke," said Larry clicking his tongue disapprovingly at my second Pernod. His hand twirled around the stem of his own virtuous glass of St. Raphael. "You keep that up," he said, tapping my glass, "and it'll blow your head off— which may be a good thing at that. Why pink?" he asked, studying my new coiffure carefully. "Why not green?"

As a matter of fact I'd had my hair dyed a marvellous shade of pale red so popular with Parisian tarts that season.

It was the first direct remark he made about the New Me and it was hardly encouraging.

Slowly his eyes left my hair and travelled downwards. This time he really took in my outfit and then that Look that I'm always encountering; that special one composed in equal parts of amusement, astonishment and horror came over his face.

I am not a moron and I can generally guess what causes this look. The trouble is, it's always something different.

I squirmed uncomfortably, feeling his eyes bearing down on my bare shoulders and breasts.

"What the hell are you doing in the middle of the morning with an *evening* dress on?" he asked me finally.

"Sorry about that," I said quickly, "but it's all I've got to wear. My laundry hasn't come back yet."

He nodded, fascinated.

"I thought if I wore this red leather belt with it people wouldn't actually notice. Especially since it's such a warm day. I mean these teintureries make it so difficult for you to get your laundry to them in the first place, don't they, closing up like that from noon till three? I mean, my gosh, it's the only time I'm up and around over here—don't you think?"

"Oh sure, *sure*," said Larry, and murmured, "Jesus" under his breath. Then he smiled forgivingly. "Ah well, you're young, you're new, you'll learn, Gorce." A wise nod of the head. "I know your type all right."

"My type?" I wondered. "My type of what?"

"Of tourist, of course."

I gasped and then smiled cunningly to myself. Tourist indeed! Ho-ho! That was the last thing I could be called—did he but know.

"Tell me about this," I said. "You seem to have tourists on the brain."

He crossed his legs and pulled out of his shirt-pocket a crumbled pack of cigarettes as du pays as possible—sort of Gauloises Nothings—offered one to me, took one himself, lit them both and then settled back with pleasure. This was obviously one of his favourite subjects.

"Basically," he began, "the tourist can be divided into two

categories. The Organized—the Disorganized. Under the Organized you find two distinct types : first, the Eager-Beaver-Culture-Vulture with the list ten yards long, who *just* manages to get it all crossed off before she collapses of aesthetic indigestion each night and has to be carried back to her hotel; and second, the cool suave Sophisticate who comes gliding over gracefully, calmly, and indifferently. But don't be fooled by the indifference. This babe is determined to maintain her incorruptible standards of cleanliness and efficiency if the entire staff of her hotel dies trying. She belongs to the take-your-own-toilet-paper set. Stuffs her suitcases full of nylon, Kleenex, soapflakes, and D.D.T. bombs. Immediately learns the rules of the country. (I mean what time the shops open and close, and how much to tip the waiter.) Can pack for a week-end in a small jewel-case and a large handbag and still have enough room for her own soap and washrag. Finds the hairdresser who speaks English, the restaurant who knows how she likes her steak, and the first foreign word she makes absolutely sure of pronouncing correctly is the one for drugstore. After that she's all set and the world is her ash-tray. If she's got enough money she's got no trouble at all. On the whole, I rather like her."

So far so good, I told myself. They neither one had the slightest, smallest, remotest connection with me. Then a thought caught me sharply.

"And the Disorganized?" I asked rather nervously.

"The Disorganized?" He considered me carefully for a moment, narrowing his eyes.

"Your cigarette's gone out," he said finally. "You have to *smoke* this kind, you know, they won't smoke themselves." He lit it for me again and blew out the match without once taking his eyes off my décolletage, which was slipping quite badly. I gave it a tug and he resumed the discourse.

"Yes. The Disorganized. They get split into two groups as well. First of all the Sly One. The idea is to see Europe casually, you know, sort of vaguely, out of the corner of the eye. All Baedekers and Michelins and museum catalogues immediately discarded as too boring and too corny. Who

wants to see a pile of old stones anyway? The general 'feel'
of the country is what she's after. It's even a struggle to get
her to look at a map of the city she's in so she'll know where
the hell she is, and actually it's a useless one since this type
is constitutionally incapable of reading a map and has no
sense of direction to begin with. But, as I say, she's the sly
one—the 'Oh, look, that's the Louvre over there, isn't it? I
think I'll drop in for a second. I'm rather hot. We'd better
get out of the sun anyway . . .' or 'Tuileries did you say?
That sure strikes a bell. Aren't those flowers pretty over there?
Now haven't I heard something about it in connection with
the—what was it—French Revolution? Oh yes, *of course*
that's it. Thank you, hon.' "

I laughed—a jolly laugh—to show I was with him.

"The funny thing," he continued, "is, scratch the sly one
and out comes the *real* fanatic, and what begins with
'Gosh, I can never remember whether Romanesque was *before*
or *after* Gothic' leads to secret pamphlet-readings and
stained-glass studyings, and ends up in wild aesthetic discus-
sions of the relative values of the two towers at Chartres.
Then all restraint is thrown to the wind and anything really
*old* enough is greeted with animal cries of anguish at its
beauty. In the final stage small discriminating lists appear
about her person—but they only contain, you may be damn
sure, the good, the pure and the truly worthwhile."

Larry paused, took a small, discriminating sip of his St.
Raphael, and puffed happily away at his cigarette.

I swallowed the last of my Pernod, folded my arms seduc-
tively on the sticky table and took a long pull on my own
French cigarette. It had gone out, of course. I hid it from
Larry but he hadn't noticed. He was lost in reverie.

Blushingly I recalled a night not so long before when I had
suddenly fallen in love with the Place de Furstenberg in the
moonlight. I had actually—Oh Lord—I had *actually* kissed
one of the stones at the fountain, I remembered, flung my
shoes off, and executed a crazy drunken dance.

The September sun was blazing down on us and the second
Pernod was beginning to have a pleasant soporific effect on

me. A couple of street arabs came up and listlessly began to try selling us silver jewellery and rugs. After a while they drifted away. I began studying Larry closely. The mat of auburn hair curling to his skull, the grey-green eyes now so blank and far away, the delicate scar running down the pale skin of his forehead, the well-shaped nose covered with a faint spray of freckles, and his large mouth so gently curved, all contributed to give his face, especially in repose, a look of sappy sweetness that was sharply at odds with—and yet at the same time enhanced—his tough, wise-guy manner. Maybe because I had been out very late the night before and was not able to put up my usual resistance, but it seemed to me, sitting there with the sound of his voice dying in my ears, that I could fall in love with him.

And then, as unexpected as a hidden step, I felt myself actually *stumble* and *fall*. And there it was, I *was* in love with him! As simple as that.

He was the first real person I'd ever been in love with. I couldn't get over it. What I was trying to figure out was why I had never been in love with him *before*. I mean I'd had plenty of chance to. I'd seen him almost daily that summer in Maine two years ago when we were both in a Summer Stock company. I had decided to be an actress at the time. Even though we were about the same age, he was already a full-fledged Equity member and I had been a mere apprentice. He was always rather nice to me in his insolent way, but there was also, I now remembered with a passing pang, an utterly ravishing girl, a model, the absolute epitome of glamour, called Lila. She used to come up at week-ends to see him.

Then I heard from someone that he'd quit college the next winter and gone abroad to become a genius. I'd met him again when I first landed in Paris. He'd been very nice, bought me a drink, taken down my telephone number and never called me.

You're a dead duck now, I told myself, as I relaxed back into my coma. You're gone. I looked at him smiling idly. I tried to imagine what was going on in his mind. I gave up and I thought of his tourists.

I had no trouble imagining the girl with all the Kleenex and Tampax or whatever. Cool, blonde and slender, she was only too easy to picture, but the thought of all that unruffled poise somehow had the opposite effect on my own—so I drove her away and began concentrating on the last one. What did he call her? The sly one. Here, happily, in my pleasantly drowsy state, I was able to dress up a little grey furry mouse with tail and whiskers in a black bombazine coat and bonnet. She was clutching a small discriminating list in her white-gloved claws and uttering animal squeals of anguish at the beauty of—what? The Crazy Horse Saloon? Oh dear, I really was too ignorant and too lazy to know what was on that list . . . something old . . . those Caves, I thought idly, the word conjuring up no picture whatever. Those Caves *anyway*, I persevered, in . . . Southern France? No, Spain: someplace with an A. Ha! Altamira, that's it. Yes, the Caves, I decided, framing the mouse in the doorway, or rather Caveway. Yes. They're very old . . . very, very old.

"The last type," said Larry, his voice suddenly snapping me out of my trance, his green eyes fixing me with a significant glare that made my heart lurch, "the last type is the Wild Cat. The I-am-a-Fugitive-from-the-Convent-of-the-Sacred-Heart. Not that it's ever really the case. Just seems so from the violence of the reaction. Anyhow it's her first time free and her first time across and, by golly, she goes native in a way the natives never had the stamina to go. Some people think it's those stand-up toilets they have here—you know, the ones with the iron footprints you're supposed to straddle. After the shock of that kind of plumbing something snaps in the American girl and she's off. The desire to bathe somehow gets lost. The hell with all that, she figures. Then weird haircuts, weird hair-colours, weird clothes. Then comes drink and down, down, down. Dancing in the streets all night, braying at the moon, and waking up in a different bed each morning. Yep," he polished off his St. Raphael with a judicious smack of his lips, "that's the lot. Hmm," a long studying glance, "now *you*, I'd say, you are going to be a combination of the last two types."

"Why you utter bastard," I gasped. "That's a dirty lie," I heard myself saying, the phrase dug up from heaven knows what depths of my childhood. Then in an effort to regain my dignity : "*Really*, of all the stupefyingly inaccurate accusations. It's a pretty safe bet I bathe about sixty times as often as *you*. . ." He burst out laughing. To accuse the American male of not bathing in Paris is merely to flatter him.

The Pernod was having quite a different effect on me now. I was wide-awake, and sputtering, and so angry I could almost feel the steam rising from my shoulders.

He put his hand over mine, the one with the dead cigarette crumbled in it, and gave me a wonderful smile. "Easy, child, easy. I'm only teasing you. Don't think I *disapprove* for Christ's sake. Live it up, I say. Don't say no to life, Gorce, you're only young once."

We were on last name terms, Keevil and I.

"I'm finding your Grand Old Man just as hard to take as your Scientific Researcher," I said as nastily as I could, and withdrew my hand.

"I like you, Gorce," he said. "I mean it. Had my eye on you that summer. High-spirited." He laughed but at the same time I knew by the way his motor had started up (you could actually *see* the engine chugging through his body) and the way he was vaguely looking around for a waiter, that the interview, as far as he was concerned, was over. And he was on his way.

"Please order me another Pernod," I said quickly.

Raised eyebrows.

"Oh, for goodness sake, I'm all right. And have one yourself. Please. Let me pay for this round." He was the sort of person whose financial circumstances were impossible to guess at, and the quick cynical look he gave me made me start to apologize, but as he didn't refuse I went on. "Please. I simply must talk to you. I'm in the most awful mess," and I sighed and buried my head in my hands, stalling for time.

He signalled the waiter and ordered another round.

"O.K.," he said. "Let's have it. What's it all about?"

"Give me a minute," I pleaded desperately. "I can't just jump in like that." My thoughts were chasing each other all over the place, but nothing seemed to sort itself out. Advice, I thought. Ask his advice. On love? Finance? Career? Better stick to love, I decided, it's what's on your mind anyway.

And with that my mind went blank.

Only one small irrelevancy finally appeared. "Why are all your tourists *she*?" I finally asked.

"Because all tourists are she," he replied promptly.

"No males at all? Don't be silly."

"Nope. No males at all. The only male tourists—though naturally there are men visitors—you know, men visiting foreign countries," he explained maddeningly, "the only male tourists are the ones loping around after their wives. A tourist is a she all right," he said, finishing it off with a lot of very reminiscent laughter.

"I can see you've made quite a study of them," I snarled scornfully.

"I get around, Gorce, I get around."

And you, I told myself, are just one of the mob.

It was no joke being in love with Larry, I could see that now; it really hit me for the first time. The waiter had brought us fresh drinks and was pouring the water into my Pernod, and ordinarily this would have had quite a cheering effect on me—its changing colour usually reminded me of chemistry-sets and magic potions, but now the cloudy green liquid looked merely poisonous and the strong liquorice smell reminded me of nothing so much as a bottle of Old Grandma's Cough Remedy, hold-your-nose-and-have-a-piece-of-chocolate-quickly-afterwards. I found that the previous drinks had turned icy cold and heavy in my stomach. I felt terribly sober and the inside of my mouth tasted sour. I sighed and picked up the chits. 120 francs.

"It's cheap anyway," I said, giving him the money. I sat staring at the drink, trying to get up enough courage to down it.

"What's eating you, Gorce? Come on, let's have it."

His words rang out like coins in the emptiness and I suddenly noticed how still everything around us had become. The students had stopped surging and gone to lunch; the Arab vendors were asleep in the sun; and the waiters, even as we watched, stopped waiting and began drifting back to their stations where they came to a standstill—or as near a standstill as they ever got—still rocking gently back and forth on their heels : heart-beats of perpetual motion gently rocking back and forth, their napkins fluttering in the breeze.

The sun shone on : the shade of the shade of the awning vanished in the hot, white, shadowless mid-day. In that blaze of heat I was loving Paris as never before.

And there sitting opposite me, stretching himself luxuriously in the sun, his eyes lazily examining his half-empty drink, was Larry, the one I loved the best . . . sensationally uninterested.

All at once I sat bolt upright and let out a yelp.

I suddenly remembered what I was doing in that arrondissement in the first place. I had been in fact on my way to the Sorbonne to meet my lover, who was attending an International Students Conference there for his Embassy. And at that very moment, as if I myself had conjured him (though I supposed I must have unconsciously registered him in the corner of my eye) he came striding along the boulevard large as life : Teddy—Alfredo Ourselli Visconti himself, looking suave and Latin and livid.

I glanced at my watch. Wow! I was just an hour too late. Then, stupidly, I tried to hide my head with my hands. It was too late, of course, and the worst of it was he had also caught me trying to hide. Being a Latin, seeing me there with a young and handsome man, he naturally put two and two together and for once in his life arrived at the right answer about me.

In a panic I knew that he must not sit down with us; if he did, he would stay and Larry would go. And that would be that. There wasn't a moment to be lost. Without explanation, I dashed over to the street-corner to intercept him.

"So I've caught you at last, have I?" he said, in that half-serious half-teasing man-of-the-world voice he always reserved for matters of the heart. Whatever guilt I felt vanished in my exasperation.

"We can't all lead a triple life as successfully as you do," I replied coolly, and saw a really desperate, haggard look come over his face. "He's an old, old friend," I added hastily. "He's brought me news of home. Very important news."

"I see," he said stiffly. "Very well. We must talk of all this tonight. At the Ritz?"

"Yop." He always brought out the succinct in me.

"Shall we say at eleven o'clock then, as usual?"

"Not later?" He was always up to a half an hour late.

"It may be difficult to get away," he said, "but I shall certainly try to be on time if I can."

He looked so pleased I could have killed him.

If I hadn't been in such a hurry to get back to Larry, I would have told him then and there, as I'd been vaguely planning to do for about a week, how hellishly bored I was with all his sophisticated manœuvres. It was partly out of necessity, of course, having both a wife *and* a mistress, as well as myself, that he jammed and juggled his days and nights with arranged and rearranged rendezvous. But that was not the only reason he always turned up so late. There was another one, as I suspected when he formed the habit of meeting me around eleven at the Ritz bar: it was that he simply refused to do anything in a straightforward way. He felt that his unpunctuality increased his mystery and desirability.

The unfortunate thing was that he had reckoned without my naïvety. I was honestly so thrilled at being at the Ritz in the first place that I didn't mind how long I was kept waiting. There were so many marvellous new things to look at and so many marvellous new drinks to experiment with; sazaracs and slings and heaven knows what else, so that at first I never even noticed the passing of time. But then as the novelty wore off and I took to bringing magazines and novels along with me, I noticed how really put out he was when instead of discovering me ceaselessly scanning the horizon for him, he found me deep in *Paris-Match*.

As I hurriedly said goodbye to Teddy, meekly apologizing for not meeting him at the Sorbonne, and promising to see him at the Ritz that evening, I had a sinister premonition of how embarrassing an homme fatal could be when his charms are no longer fatale to you.

I turned round to find Larry quietly taking in the scene. When he caught my eye he began grinning from ear to ear. I felt my ankles wobble under me.

"Watch out," he shouted as I walked towards him, "you're going to knock over that chair!"

But of course it was too late.

Larry was really enjoying himself now. He laughed and laughed when I returned. "Gorce, oh Gorce," he chortled, neighing like a barnyard in uproar, "if you're his mistress, and I *think* you are, you've skipped a grade, honey." A waggle of his forefinger. "That's not for first-year tourists, that's for the second-year ones, you know."

At this point, I now realize, there were several things I could have done. For instance, I could have nodded sheepishly or good-naturedly, or whatever one does with 'good grace'. I could have said, "Well, there you have me, I guess," and he would have said, "Now never mind, and what was it you wanted to tell me?" and I would have said, "Nothing, forget it" and he would have replied, "Well, cheer up, see you around sometime" and he *would* have, I suppose—sometime. Our Paris, after all, was really very small. And I would have at least been spared one of the most embarrassing moments of my life. No honestly, I don't think *anything* has embarrassed me so much since.

It's crazy but I wonder if all the rest of it—and I mean *all* the rest of it—would have happened if our meeting had ended then and there and in that way. Who knows? But, anyway, seeing myself and the affair with Teddy suddenly through Larry's eyes, and realizing that whatever I had done, however original I had thought of it as being before, I was only remaining strictly within the tourist pattern, and having

Larry *know* this—well, at the time it was too much to bear.

To have an affair with a man, and one's very *first* affair at that, just because he picks you up under rather romantic circumstances on the Champs-Elysées, takes you to the Ritz and things, and above all, because you're impressed with the fact that he has a wife *and* a mistress already, what could be more predictable? Tourist Second-Year Disorganized.

No, dammit, I wasn't going to be stuffed into that category no matter what. Not in Larry's mind anyway.

"Here's my advice to you, and you're old enough to give it to yourself," Larry was saying sagely. "Stay away from married men. I mean it, stay away."

"How *can* you think such things of me? It's not that way at all," I moaned. "We love each other. There's no wife in this at all. How *could* you think such a thing of me? There's something much worse though. A crackpot at the Italian Embassy who's always hated Teddy. Do you know what he's done? He's broken into Teddy's flat and burned some important papers so that Teddy got into the most awful trouble and he's been recalled! He has to leave any day now. God knows if he'll ever be able to straighten this out. It's torture. We can never meet except briefly like you saw us now, and in the open, as if there were nothing to it, for fear of getting that man on to *my* trail. Lord knows how he'd use me against Teddy! All I know is that Teddy is going back to Italy and that I'll probably never see him again." I was getting worked up by then. "And I love him so much, Larry, I really do. What shall I do?" Lies, from beginning to end.

"You poor kid," said Larry. He said it so nicely, so sincerely. I was absolutely staggered by the difference in his tone. I was feeling more than a little sorry for myself at this point, but I was also feeling more than a little elated at the way I had cleared myself of the dreaded tourist charge, at the same time getting rid of Teddy so neatly, or at any rate disposing of him in the near future.

"We've been desperate these last months. We try not to see each other but it's no good. I'll . . . I'll die when he goes."

By now I was really moved. My eyelids stung and tears began to roll slowly down my cheeks.

"Poor kid, poor kid," he kept repeating. How nice Larry was now. Not mocking, not bored, not restless. I looked into his eyes, soft eyes, interested and sympathetic. He gave a short little laugh of encouragement. It stirred me to my roots. I took a long heady swig of Pernod right into the hot molten sun, and brother, that was my undoing.

"Take it easy, take it easy," he was saying. "Everything's going to be all right." He took my hand away from my drink and held it gently in his own. By now I was maybe drunk, I don't know, but in such a state of uncontrolled passion that the mere touch of his hand on mine charged through my body like a thousand volts.

You know how it is. Some people can hack and hack away at you and nothing happens at all and then someone else just touches you lightly on the arm and it happens . . . yes, I mean I came. I mean that's what happened.

I remember looking down at the table and seeing my fingers clinging and curling around his. I remember being quite aware of this but at the same time quite unable to stop myself. Then I put his hand up to my cheek and caressed his knuckles with my mouth. A split second suspended itself into infinity in the air while my heart pounded furiously and I kept kissing and kissing his knuckles. And then it was over.

I jerked my head back sharply. I tried to pull my hand away from his. He held on tightly. His voice was very close to me, mocking and smooth. "Why you little fraud." Very softly, very clearly. "You shabby little fraud. You'll die when he goes, will you? Now how do I know you've been lying?" He was quite simply torturing me.

My eyes dug a hole in the table, unfortunately not large enough to crawl into. "You *don't* know——" I began but the whole thing was too much for me. There was one moment while I counted the seconds and then I resigned myself. With a sigh I forced myself to look at him and he looked back at me hard and down and through and I yielded up without a struggle my badly kept secret.

"Isn't it awful?" I said, my voice faltering into a miserably insincere little giggle.

He held his head on one side. He was, I could see, overwhelmingly puzzled. And so, in a word, was I. Had playing with fire for so long without getting burned heated me up for this almost spontaneous combustion? Why, why, *why*, was the question burning in his face. As there was no reason that I could figure out, he wasn't going to get an answer. And maybe he didn't really want one anyway. At any rate he let go of my hand. And his motor started up again. The implications of these acts should have made me feel worse but somehow they cooled me down, and I reached around for my tattered cloak of carelessness. I said casually, "I saw this stinking little Art film last night. All about the simple life on a barge up and down the Seine. How about that? Not a bad idea." I was really talking to myself. In times of stress when I'm not coming out of things too well the simple life has a tremendous appeal for me. Picking strawberries off a deserted wind-swept coast on the Atlantic ocean when I was seven is an image I frequently and yearningly return to.

We began talking of other things. Although I had been the one to make such a fool of myself I was the calmer. It was Larry who was flapping about, searching for conversation.

At one point I noticed his eyes had found their way back to my bosom again. "I think that dress needs something or other around the neck, you know," he was saying helpfully. "Haven't you got anything?"

"I had a pearl necklace," I answered, by now really wishing he would go. "I lost it or something. Anyway it's gone. The hell with it."

"What a shame. It wasn't real, I hope?" he asked with a sympathy he couldn't feel.

"As a matter of fact it was. Who cares? The hell with it I said." I was really getting annoyed at the trivial turn in the conversation.

"Oh come now," he persisted. "You don't often lose things, do you?"

"All the time," I said defiantly, wondering how long we

were going to toss this around. "I don't like possessions. I travel light so I can make my getaway." Bitterly I was thinking that he was going to incorporate this, too, in his tourist research. O.K. O.K. I was it all right. I was practically the prototype. Getting drunk, having affairs, losing money, losing jewellery, losing God knows what. Whoopee, twenty-three skidoo, and Oh you kid!

"You don't give a damn, do you?" he said finally.

"No. I don't."

A long pause. "Gorce, I'll tell you something. You know what? You've got to stop all this drifting. You've got brains and looks and talent. Things could really happen to you. What's become of your acting? You weren't bad. You'd be sensational if you could project that off-beat thing that's you —really you. And what are you doing instead? Wasting your time bumming around with a tourist-trap Casanova!"

"Well, but *living* you know . . ." I said warily, at the same time trying to project that off-beat thing, whatever it was.

"Oh no. Not that please," he cut me off briskly. "Look, I tell you what. I'm going to direct a programme of one-act plays at the American Theatre. You know, that little one around Denfert-Rochereau they keep trying to get started. It's just possible that you might be right for something. You might fit into the Saroyan play. We're playing safe and starting off with the usual stuff: Saroyan, Shaw, Tennessee Williams——"

"Which ones?" I asked breathlessly.

"Haven't decided yet. Anyway, come over there sometime. We'll be casting soon."

Then, having made this decision and having wasted enough of his precious time that should no doubt have been spent geniusing, he shot to his feet and faced the cluster of waiters with such imminent departure in his manner that two of them came running.

But I didn't care any more. The whole flock of them could have come. The Pernods melted in my stomach in one glorious swooshing splash and all was gaiety and song and dance.

Larry paid the bill and stood up, looking down at me and grinning.

"Gosh, I'd love to act again," I said. "I really would. I'm dying to—but when?"

"As soon as you get your laundry back," he said, and left.


Larry had gone. I drifted into the street lit with love and began turning imaginary handsprings. I hadn't the faintest idea where I was going. I found myself in front of the Métro Odéon and began playing with the metro map, pushing the buttons en toutes directions. Porte des Lilas–Châtelet, Mairie d'Issy–Porte de la Chapelle, Vincennes–Neuilly . . . how beautiful they sounded. "To the end of the line," I murmured. A virtuous thought crossed my mind that in this new life dedicated to Art I should take the metro, not taxis. But I found I couldn't bear to go underground into the dark. Not on a day like that.

A taxi came by and I hailed it, suddenly knowing where I had to go. I told him to go directly to the American Library in Saint-Germain. There I would get out the Collected Works of Tennessee Williams and William Saroyan. Then I would go and see about my laundry. As if to emphasize the miracle of the day the taxi-driver actually conceded the quartier to be in his route.

With many a 'bon, bon, ça va' to commemorate our fellow-feelings we drove off. Upon arrival I glanced at my watch and saw that it was one o'clock. Everything would be closed until three. The little hotel to which I had recently moved was on the Rue Jules Chaplain in Montparnasse, and so was the teinturerie where my laundry was marking time. It was a matter of three minutes away. Three minutes *au maximum*, a mere flicker in the eternity of a taxi-driver's life, you would think, but the doughty old Parisian at the wheel refused to budge another inch with me in the cab.

One o'clock. Two hours to go.

I found a table at the Royal Saint-Germain, ordered an omelette au jambon and a café noir, and stared across at the church with its towers encased in scaffolding. I wondered why I'd never seen any workmen on it. Maybe I *was* up and about for only a few hours every day, after all. Boy, I'd better pull myself together.

I made a mark with my knife on the paper table-cloth to underline my decision : *Teddy would have to go.* I probably really didn't have the true courtesan spirit anyway. How in hell had I got into all this in the first place? I tried to figure out how the whole thing started. Well, first of all, of course, I came to Paris. And the reason I had a chance to come to Paris was because of dear old Uncle Roger. . .

The week before I became thirteen—two days after I'd run away for the fourth time—my uncle Roger had sent for me. He was then living in lofty majesty, in a big, white clapboard house overlooking the Hudson Valley, and spending most of this time in the enormous living-room he'd had converted into an observatory. A giant telescope was rigged up right smack in the middle of the room, the original idea being that it would give him something to do when he got bored at one of his parties, but gradually it had come to obsess him and he was never far away from it. He even began using it to punctuate his conversations, to gesture with, the way other people use their spectacles and pipes. Uncle Roger had invented a special kind of screw which made him very, very rich, and a special kind of oracular noblesse oblige in distributing his largesse, which made him very, very godlike. The telescope helped too. He was hard at it when I was announced.

"They tell me you were heading down Mexico way this time. What for?" he asked me over his shoulder, apparently unable even for a minute to tear himself away from the stars, or whatever you see through a telescope in broad daylight.

"I wanted to be a bullfighter," I mumbled.

"What were you going to be last time?"

"You mean last year when I ran away?"

"Yes."

"A singer in a jazz band. Why?"

"Nothing, nothing. Just curious." He twiddled a few knobs and had another look at—the sun—I suppose, and finally turned round and looked at me. I was staring down at my saddle shoes. One shoelace had been badly tied and I was trying to re-tie it in my mind.

"My dear child, what a face! What a face to put on. Why so broody?"

"I am in mourning for my life," I said, still staring at my shoes, wishing they were black, at least, and wondering if he'd ever read the play. He hadn't.

"Good heavens, is that what they teach you at that school?"

"No."

"Well, never mind. Let's see what we can do to cheer you up, shall we? The reason I've asked you to come—now don't be afraid, I won't scold you. I'm sure you've been scolded quite enough—sit down, child, sit down anywhere, just throw all that camera stuff on the floor, we're shooting Venus tonight, getting her quarter phase—the reason I asked you to come, is to find out what you'd like for your birthday this year."

"I want my freedom!" I said, tears stinging my eyes at the word.

"Your freedom? Ah yes, of course. What are you planning to do with it?"

I hesitated. I had to think for a moment. I hadn't really put it into words before.

"I want to stay out as late as I like and eat whatever I like any time I want to," I said finally.

"Is that all?"

"No. I think if I had my freedom I wouldn't allow myself to get introduced to all the mothers and fathers and brothers of the girls at school. And all that junk. I wouldn't get introduced to anyone. I've never wanted to meet anyone I've been introduced to. I want to meet all the other people . . . I can't explain. . ."

"Try. There must be some reason for your ambulatory urges."

"It's just that I *know* the world is so wide and full of people and exciting things that I just go crazy every day stuck in these institutions. I mean if I don't get started soon, how will I get the chance to sharpen my wits? It takes lots of training. You have to start very young. I want them to be so sharp that I'm always able to guess right. Not *be* right—that's much different—that means you're going to do something about it. No. Just guessing. You know, more on the wing."

Uncle Roger went back to the telescope and swung it around a bit, back and forth. Finally he came over and sat down beside me. For the first time he spoke to me man to man. "I think I understand your predilection for being continually on the wing, or rather, to put it more precisely, on the lam," he said seriously. "It's difficult to know nowadays where adventure lies. There are no more real frontiers. Funny how these things work out. I came roaring out of the Middle West, you know, and my greatest ambition was to conquer—that's how I saw it—to conquer New York; New York and the mysterious, civilized East. Now my father before me had set his sights on conquering the Middle West. That was his adventure. I wonder what you will try to conquer? Europe, I suppose, since our family seems to be going backwards."

I don't know why but at this moment I had one of those aberrations where people say one thing to you and you take it to mean something quite different. I fully expected Uncle Roger to put a steamship ticket in one of my hands, a bouquet of flowers in the other, and wish me Bon Voyage.

I drew myself to attention, trying to look alert, composed, above all trustworthy, and I said, "I should like to go to Europe very much, Uncle Roger. Could you write to my school and explain that you've decided to send me away?"

"Good God, this is impossible!" exclaimed my uncle, horrified. "See here, young lady the world may be very wide, but you also are very young and don't you forget it. Now then," he said, and he took me by the elbows and looked earnestly into my eyes, "I have a proposition to make to you. The more I see of the world the more I realize how much we are haunted by our childhood dreams. We have been having a serious conversation just now, whether you know it or not. I want you to remember every word. And when you've graduated from college——"

"Oh no!"

"——graduated from college, and if you haven't run away in the meantime, I'll give you your freedom. Two years of it. Upon graduation you'll receive in monthly sums enough money for you to go anywhere you like and do anything you like during that period. No strings. I don't even want to hear of you in those two years. Afterwards come back and tell me what it was like. . ."

When I first arrived in Paris I got sick. Then I got well and began walking everywhere round and round and round, crossing and re-crossing the river, hardly knowing where I was going or where I'd been. Hardly caring, it all seemed so fine.

And then one day, one memorable day in the early evening, I stumbled across the Champs-Elysées. I know it seems crazy to say, but before I actually stepped on to it (at what turned out to be the Etoile) I had not even been aware of its existence. No, I swear it. I'd heard the words 'Champs-Elysées', of course, but I thought it was a park or something. I mean that's what it sounds like, doesn't it? All at once I found myself standing there gazing down that enchanted boulevard in the blue, blue evening. Everything seemed to fall into place. Here was all the gaiety and glory and sparkle I knew was going to be life if I could just grasp it.

I began floating down those Elysian Fields three inches off the ground, as easily as a Cocteau character floats through Hell. Luxury and order seemed to be shining from every street-lamp along the Avenue; shining from every window of its toy-shops and dress-shops and car-shops; shining from its cafés and cinemas and theatres; from its bonbonneries and parfumeries and nighteries. . . Talk about seeing Eternity in a Grain of Sand and Heaven in a Wild Flower; I really think I was having some sort of mystic revelation then. The whole thing seemed like a memory from the womb. It seemed to have been waiting there for me.

For some people history is a Beach or a Tower or a Graveyard. For me it was this giant primordial Toy Shop with all its windows gloriously ablaze. It contained everything I've ever wanted that money can buy. It was an enormous Christmas present wrapped in silver and blue tissue paper tied with satin ribbons and bells. Inside would be something to adorn, to amuse, and to dazzle me forever. It was my present for being alive.

As I say, I'd started at the Etoile and was working my way down to the Place de la Concorde. Somewhere around the Rond-Point I floated off the kerb and into an oncoming car. The scream of brakes that had at first seemed so dim and irrelevant was now screeching into my ears. All in all it was a very near miss. The driver leapt out of the car and rushed over to the lamp-post against which I was limply draped. "Are you all right?" he asked anxiously. I could have kissed him for not yelling why the hell hadn't I looked where I was going. I nodded and started to leave but found that it was quite impossible to put one foot in front of the other. The upshot of the matter was that this extremely charming man, his arm firmly under my elbow, suggested we both take a spin in his car for a little while to unwind.

The next thing I knew I was ankle deep in martinis at the Ritz Bar, and he was calling me Sally Jay and I was calling him Teddy.

I sighed nostalgically, drained my coffee to the grounds, and unrolled l'addition from the tight little scroll in my hand. If I was going to break off with Teddy it wouldn't do at all to remember those early days and what fun they'd been. After all, he was madly attractive dans sa façon. No question. Was

I being wise or merely rash? Oh dear. By now I was completely uncertain. Two of les boys flitted past. They certainly wore their jeans with a difference. One of the differences between Saint-Germain and Montparnasse, I decided, was that Saint-Germain was queerer. And that was the only decision I seemed likely to make for the time being.

# CHAPTER TWO

Six o'clock that evening found me back at my hotel, exhausted from an enervating battle fought and lost over my laundry. I had the books of plays, though. That much had been accomplished. Three were on the table beside me and one, appropriately enough, was open in my hand.

There was a knock on my door. I called out for whoever it was to come in and Judy's head, wiggling on its long stem of a neck, poked itself into the doorway. "Oh, I hope I'm not interrupting you," she said, backing out as soon as she noticed the book in my hand. Judy lived in my hotel. She was just seventeen, and what she was doing in Paris was supposedly chaperoning her younger brother, a fully-fledged concert pianist of fifteen, who was studying there with one of the leading teachers. In view of their combined and startling innocence, however, this was a rather useless arrangement. Their last name was Galache, and they were the issue with which the highly unlikely union of a Quaker woman from Philadelphia and a dreadfully dashing Spaniard (now, alas, dead) had been blessed. Naturally their upbringing, up to this point, had been strict and very sheltered.

"No, of course you're not interrupting me," I said. "Come in. Sit down, my child. There is almost no time in the world when I wouldn't want to see you."

Judy was so different from me that it was really ludicrous. Whereas I was hell-bent for living, she was content, at least for the time being, to leave all that to others. Just as long as she could *hear* all about it. She really was funny about this. Folded every which way on the floor, looking like Bambi— all eyes and legs and no chin—she would listen for ages and ages with rapt attention to absolutely any drivel that you happened to be talking. It was unbelievable.

"And *then* what did you do?" she would ask with real avidity at the end of a dreary, over-long and absolutely pointless anecdote.

"So, then I simply left."

"But where did you *go*?"

"Back to the dance."

"And then what?"

"I began dancing."

"And then what?"

"Why, that's all."

"But what did *he* do then?"

"Oh Judy, *please*. That's all, I said."

"Oh," she would sigh, resigning herself to the inevitable, but unable to conceal her disappointment. And this 'oh' always escaped with the most heartbreaking, dying fall.

Ridiculous as the idea may have been for her blue-stocking mother to send brother and sister over alone like this, the fact was that Judy was protected as much by her curiosity as by her innocence. And then there was this other thing about her, too. You know all that razzle-dazzle about people being born in Original Sin and all that rot? Well, maybe it's rot and maybe it isn't. I mean I wouldn't slit my throat from ear to ear, just because I'd found out for sure that most people *are*. But she wasn't. That was the thing. She simply *wasn't*. I'm positive of that.

She was terrifically excited at this moment because she'd just been to see the paintings of a young artist called Jim Breit. He was, she explained to me, one of the Hard Core. The Hard Core was what we called a group of rugged individualists who circled around an old satyr, a sort of archetypal poet-painter nicknamed the Ancient, and made their headquarters in the cafés of the Dôme, the Rotonde, and, especially, the Select in Montparnasse. A rowdy bunch on the whole, they were most of them so violently individualistic as to be practically interchangeable. For instance, there was a pair of identical blue-bereted brown beards, and although each of them had markedly different personalities—one boring and pompous, the other gay and positively skittish—Beard Boring and Beard Bubbly, in fact—I found myself avoiding them both, as I was never sure which was which. The ones who Did Anything (and there were plenty not averse to Taking it Easy—or whatever the course was called at the Sorbonne), mostly painted. That any of them would actually be *talented* had never occurred to me. Another essential difference between Judy and me.

"Which one is Jim?" I asked.

"The rather short one with very blue eyes who has dimples when he smiles."

"The one who's so shy and polite?" She nodded. "I'll be darned. He certainly doesn't look like a painter, does he? Still that's probably in his favour. What is he—G.I., Fulbright, Guggenheim, or Rockefeller?"

"I don't think he has a grant," she said. "I think he's just here on his own."

"That's original, anyway. What are his paintings like?"

She thought this over for a moment, very seriously. "They're *good*," she said finally. "I can't describe them, but, you know," she said suddenly, "I'd like to *own* one of them."

That *really* impressed me. "By the way," I said casually, "I'm going back to the stage. See?" And I held up my book of plays.

"Oh Sally Jay. Are you an actress? Why didn't you tell me? How exciting. I'll bet you're perfectly marvellous. What have you been in on Broadway?"

"Well, nothing, really." I had to admit that there was only that season in Summer Stock. Then I told her about my meeting Larry that morning, and how he was going to produce some one-act plays here. I had quite a time trying to answer all her and-then-what's in describing what actually *had* taken place during our encounter. "So anyway," I finished, pointing at the books, "I've got to get through all of these and practically memorize them by next week. I'm going to be in this damn thing or bust."

My telephone rang and I jumped a mile. I thought it might

be Teddy and I still hadn't made up my mind quite what to do about him. Should I let him suspect things were not too well by the tone of my voice *now*, for instance, or spring it on him later as a surprise? It seemed a very hard thing even to pick up the receiver. I just didn't want to answer it.

When I did, it wasn't Teddy after all. It was the concierge who wanted to know if Miss Galache was there with me. Someone was waiting downstairs to see her.

"Oh heavens," exclaimed Judy. "It's Claude—Claude Tonnard. I'd completely forgotten about him. He's a painter too, but *French*." We both giggled at the absurdity of knowing a Frenchman in France. "We're going to have coffee at the Select. Please come along. You'll like him. Honestly. And he doesn't speak a word of English so he'll be awfully good for your French, because you'll probably want to act in French too, won't you? Oh dear, I forgot all about my pills. Oh well, it doesn't matter. I'll take them later."

"Judy, you *must* have them now."

Judy had some mysterious ailment which she either didn't know about, or wouldn't talk about. She was extremely delicate, and she tired easily.

"All right, I'll run up to my room and get them. But please come to the Select."

"Nope. Absolutely not. I've got *much* too much work to do," I assured her as she left.

I went to the window and looked out at the September evening. Though still hot with the vanished sun, the dusk, with its suggestion of autumn and nights drawing in, sent shivers of excitement up and down my spine. I thought of sex and sin; of my body and all the men in the world who would never sleep with it. I felt a vague, melancholy sensation running through me, not at all unpleasant. If I could only figure out if it was Larry I was in love with, or just love, then I'd be all set, I told myself. It had certainly seemed to be Larry that morning, especially after that scene at the Dupont, but if I was so sure of it then, why not now? After twenty minutes of this soul-searching, or rather tail-chasing, and after reaching the same conclusion over and over, with the same lack of conviction, I left the window and began pacing around the room. When I felt the horns of my dilemma actually toss me into the air, I lit out of the hotel and landed in the street.

When I got to the Select, I saw that the Hard Core, already assembled, were, as usual, surrounding the Ancient and hanging on to his every obscenity. I picked out Judy's 'good' painter, wedged in between the two Beards, and smiled at him encouragingly, noting as he dimpled back, what a pleasant-looking boy he was. The vague nymphomania I had experienced at the window returned. What an awful lot of possible people there seemed to be around all of a sudden. All on the same day, too. I told myself that this must be part of some pathetic fallacy, whereby if you fall in love with one man, *all* men instantly become desirable, whether they actually are or not. But as soon as I laid eyes on the Frenchman with Judy, I realized how ridiculous this was. I didn't need any pathetic fallacy to tell me that taken all in all—age, weight, shape and colour, this was really le jacque pot! It isn't often that one sees so pure a type of Ladies' Man, so distilled an essence of temptation. I imagined every woman for tables around going mad with desire.

Only Judy, plying him with questions about which art gallery would be the best for a young artist to exhibit in, seemed unaffected. What amused me most was the expression of grave respect sitting so awkwardly upon his features, as he listened to her. It's amazing how right you can sometimes be about a person you don't know; it's only the people you do know who confuse you. I had guessed at once that this wasn't his everyday expression, and sure enough, as I approached, I saw it relax slowly into an entirely different one. Close up he was even more devastating. The eyes, smouldering lazily under their bushy, beetling brows, almost seemed to be lying down, while the magnificent head leaned forward, not *eagerly* exactly, but alertly. My heart raced. If he wasn't unaware of his power, he certainly wasn't bored by it either. He looked carefully at me. I-feel-as-if-we-*have*-already-so-why-waste-time? the look stated unequivocally.

Unexpectedly, I felt my interest drop. There was something about this that rather bored me. Something harrowingly familiar about him. I sat down rather shaken, all sorts of things rattling along the corridors of my mind.

"Mademoiselle Galache is doing me the honour of seeing my paintings tomorrow," he said in French. "Perhaps you would care to join her, Mademoiselle. . ." He turned to Judy. "Excuse me, but I don't believe I heard your friend's name." So we were introduced again. I didn't blame him. What with all that had been going on between us, I hadn't been aware of our being introduced either. I mean, how many things can you concentrate on at once anyway?

"Oh Sally Jay, do come. Please," said Judy.

I sighed. "I'd like to very much, but I'm afraid I can't. I'll be too busy."

"Alors vous prenez du thé chez moi le jour prochain. C'est dimanche," he said promptly.

I considered. That he meant tea to be just us deux and chez lui, was painfully clear. On the other hand, it was also true that he spoke no English at all, and that, what with one thing and another, would be mighty good for my French. He possessed such ravishing good looks—the stylized good looks of the hero on a French cinema-poster, true, but ravishing quand même. No. I must get off this sex kick, I thought, or I'll be turning into some sort of maniac. *"Pushover, Gorce. Pushover is the word,"* the grinning ghost voice of Larry snickered in my ear.

Turning to the Frenchman and disciplining myself, I said no, that it wasn't possible. I said it firmly, and I explained that I had only a very short time in which to study for some rôles that I wished to audition.

I could see he wasn't used to being refused anything and that my refusal had seriously put him off. He looked offended and proud and huffy and at that very moment I was able to put a name to the aura of familiarity enveloping him. The name was Teddy.

For some reason that did it. That absolutely clinched it.

If I didn't even want to be reminded of Teddy, I certainly didn't want Teddy. That was logic.

"Oh gosh," I said in English, leaping to my feet. "Just look at the time. I've got to get back. G'bye, Judy. G'bye—oh—Enchanté, Monsieur. . ."

"Tonnard," he supplied, rising quickly, "Claude Tonnard. Alors une autre fois, je peux espérer? Je peux vous donner un coup de téléphone? Vous habitez ce quartier?"

"Oui, je suis au même hôtel que Mlle Galache. Au revoir." And I fled.

I went back to the hotel and had a bath.

As I lay there, washing myself, the mirror covering the wall around the tub began to steam up. I remembered how I used to count the times I'd been to bed with Teddy on it, keeping score like in a game of bridge: one, two, three, four upright sticks and a diagonal slash for five. And so on. . .

I find I always have to write *something* on a steamed mirror. Only this time, I couldn't think of anything to write.

So I just wrote my own name, over and over again.

# CHAPTER THREE

AT ELEVEN O'CLOCK that night, in one of my dangerous moods—midnight-black, excited and deeply dreading (as opposed to one of my beautiful midnight-blue ones, calm but deeply excited), my nerves strung taut to singing, I arrived alone at the Ritz, only to discover all over again what a difficult thing this was to do. I tended to lose my balance at the exact moment that the doorman opened the cab door and stood by in his respectful attitude of 'waiting'. I have even been known to fall out of the cab by reaching and pushing against the handle at the same time that he did. But this time, however, I had disciplined myself to remain quite, *quite* still, sitting on my hands until the door was opened for me. Then, burrowing into my handbag, which suddenly looked like the Black Hole of Calcutta, to find the fare, I discovered that I needed a light. A light was switched on. I needed more than a light, I needed a match or a torch or special glasses, for I simply couldn't find my change purse, and when I did (lipstick rolling on the floor, compact open and everything spilt—passport, mirror, the works) I couldn't find the right change. We were now all three of us, driver, doorman and I, waiting to see what I was going to do next. I took out some bills, counted them three times in the dark until I was absolutely certain that I had double the amount necessary, and then pressed it on the driver, eagerly apologizing for over-tipping. Overcome with shyness I nodded briefly in the direction of the doorman and raced him to the entrance. I just won. Panting and by now in an absolute ecstasy of panic I flung myself at the revolving doors and let them spin me through. Thus I gained access to the Ritz. I had once seen a man in the taxi in front of mine jump out and with a lordly wave at the doorman say something like, 'Pay him for me Guillaume, my good man,' and stroll inside. I have never arrived there alone since, without devoutly wishing I was sharing that cab.

Inside, confronting the long vista, at the end of which bellboys in the lobby began to reshape themselves, I paused to recover. On my right was the small bar, I think it has some special pet name like the Club Bar, or the Bar Bar, something like that but I can't remember, where the men habitués, ex-kings and things, and brokers and bankers and art dealers, whiled away their hours gambling for drinks with those dice in sort of hour-glass cages, sometimes with one another, sometimes with the waiters, the whole atmosphere exuding that special phoney bonhomie of men among men among waiters. This, it occurred to me, was probably what Larry would have called the *real* bar. It had no interest for me whatever.

But just across the way was the large regular bar and that was décidément autre chose. Here all was laughter and confusion. Here beautiful women, their hair dyed gorgeous colours, squashed soft, pale furs into golden chairs, crunched diamonds around glasses of iced drink, jammed bright lipsticked cigarettes into their mouths, and exhaled a heady perfume, while high above them the crystal chandeliers sparkled and tinkled in accompaniment. Jewelled and bejewelled from youngest to oldest, they all had one thing in common : they actually seemed to *own* their jewellery. It belonged to them; they'd earned it.

Always before in my past, at a school or country club dance, the jewellery was worn with a smile, so to speak, the implication being that it was really on borrowed time—or at the most, Daddy's birthday present. And this was true not just of the young girls but of their mothers as well. I mean it always looked as if *their* mothers had loaned or left them the stuff, or as if their husbands had diffidently kicked through with the donation. Not so with those at the Ritz. Ho, no. These were no mere jewels of indulgent relatives. These had been acquired in some much more serious, mysterious and complete way.

39

Thus was I reflecting, standing there at the entrance of the bar that night, looking around for Teddy and painfully conscious of myself again. I was still wearing the evening dress I had on when I'd met Larry that morning and the funny thing about it was that, even though twelve hours had elapsed since then, it still wasn't particularly appropriate. I mean I really felt I could expect it to be correct attire at *some* point of the day—like a watch that has stopped, eventually just happening to have its hands pointing to the right time. I can't understand it. I have quite a lot of clothes and go to quite a lot of places. I never actually seem to be wearing the right things at the right time, though. You'd think the law of averages. . . Oh well. It's all very discouraging. Nevertheless this dress that I had on at the time, I encouraged myself, wasn't actually *unbecoming*. It was a sort of blue and silver and of course I'd taken off the red leather belt and was wearing the proper belt—which pleased me as well. It was one of the few I hadn't lost.

Very jeune fille, I was, jewelless and all (the pearl necklace that I'd lost had been given to me, as a matter of fact, by Uncle Roger), and as full of safety pins as ever. I probably had one safety pin to every two of those gorgeous creatures' tiny, gleaming, well-sewn, well-hidden hooks-and-eyes. But what the hell, I told myself, it wasn't as if I were *one* of them or even competing with them, for heaven's sake, I was merely a disinterested spectator at the Banquet of Life. The scientist dropping into the Zoo at feeding-time. That is what I told myself.

I looked around. Teddy had said he was going to be on time and I saw that he was as good as his word. He was over by a corner, and when he spotted me, he stood up and began waving his hands in short, choppy, excited gestures, trying to attract my attention. At the same time he gave me the impression that he was *standing on his toes*. All this unconfined joy was deeply unsettling. I was experiencing that terrifying thing of suddenly seeing someone you know terribly well as if for the first time. Even his name seemed to be forming itself in my mind for the first time, and I thought what an utterly dopey name it *was* for a man of forty, the name of what they used to refer to in the newspapers as 'a playboy'. He was a large, neat compact man with a smooth olive complexion, well-groomed sort of tan-coloured hair, a sensuous mobile mouth and large white teeth; impressive enough, but let's face it, there was nothing—well—*spontaneous* about his looks, if you know what I mean. I mean he had none of Larry's careless, lazy, crazy animal grace. There he was over in the corner, flashing away this charming, ingratiating smile that I'd never even remembered *seeing* on him before, and then he began to rub his hands together. For no reason at all, I was suddenly reminded of Charlie Chaplin. Oh Christ, I thought, what have I let myself in for? I could feel myself working up into a large-scale panic and I tried to clamp down on it before it rode away with me. I will *not* have his blood on my hands. I will *not* have his blood on my hands, I kept repeating over and over again. This calmed me down a bit and I managed to zigzag my way through all the gorgeous women over to his table. He could have bought me their clothes and their jewels and their lives, I supposed, but the hell with the Ritz—what I wanted was to live among us artists.

"Well, well. I see you did get here first after all," I said upon arriving at his table, feeling ages older than him.

"Yes," he murmured, bending down over me, attempting to kiss my hand and only just succeeding, as it was offering its usual resistance at the wrist. "I thought it would please you," he said, and he gave a sigh at the whole homme-du-mondeness of having to please women. We sat down. He snapped his fingers imperiously at the waiter in that undemocratic manner that could still make me want to die of shame, and ordered, without consulting me, two champagne cocktails. I hate champagne more than anything in the world next to Seven-Up.

"What are we celebrating?" I asked at the same time as he said: "I think a celebration is called for. . ."

"I must tell you something," I blurted out, just as he began: "Because I have something important to ask you..."

I had intended letting him down gently when we got back to his flat. You know, telling him how I thought it was all a great mistake for me to get involved with a married man, how it might become too serious, how I might even go off the rails, how he might spoil me forever for anyone else—all very touching and flattering and *crippling* one hoped, but now, what with all this loose talk flying around, I could see that if I didn't take the plunge immediately I wasn't going to get a word in edgeways, and maybe I'd lose my nerve and would never get it over with. At the same time I had this mad notion that if I wasn't back in my hotel room and studying all those plays in two minutes flat I wasn't ever going to see Larry again.

"Now look, Teddy," I said, interrupting him, "you may as well tell me what's on your mind here and now because I'm *not* going back to your place tonight or ever again."

This unfortunately coincided with him saying: "But I can't talk about it here. Will you please come back to the flat where we can discuss it?"

It looked like I was going to spend the rest of the night one line ahead of the dialogue and this brought on one of my fits of nervous laughter. Especially since I couldn't help remembering a similar situation. It occurred at the beginning of our affair when, in my eagerness to get things rolling, when the thought of sleeping with someone occupied the entire area of my brain, not to say my body, twenty-four hours a day, I had said to him, it just sort of slipped out: "I am *not* going to bed with you *tonight*, you know," and Teddy had replied in honest bewilderment, "I was thinking of asking you, but I haven't *yet*." I have this awful tendency to jump the gun.

Anyhow he managed to get us out of this particular conversational snarl by saying "Very well then," and waiting for me to go on. So I finally pulled myself together and took the plunge feeling a sort of drowning-on-air sensation as I went, my whole life whistling past.

"I'm sorry, Teddy, but I can't see you again. I know it's going to sound totally and completely insane but it's just that I am madly in love with this boy. You know, Larry, the one you saw me with today at the Dupont. And so I don't think I ought to see you any more."

I have no idea how he took all this, for the simple reason that I kept my head well down, eyes on the potato chips the whole time I was talking, and for quite a while after that. Also I'm not exactly sure what he *said*, either, because my own words kept thundering back into my ears like waves crashing against the shore. But I think he must have said, "You're not serious," or something like that. Something expressing incredulity.

"I am," I replied. "No kidding. I mean I'm in love for the first time in my life. I've been meaning to tell you about it but the opportunity just never seemed to come up."

"I see," he said, and then after a while : "How long have you known this man?"

"Oh, ages really. Like I told you this morning, I knew him in the States first, you see. But we really didn't get to know each other well, that is—um—until—oh—just about two weeks ago." I pulled those weeks out of thin air.

"Ah-ha. Yes. I could see something was going wrong with us just around then," he said, incredibly enough. "I am afraid you are not very good at deceiving or even concealing things, my dear." And I could feel, positively *feel* his satisfaction at being 'right' overcoming for the moment his chagrin at what he was hearing.

I nodded with relief and sneaked a quick look at him. It seemed to me that he was looking pretty composed, though a bit green. Was this possibly going to be easier than I thought? Hot dog. Mentally I was already over the hills and far away. Back at the old homestead.

But he went on to say, "Nevertheless, my dear, I must try to make you change your mind about all this. Since you have decided so dramatically that it is to be all over between us, since you will not even come back to the flat with me to discuss it calmly, I must try to say what I have to here.

It is most difficult, I assure you, but most important to your future. You are making a grave mistake, my dear. I know. You see you are still, forgive me, very young—a mere child——"

I felt my attention wandering off. It generally does at the phrase 'mere child'. It generally wanders off to see if it can't find some really lurid thought that would shock the pants off the other person, if he only knew. Teddy was saying something about how when he first met me he thought I was just another wild Indian American (his words not mine), but that actually I wasn't. *That*, apparently, was the trouble with me. The trouble with me was . . . So then I perked up the old ears and started listening carefully as I always do when anybody is about to say anything unpleasant.

"I must admit it to you now," he said, "though I think you may have suspected it at the time, that I was a bit shocked and a bit, yes a bit displeased when I discovered that you were a virgin. This being the case, you should not have behaved the way you did when we first met, so—forgive me —so almost like a guttersnipe. It was not proper. I saw of course that you were very young, but your whole manner was so dégagé, so sophisticated, so cynical, so—" Here he broke off and shook his head in despair, as if the exact word would eternally escape him, but he managed to catch it just in time, "—so *debauched*, even. And yet—" this next thought amused him so much he had to laugh right out loud as he said it, "—and yet like all your countrywomen, so profoundly inexperienced."

The fact that this was probably true did not prevent me from noticing that Europeans can never resist a dig at America when at a sexual disadvantage with one of its 'countrywomen'.

Suffer him his little sally, I was counselling myself. After all he *is* going to lose you in the end. But I did get mad all the same. I probably shouldn't have. He'd probably said things like that to me a million times before. But I did. I was just so terribly jumpy at this point. A bundle of nerves. The thing was, I was afraid he was in love with me. Seriously.

44

And I didn't want to hurt him, you see. I wanted to pick a fight with him.

So I sneered and said, trying to make it sound very tough: "Listen, Buster, don't give me any of that bull. There's only one reason you were so teed off with me when you found out that I was a virgin. You just couldn't bear the thought of *any* woman deceiving you on *any* grounds. Even those. Don't kid yourself, mon vieux. It was just a matter of pride."

"It is always a matter of pride." He said it very mildly, with a sort of shrug in his voice. I tore myself away from the potato chips and finally took a good look at him. I was right the first time, he did seem perfectly composed.

There was a pause and suddenly he leaned forward, shoulders hunched, head to one side, in a manner that I saw was meant to be at once jaunty and serious, and said: "I wish to ask you something. In your answer a lot can depend. Please make an effort to reply with honesty."

Thinking this the very last way to worm the truth out of me I squirmed and tried to look co-operative. I said, "O.K. Shoot," and made guns of my fingers. I noticed that he looked pained, but he went on:

"Exactly why, since you were a virgin, *did* you acquiesce to me so easily in the first place? Why me, since it is all too clear you were not in the very slightest in love with me? It is most unusual. Why? Be honest now." And he looked me first in one eye and then the other, very quickly, as if to catch out any deception that might be lurking there.

"Why? Oh, Holy Cow!" I groaned.

"*Please* not to use these ridiculous expressions," he exploded in exasperation. "I have never heard any other Americans use them except those—what do you call them—those cartoon animals. Mickey Mouse."

"Micky Mice," I said firmly.

"What?" he demanded irritably.

"Nothing. Sorry." But really I was quite pleased with myself. I had at last provoked him to some kind of temperamental display and if I could just ride in on that, building it up to the sharp exchange of words and some offended dignity on my part, I'd be sailing out of the Ritz in no time.

Incidentally I haven't the faintest idea why I do talk the way I do. I probably didn't do it in America. After all, I hardly ever read the funny papers as a child or anything like that. Maybe I just assumed it in Paris for whatever is the opposite of protective colouring : for *war-paint*, I guess.

Whatever unpleasantness I had hoped was brewing seemed to have blown over. "You haven't answered my question," he said gently.

It was a good chance. At first I thought I'd let him have it about being so impressed with his wife and mistress. I knew that would go over like a lead balloon, but as I'm every kind of coward I also knew I wouldn't be able to bear his mighty fallen crest. Then I thought of the obvious thing, which was simply that I'd never really met a man-of-the-world before, and when I did it struck me that he was just the one who would be best qualified to teach me—oh, you know what. But somehow that stuck in the old throat as well. He'd say I'd been using him. Which was true. Well, hell, we'd been using each other, I could have said—and honestly too, I did it because I thought I'd like his body, but even though I didn't know one thing about men I knew that wouldn't do. Too something or other.

There are, I know (it was in our philosophy course in college), at least a hundred different reasons why some particular event takes place. So I thrashed about again trying to find some other truth and in the instant that it flashed through my head, I think I got as close to my raison d'être as I ever have. At least I'd never put it to myself so clearly.

"I only did it," I said, "now this *is* going to be the truth, Teddy, I only did it because it seemed to be the glamorous thing to do at the time. It was my *ideal* of glamour."

Nothing changed in his face, but I could see from the way he kind of switched off and the light went out of his eyes and his eyelids fluttered downwards listlessly, and from the way one hand slid from the table and began aimlessly rubbing his knee, that for two cents he'd abandon the whole project. But the strength and tenacity that had placed him where he was, high in the Diplomatic Corps, refused to desert him in his hour of need, and after a moment or so of resolute breathing he started lecturing me on the error of my ways.

"That is the answer I would expect of a midinette," he began "or, as you would say—of a *bobsy*-soxer. . ." There are few things as tenuous as a Latin's grasp of the American Idiom.

I interrupted him. "Yes sir," I said. "That's me, kiddo. Just a bobby-soxer at heart."

So he gave up. And in a way I kind of gave up myself. I gave up wondering if anyone was ever going to understand me at all. If I was ever going to understand *myself* even. Why was it so difficult anyway? Was I some kind of a nut or something? Don't answer that.

"Well now," he said in quite a different tone, getting back to what he supposed to be first principles. "Since you are capable of doing things for such extraordinary reasons, why should we break off now? Why can't we continue our little intrigue just as we have been doing?"

"Because now I'm in love," I said. "Now I should hate it."

"Ah yes," he said quickly, "that is what you must try to understand about yourself. You are not promiscuous. That is exactly what I want you to see. You waited twenty-one years before you accepted a lover——"

"You make it sound so——"

"*Please*. You waited twenty-one years before you accepted a lover and, whatever you may say now, you chose very carefully." He shifted in his chair and his hand flew to the immaculate knot on his tie. "My dear, permit me to know a bit more about you than you think. You are emotionally extremely deep and still not wholly awakened. Yes, it is true. One must go slowly. With someone as passionate as you there is always the danger of her going off the deep end, and you must not be allowed to go drifting from one affair to another. It would be disastrous for you."

It occurred to me that this was the second time that day

that I'd been cautioned against drifting. Three times and I'd get a parking ticket.

I glazed my eyes and thought, I'll just sit tight until he runs down. There was nothing else to do. I'm not listening, sang my mind—not listening, not listening.

"——like your American friend at the café today," he was saying. "I studied him very carefully. Yes, I was looking at you both for a long time before you saw me. Believe me, and do not simply put it down to the jealousy of a rival—taking into account his youth and good looks—I admit them, you see, though I find him almost *too* good-looking. I will tell you, and I am sure that this is true, there is something not quite right about him." He broke off abruptly, and then said, "Tell me, what does he do?"

"Well, he's a sort of student. Oh I don't know. He does lots of things. He was an actor when I first met him. Now he's a director, and writer I think. What's wrong with that?"

"Nothing. What does he do for money? Is he one of your rich Americans? I do not think so."

"I don't know."

"Considering that you are so much in love with him you know remarkably little about him," he pointed out.

I drew myself up. "We Americans do not think all that sort of thing important," I retorted huffily. "I don't know if he has any money or not, and frankly I don't care."

"Perhaps he wishes you to supply it?"

I appreciated that Teddy was one of those naturally, almost helplessly charming people who, when prevented from exploiting this charm, flip with chagrin and show you the other side of their coin. Nevertheless, I felt it the moment for my getaway.

"Look, I've got to go," I said and tried to suit action to word.

"Come, come, please. It is only my little joke. You Americans take things so seriously. I was only teasing you. Please tell me more about this Larry. I should very much like to know."

"Well, he's going to direct some plays at the new American

Theatre up around Denfert-Rochereau. And I'm going to be in them, I hope. I think he's probably a genius. I wouldn't expect you to understand him even if you did know him, which of course you don't, do you?"

Teddy was imperturbable. "He strikes me as a person who is not quite talented enough for his ambitions. And he is morally lazy."

"Oh really? How interesting. Now what makes you think that?"

"He did not rise either when you left the table or when you came back."

I suddenly felt afraid. There was no doubt that Teddy's life in the Diplomatic Corps had trained him well for these snap judgments. Looking back, I didn't know anyone he'd actually been wrong about—except of course me, but then as we know I am totally incomprehensible to everyone including myself.

"In any case," Teddy was going on, "getting back to you, what I have been meaning to say is that you need a steadying influence. A husband, even, and this boy is certainly not to be that to you. No, I do not think there is any danger of that happening. In fact, I should say that it is highly unlikely that he'll marry for a long time—if ever."

I was feeling terribly, terribly tired. Champagne has never done anything but depress me unutterably, and I now saw my hope of studying those plays that night slipping further and further away. It would have to be abandoned. The thing to do was get some sleep and start fresh in the morning.

"O.K., O.K.," I said. "What has all this got to do with me?"

He raised his eyebrows. "But everything! I have a plan, you see. I will tell you——" Only he didn't. He sucked in his breath as if holding it in readiness for the next big surprise sentence, and in spite of myself I leaned forward genuinely agog, and then he simply exhaled and smiled instead. It was a very animated smile, teeth flashing all over the place; the old charmer again.

"No," he said slowly, shaking his head and making his eyes

heavy-lidded and mysterious—I even think he might have taken a long drag from his cigarette; anyway, the effect was very corny. "I cannot tell you here. You must come back to my flat. Please. Only for a little moment. I promise I will not touch you. You have my word."

He had, at any rate, my curiosity, which is far more fatal. The sleeping beast was finally roused and I knew I would have to wait, standing by helplessly, while it rampaged around the town. That's my answer to the question what is your strongest emotion, if you ever want to ask me : Curiosity, old bean. Curiosity every time.

And so, wearing an aggrieved and, I hoped, slightly *black-mailed* expression on my face, and altogether putting up what must have been for him a most distressing display of reluctance, I eventually allowed myself to be persuaded back to his flat.

We made ready to go, and he signalled the waiter again with the enchanting little series of finger-snaps he'd used earlier on, and although he was none of these things I suddenly saw him as fat, ageing and silly. The phrase 'Old World' flashed through my mind. He was no match for my American callowness.

I caught him watching me as we rose and saw with surprise that there was real pain in his eyes and the tight set of his mouth. The moment was duly noted and marked down as savagely thrilling to my twisted soul. I think that was the first time I really felt like a woman. Hey, hey, I wanted to shout at the mad gay assemblage drinking their heads off around me, I must *have* something after all. What do you know about that?

But don't think I had it all my own way. Suddenly walking through that gilded cage of a Ritz bar, through all those exotic perfectly mated birds-of-paradise chirping away so harmoniously, I experienced a terrible pang of conscience. It seemed to me that all the women loved all their escorts, and all the escorts loved all their women, and if they were in groups of more than two they all loved one another or at the very least were extremely *well* pleased with one another.

That's what made me feel sad and guilty all of a sudden. The men were smooth and worldly and successful and happy and they all looked so much like Teddy. These were the people he should be having witty, elliptical, sexy conversations with, instead of wasting his time with a sulking, skulking, bad-tempered and very recent schoolgirl. I mean when *their* love affairs were over they would have the sense and savoir-faire to let each other down so gently they'd never even feel the bump while I—Oh Christ. What an impossible situation.

And then I became impatient. It was all too ludicrous, for God's sake, *I* should have been the abandoned one. I mean I was the one seduced, I was the virgin wasn't I? It shouldn't have been me trying to wiggle off the hook. Surely it was up to Teddy to do the discarding after he'd taken my 'all'. I'd read enough books and listened to enough college girls moaning in the Spring to know that. Hourly I should have expected the axe.

There is a terrific movie which gets shown a lot around Art cinemas, even though it's a very old one, and I always try to see it if I can. It's called "The Scoundrel", and it has Noël Coward in it as this great Wolf. At one point when his latest victim comes round and begs him on her knees to take her back, he removes the boutonnière from the lapel of his dinner-jacket and murmuring Forgive-me-my-dear-for-stooping-to-symbolism, he tosses the flower into his highball and drowns it with a squirt of the soda-syphon. So you know what I mean? *That's* the sort of thing I brought myself up on. I mean that's more like it.

I mean how *can* Life be so contrary to—never mind Art —just to general information and what's called Common Knowledge? And how the devil did our rôles get reversed like this, with me playing the Fatale and he the . . . well, whatever you call it. I don't know. It was too much for me.

And what was this plan all about? Was I meant to supplant the old mistress in the set-up of his hierarchy—or to open another branch of the establishment?

Lost in our separate thoughts, we hardly talked to each other on the way back.

Considering the amount of time I had spent there on and off for about three months, it is amazing that I have practically no recollection at all of Teddy's flat. It wasn't his real home, you see. It was just a very small *pied-à-terre*, and he kept it of course for only one reason. Frightfully suave, and mature, and expensive, and I admit to having been breathlessly impressed by it at first. But after a while I found that if I ever thought about it for long it always made me laugh. I wonder what there is about deception, I suppose I mean discretion (do I?), when it gets organized to the hilt like that, that always makes me laugh?

Anyway this Organization was just off the Rue de Rivoli and do you know I can't even remember the name of the street? Let's see, as you turn off the Rue de Rivoli first there is the American Embassy (where I was later to spend so many frenzied hours), then—hah—wait a minute, it's all coming back with a whoosh . . . the Rue Boissy d'Anglas, of course! It was on the second floor and it had a large window that looked out on to the street. Only there wasn't much to look out at. There wasn't much to look in at, either, for that matter. It was businesslike as hell. It consisted of two rooms, the main one and a tiny kitchenette leading off it. The main room had a dining-room table, a large red leather sofa, a few shelves for a very few books, a phonograph for a very few records, a radio, a coffee-table, a drink-cabinet— and a divan. Tout confort. Stripped for action and strictly anonymous.

We arrived in full sail, Teddy fumbling with every latchkey in sight and me racing from minuterie to minuterie to keep the stairs in a blaze of 40-watt bulbs. Even when we got inside I didn't stop. I turned on every light I could find (there weren't very many) and then headed straight for the sofa. I didn't sit in it, though. I sat primly on one of the arms and refused a drink. Also I began tapping my feet.

"Do you mind if I have a drink myself?" he asked.

I nodded assent.

At long last he stood before me, his drink in hand and a certain look on his face. With his free hand he reached for mine. It was so entirely *expected* (even though he had promised not to touch me), that I just lost my head. I jumped up and with a sudden movement knocked the drink out of his hand. I'd been saying to myself poise, baby, poise, all this while, but I simply couldn't help it. I really frightened us both.

"Don't touch me!" I said.

"I am sorry." This very humbly.

I remember all this part so very clearly. And I remember a little later wondering why things always turn out to be diametrically opposed to what you expect them to be. It's no good even trying to predict what this opposite will be because it always fools you and turns out to be the opposite of *that*, if you see what I mean. If you think this is geometrically impossible all I can say is that you don't know my life.

I mean never in a million years could I have worked out what he was going to say to me next. There was his glass lying on the floor, the drink seeping into the carpet. He bent down to pick it up and he noticed an ice-cube on the carpet and he picked that up as well. He looked at it. He started to put it into the empty glass, but some threads from the carpet had stuck to it and I could see him deciding not to. So he just held it in one of his hands. And he sighed.

"It is most difficult," he began, and then squared his shoulders resolutely. "Very well. This is my plan. It is that I wish to marry you. That is all. Will you marry me, Sally Jay?" He was still holding on to that ice-cube. It must have been freezing his hand off. God, I can see that ice-cube perfectly, carpet-hairs and all.

"Howling hailstones!" I exclaimed. I let that out quite unconsciously. He really had knocked me for a loop. "But what about your *wife*?" I asked when I could.

"I haven't got one," he said.

"You haven't got one." The room was spinning. "What d'you *mean*, you haven't got a wife?" What did he mean, he didn't have a wife? He probably didn't have a mistress either.

"Listen, Teddy, you said you had one. You definitely said

you did. You *must* have one." I was beside myself. Even he was taken aback at my vehemence.

"Yes, I had one. But she is gone."

"What happened to her? Where *is* she?" I accused him. I was ready to try him for murder.

"She left me." He put the ice-cube into the glass and the glass on to the coffee-table and sat down heavily. "She left me about three weeks ago," he continued. "She has gone back to Rome. She will try to get an annulment. I think she may be able to. We have not been able to have children."

When the smoke cleared away and I was getting used to yet another one of the thousand natural shocks that flesh is heir to, there was a new Teddy sitting there beside me—a new Alfredo if you like. This was the first time in all the while I'd known him that he was confiding in me instead of elaborately concealing his private life, and the revelations in those few words changed everything. Suddenly I remembered the desperate look he'd given me that morning when I joshed him about successfully leading three lives. The homme fatal, fond and foolish as the pose had been from time to time, was gone forever; the bourgeois manqué sat firmly in his place. Looking at him there I knew I would never again see the foolish philanderer; the conscious charmer. Instead he had become permanently one half of a *family*. I saw them together, he and his wife, round a dinner table: silent, dreary and childless.

I tried to pity him. It was just about the saddest thing on earth really, and certainly I should have shown some compassion. But there is no point in telling this at all if I don't tell the truth, and the truth was that now that I felt I *completely* understood him, I completely despised him. From my standpoint what he had just told me was just about the worst thing he could have said to me. The main trouble with being an homme fatal, the really, *really* crux of the matter was one was so entirely dependent on every single prop. Take one away and the whole structure collapses like a house of cards. If his *wife* doesn't want him, *I* certainly don't, was my way of putting it.

54

I think he actually had forgotten me for the moment, thinking about her, for he seemed a long way away when I next spoke.

"What about your mistress?" I had asked.

"Yes," he said nodding vaguely, a million miles away.

"Your mistress. Why don't you marry her?"

He shook his head. "She is too old," he said. "It is too late for her to have children."

Crash went another prop. Boy, this really wasn't one of his days. He just couldn't put a foot right. It was a situation all too familiar to me, this business of setting off on the wrong foot and doggedly remaining there. Only I'd never watched it from the outside before. It was fascinating. Poor bastard, it should have made me want to reach out and yank him on to the other foot. It should have given me a fellow-feeling. But it didn't.

Eventually we both became aware that I hadn't answered his original question. I think we both knew the answer. It was just a matter of how I was going to phrase it.

Basically I am a Space person, especially when up against it, and now I began hopping all over the room from corner to corner.

"Well," I said finally, over by the bookshelves. "Well, I'm awfully sorry to hear about all this—I mean your——" I was over by the window by now. "I mean I didn't dream that you'd be so easily. . ." Back to the mantel. "Oh, hell. Of course I can't marry you. It never occurred to me you'd ever want to. I just thought you'd be the ideal teacher to—you know, the ideal person to sharpen the old teeth on," I finished, drifting back to the arm of the sofa and bending over him to see if he understood.

"I see," he murmured sadly into the floor. "I see. You were using me."

"Hey, do you know that's just what I *thought* you'd say?" I exclaimed excitedly.

"Ah, so?" This didn't cheer him up any.

"But we were using each other!" I said triumphantly.

55

At this he turned and looked up at me shrewdly. "Using each other," he mused. Suddenly his manner changed. It became brisk, businesslike and determined.

"Yes, that is it, of course," he said, and he swung three-quarters round and crushed out his cigarette.

"Now see here, Miss Gorce—" he began masterfully, but instantly realized he would be spoiling his effect by having to look up at me on that sofa-arm. Abandoning this position forthwith he began complaining about my name. "Gorce," he said, staring into the middle distance and shaking his head in wonder. "Gorce! You Americans. . ." (People really *do* say You Americans, by the way.) "Nevertheless, charming, enchanting Miss Gorce, please do not be offended if I tell you that you still have much to learn. You may find it amusing now, at your age in life, to be this—this—ragamuffin—but it will not always be so. You will understand what I mean when I take you to Florence to meet my family. You should know that we are one of the oldest families there—and one of the proudest. Ah yes—I know you Americans like to sneer at background, but wait—after you are among us for a while you will soon discover how barbaric most of your compatriots will appear to you, and you will realize how important it is. That is something I can do for you."

"Why that's great, man," I said. "That sounds just great. But why pick on li'l ole me?"

"Because you are not stupid," he replied gravely. "You can learn. You could become a remarkable woman some day. And you are young and obviously healthy. I am sure I do not have to tell you how proud I am as well of the name and how I wish to see it continued."

I don't know why, but somehow that gave me pause. "Tell me something," I asked him, "tell me exactly how we would live. This isn't just idle curiosity. It's difficult to explain, but I just somehow feel that I never really *have* lived; that I never really will live—exist or whatever—in the sense that other people do. It drives me crazy. I was terribly aware of it all those nights waiting for you in the Ritz bar looking around at what seemed to be real grown-up lives. I just find everybody else's life surrounded by plate-glass. I mean I'd like to break through it just once and actually touch one."

He smiled. "Well, my dear, I am afraid those lives at the Ritz will have to remain under plate-glass for a while. You see, most of the money was my wife's. As you may know, the Diplomatic Service does not pay very well even in its highest positions. Oh, we shouldn't starve. I have good prospects and good contacts, while you as an American would be invaluable should we be transferred over there. An excellent post. The living-allowance is double that of any other place. And you will have some money of your own, of course, will you not? Surely this uncle of yours will supply you with the equivalent of what we call in Europe a dowry?" He said this perfectly seriously, and then broke off, puzzled to find me roaring with laughter.

I howled and howled. In fact, I fell off the arm and into the sofa almost on top of him. "Oh, no, no, no," I gasped. "This is too much."

"What is it?" he asked. He was getting worried.

I tried to tell him three times and each time I collapsed. I finally pulled myself together.

"Please forgive me, but I've never had to change my mind so often at such short notice in my whole life. It's quite breath-taking. You see, first I thought you wanted my body, then I thought you wanted my love, then my *life* even, happily-ever-after and all that sort of thing, and now it turns out it is merely my money. Oh, Teddy, darling, thank you, thank you." I was practically sobbing.

"For what?" he asked patiently.

"For restoring my cynicism. I was too young to lose it."

He laughed at that and I laughed. We both laughed. We shared a moment of mutual omniscience; we had each other's number.

"Delicious," he murmured. "My dear, you are delicious. There is no one quite like you." And we smiled at each other.

Now here is what gets me. With anybody else I know, it

would have all ended in a lot of civilized laughter and exchanges of everlasting friendships. But not with me. I may be carping but I don't seem to be let off anything; if a bad time is to be had, I *have* it.

So what happened was, he stood up and took me by the shoulders and the next thing I knew, instead of being chastely kissed on the forehead and decorously wished a good night, I was being savagely pressed against his chest and peremptorily ordered to get into bed.

"Hey, wait a minute," I protested. "Now just take it easy——" And in less time than it takes to tell we were at it tooth and claw. Or rather I was at it tooth and claw. He was growing violent and it was becoming harder and harder to defend myself. The strange thing was that we were still more or less *laughing* through all this, until suddenly as his hand, ice-cold like that damned ice-cube, slid under my dress, I panicked and bit him very hard on the nearest available piece of flesh. It turned out to be his ear.

To my amazement, and no doubt his credit, he didn't cry out in pain. He fell softly against me for a moment, his arms limp at his side, and then he straightened up. He appeared to be thinking, at least that's what I could have sworn, but before I knew what was happening he had struck me across the face. Then, cool as a cucumber, he walked towards the door and held it open for me.

I didn't quite see why I, who had done nothing wrong, so to speak, who at any rate most certainly hadn't started all this, should wind up crushed and dishevelled, with a torn dress, a burning cheek and lipstick all over my face, while he, the real culprit, was suavely ushering me out, and I strove to correct this injustice.

"Now that you're free," I said on my way to the door, "you must come to America. I'm sure you can fortune-hunt on a much larger scale there than you've been able to over here. Only you'd better start quickly before you turn into just another dirty old man."

The blow commonly described as below the belt really went home. "You little slut, get out," he shouted, his face all awry, "and take care. Nobody insults me like that and gets away with it. You will see. I can promise you."

With these words singing in my ears as I felt my way down the stairs, too discouraged to find the minuteries, I reflected wearily that it was not easy to be a Woman in these stirring times. I said it then and I say it now : it just isn't our century

# CHAPTER FOUR

AFTER ALL THAT, getting down to work seemed like a pretty good idea.

Frankly, there didn't seem to be too much else left to do. "Fame is the spur," I kept saying to myself, "that the something something doth raise, dot, dot, to scorn delights and live laborious days," though not entirely truthfully, for I knew that the thought of Larry was as much a spur to me as fame.

The day my laundry came back, I took out all my clothes and spread them around the room for Judy and me to look at. I was determined that for once, for just once in my life, when I went to those readings, I would be wearing the 'right' thing. The right thing in this case had to be something general; something that wouldn't type me. To my chagrin, I found all my clothes stubbornly resisting this desired neutrality, splitting themselves resolutely up into three categories : Tyrolean Peasant, Bar Girl, and Dreaded Librarian. It looked hopeless. Fortunately, I did have a black cotton skirt, and Judy, by some coincidence, had a black cotton blouse with a white collar. So, the problem at last solved, I climbed happily into the outfit, and pranced off in the direction of the theatre.

I had assumed the readings to have started the week before. My strategy was to give them seven days grace to stew around in, and then, very over-the-shoulder, off-the-shoulder, daintily treading all over everybody's toes, in I would waft, impress the hell out of them, and win the day. But when I got to the theatre, it turned out, quite unexpectedly, to be empty. I finally managed to uncover one of those mysterious old women, who inhabit deserted buildings in France like mice, and who, under my relentless inquisition, was forced to confess, not only that it was a theatre, but that it was going to open up soon for some company to begin its casting. Wrenching the exact day and time from her unwilling lips, I returned chez moi, carefully hung up my neutral clothes to preserve them, and held my breath for three days.

And so it came about, that, instead of drifting over to the theatre in that casual off-handed manner planned, I was actually camping on its doorstep when Larry arrived. And a good thing too. The competition was fierce.

I won't drag you through the quarter-finals, the semi-finals and the finals. The only relevant question is, did I or didn't I. And the answer, in a word, is Yes! In two words really, Yes, Yes! Because I read so brilliantly, not to say inspiredly, that I came out with *two* rôles. In the first, the Saroyan one, a waif who sweeps out the jail, and in the second, the Williams one, a batty prostitute.

"We'll get you a wig to wear for the first one," said Larry, "but I want you to use your own hair, or whatever that stuff is you've got on the top of your head now, for the other, Pinkie." Then he said, quite seriously, "You more than surprise me, screwball. I had no idea you were good."

I could have died of happiness. I went back to Montparnasse and flung myself into a celebration which lasted two nights and from which it took me three days to recover.

The night before we went into rehearsal, I was determined to get to bed early. When I got into my bath, I was singing. Gradually, deliciously, I could feel myself relaxing. In a sudsy dream I floated off, unknitting, unknotting, unravelling. I was so sleepy I could hardly put my pyjamas on and get into bed. I curled up into the pillows and was just dozing off when I noticed that the script that we were going to start off with was by the bedside table. I thought it might be a good idea to have one last look at it, making a few notes along the way if necessary. Five seconds later, I was crawling under the desk looking for my pencil. When I retrieved it, I saw that it was broken. I tried using my eyebrow pencil, but it was impossible to read my writing. I finally·got a razor blade, sharpened the pencil, popped back into bed again, and re-curled myself into the pillows. The script was opened, the pencil poised.

All at once I rolled over on to my side. For no reason at all, I was in the middle of a black depression. I turned off the lights and lay back in the darkness, tired but wide awake, sleepy but unsleepy, too sleepy to read, not sleepy enough to sleep, my eyelids pinned back from my eyes, my spine rigid. I remained like this for I don't know how long until I be-came aware of something else that was furthering my dis-comfort. I was beginning to be hungry. In no time at all, I was ravenous. Cursing myself for having forgotten to eat supper, I turned on the lights and looked at my clock. One o'clock in the morning. This made me at once more hungry and more tired. The hunger won. I rolled up my pyjama-legs, pinning them with the safety pins I found on a skirt, put on my raincoat and went out.

At the corner of my street I could see the lights of the new nightclub that Shugie Jackson, the coloured singer, had just opened. She was a friend of mine and I was dying to see what it was like inside. Sternly I drove myself past it, past the statue of Balzac in his bathrobe (presumably unable to sleep either), past the Rotonde where I could hear the strains of the Hard Core at their carousing. I bunched my fists into my pockets and dashed across the street. At last safely past the other temptations of Dôme and Coupole, I came upon a tiny, steamy, all-night café which still had up its last year's decora-tions. Snowballs, Santa Clauses and champagne bottles were painted on the glass doors and windows in honour of their New Year's Eve Réveillon and to commemorate the Quatorze Juillet, red, white and blue streamers hung from the light fixtures on the ceiling. The joint, even at this late hour, was jumping. I sat down at one of the few empty tables, and ordered a hot chocolate and a croque-monsieur, reflecting moodily that cheese would probably give me bad dreams if I ever did get to sleep. Slowly, I realized that my table was becoming the focal point of attention. A lot of men began hovering around, looking me over rather carefully, not to say boldly. Two of them came right over and thrust cigarettes at me. It was the way they were *thrust*, rather than offered, that suddenly made me come to.

When the third man strode up, I told him to go to hell and leave me alone. Instead, he sat down next to me and asked me what I thought I was doing there in that case and a lot of other stuff which, thank goodness, my limited knowledge of argot prevented me from understanding. Desperately, I looked around for help. Everyone was minding his own business. I saw that there wasn't another woman at a table who wasn't a prostitute. My friend sat on, glowering at me suspiciously. Instinctively, my hand flew up to my coat collar. I clutched it close to me protectively. When I discovered that it was already buttoned, I tore my hand away in anger and the button, of course, came away. So the coat flew open and there I was—unmasked in my striped pyjamas. Oh *killing* stuff really, haw, haw, haw. That's what I mean about being appropriately dressed. My clothes. I mean, is it *worth it*? I ask myself.

The old boy at last had my number. "Merde, ces fous Americains," he mumbled to himself disgustedly, and spat on the floor. Then he left. But I stuck it out. As a point of honour, and also because I was starving. I assumed, in turn, my most haughtily aristocratic, my most toothily intellectual, and finally, my just plain most humble expressions. None of them made the slightest difference. I was still the greatest phoney of them all—the unavailable prostitute.

In an atmosphere of open hostility, I gobbled up my sandwich and hot chocolate as fast as I could; the hot chocolate burning my tongue, a revelation burning my soul. I had always assumed that a certain sense of *identity* would be strong enough within me to communicate itself to others. I now saw this assumption was false. Tout simplement, in a tarts' bar, I looked like a tart. I tried to cheer myself up by thinking that after all this was really a very good thing for an actress. But it was depressing, anyway. Not so much the thing of looking like a prostitute. I mean, except for the inconvenience of the moment, I found *that* rather thrilling, but the whole episode was forcing me to remember something that I'm always trying to forget and that is, that in a *library* as well, I'm always being taken for a librarian. No kidding. My last Christmas in New York, I had an English paper to write over the vacation, and there was this public library I used to go to, and no matter *where* I sat, people were always coming up to me and asking me where such and such a book was. They were furious too, when I didn't know. It was eerie. I began to feel that I actually *was* a librarian. The wood growing into my soul and stuff. I suppose I am rather an intellectual.

I left the café and walked down the empty street, keeping close to the buildings, hiding in their shadows. I didn't want any more trouble.

In the hush of the night, I reached the Dôme, dark, chill, and still, tucked away for the night. The chairs and tables were piled up against the entrance, and the awning folded away; they had literally rolled up the sidewalks. So that's what it meant, I thought, to roll up the sidewalks. I began turning this over in my mind, again and again, in that obsessive way that told me sleep was near, when all at once two quarrelling voices pierced the air.

"Like hell I will !"

"Like hell you will ! You'll do exactly what I tell you."

"Go —— yourself." A female voice, American and very sullen. I hadn't heard the phrase since I left college.

"Thanks, I'd love to. Just tell me how," was the snappy comeback : as good as any, it seemed to me. I made a note of it.

The footsteps kept approaching. They would be upon me any moment. I cowered behind the nearest pyramid of chairs, and from this vantage point, watched the night cough up its second revelation. . .

There under the light of the street lamps, the disembodied voices revealed themselves as belonging to Larry—Larry and a girl. I held my breath, and crept further into the chairs.

64

When I peered out again, the girl was leaning against a chestnut-tree, swaying a little and tugging at something around her neck. As the necklace broke and the pearls, catching the light, went spilling on to the pavement, bouncing along the street and into the grating around the chestnut-tree, she began giggling wildly; it was an absolutely frightening sound. She made no attempt to recover her pearls.

"Let 'em go, let 'em go," she quavered through her giggles. "Girl I shared the cabin with coming over said never, never wear pearls when you travel. Said pearls are for tears. Well, I'm travelling, you bastard. I'm travelling . . ." and the giggles turned to sobs.

Larry was tender, comforting her. "There now. Please. That's a good kid. Now, baby, don't upset yourself. Wait a minute." He disappeared out of my sight, on all fours, I imagined looking for the pearls. "There now," he said after a while. "That's all I can find now. Come along. Let's get some sleep. You want to look your best when you meet those people tomorrow."

She jerked away from him. "Let's get it straight once and for all, you bastard. I'm not working while I'm over here."

She had moved further away from him, into the light, and now I got my first good look at her face. It was another jolt. A big one. To my astonishment the girl with Larry was that ravishing model Lila, the one that was always coming up to visit him on the week-ends in Summer Stock. She didn't look very ravishing just then, though, out there in the lamplight at three in the morning, tear-stained and so much the worse for liquor. She looked a mess, in fact. I felt sorry for her. She seemed so sad and a long way from home.

"Be your age," Larry was saying. "You can't stay in Europe without working, who do you think I am? And it's not so easy to *get* work over here. Believe me. I worked damn hard to get these people interested in you. How can you run out like that? I tell you there are hundreds of good-looking babes around. American too. It's coals to Newcastle."

"I came to see some bright lights," she whimpered. "Now that I've got this chance to go to Biarritz, I'm going whether you come or not. It's all paid for. This guy . . . Aw Larry, I'm young. I just want to have some fun."

"O.K. I give up. Go to Biarritz, for Christ's sake and have fun. You manage your own life, you do it so well. You'll end up back in Sheldon, Iowa. You'll end up in the gutter. I don't care. But don't come back to me. I've tried to straighten you out for the last time. Come on. I'll take you back to your hotel." He began to look for a cab along the boulevard.

She followed him. "Oh baby, don't be angry," I heard her say. "You're not jealous?"

"Jealous, no; just sore that I wasted all this time and trouble."

"I'll be back in a month."

He'd found a cab by then. "Don't tell me about it. I've washed my hands of you. Hurry up, get in."

"Don't bother, I'll find my own way."

"Oh, get in," he said wearily, "you don't even know how to pronounce the name of your hotel."

I shut my eyes, and when I opened them again, the cab had gone. I stayed crouched there for a while, trying to make sense out of the little slice of life I'd just witnessed. But I couldn't. I just couldn't dig the relationship, for one thing. Anyway, she was off to Biarritz, so I wouldn't have to worry about it for a whole month. Meanwhile. . .

Making sure the coast was clear, I dodged back to my hotel. I was dead tired and fell immediately into a dreamless sleep.

# CHAPTER FIVE

RETURNING FROM REHEARSALS one evening about two weeks later, I arrived in my room just in time to catch the telephone ringing. There at the other end, purring away into my receiver, fur all over his smile, was Teddy Visconti—God rot his blackened heart, the Machiavellian Monster. Only of course I didn't know any of this at the time. All I knew then was that I had to think for a moment to remember who he was.

I was rather cool to Teddy at first. I hadn't recalled our previous encounter with much pleasure, and I couldn't imagine ever really wanting to see him again. Systematically he set to work disarming me. Beginning with his congratulations on my good fortune (he'd read an item about the American Theatre in the *Herald-Tribune*), and his best wishes for my success, he went on to sweep the floor with himself for his disgraceful, unspeakable and totally unjustified behaviour at our last meeting. By the time he had waltzed into a heady tirade on the saintliness of allowing bygones to be bygones and finished up with a passionate proposal of eternal devotion (along strictly platonic lines), I was pretty well softened up.

But the *main* purpose of his call, said our wily old gift-bearing Greek, sailing to his climax, the main purpose was to wonder whether we, that is *both* of us, Larry and myself *of course*, would be kind enough to allow him to arrange a small dinner-party in our honour that Saturday—a sort of send-off to our joint venture. It was, in fact, simply the only way he could think up to secure my forgiveness. I couldn't refuse—could I? It would be too unkind. He would be giving it at his old flat, the one I knew in the Boissy d'Anglas—he was moving out, it held too many memories for him, but he had specially secured the landlord's permission to stay on that week-end if he had the party. He knew that the whole thing was ridiculously sentimental, of course, but that was the way he was, and what could he do? My head was spinning by now from all this rich, powerful prose, and apart from everything else I looked forward to the chance of spending an evening with Larry on a basis other than professional. So into the trap I marched, eyes shining, mouth open, ears flapping. I do remember thinking it all a bit odd, somehow, after I'd hung up. That's the story of my life. Someone's behaviour strikes me as a bit odd and the next thing I know all hell breaks loose. I don't always understand other people's motives. I will repeat that for my own benefit, if you don't mind. I don't always understand other people's motives. I wonder why? I'm very bright really. For instance, Doctor Long gave me an A in Seventeenth Centch. Eng. Poetry at college, and he was known to be one of the toughest professors we had. He'd been teaching there for eight years, and he'd never given anyone above a B plus. But he gave me an A. A straight A too—not minus.

"So *that's* the plot," said Larry when I told him on our way over to the party exactly who Teddy was. "I'll be damned. You had me thinking this was some official diplomatic function we were gracing. Some project of the Italian Government. I don't know what I thought. . ." He paused for a moment to consider, crossed his legs, jiggled his foot and sent the air hissing through his teeth. It made him seem more like a steam-engine than ever. "Come clean, Gorce," he said finally. "I smell a rat here somewhere. I remember this type Visconti. He's the one you were going to die without—isn't he? So what am *I* doing here? Maybe some kind of bait? Come on, you can level with me. Who am *I*? The jealous rival? Heavy father? Let's have it."

His analysis of the situation was so staggeringly wrong, I could only shake my head in wonder. I had been terrifically excited when Larry accepted the invitation. I had counted on the sight of an impressive discarded lover like Teddy, in an atmosphere drenched and scorched with his hopeless passion, to stimulate Larry's interest in me. I wore for the occasion an evening-dress limp with sophistication, and an expression to match—or so I hoped.

"As long as he doesn't decide to take a pot-shot at me," Larry went on. "These Corsican bandits are a hot-blooded bunch, you know. They don't stand for no messin' around with their wimmenfolk."

"Larry, you haven't the faintest idea what you're talking about. In the first place he's a Florentine nobleman, not a Chicago gangster. In the second place I swear there is absolutely *nothing* between Teddy and myself any more. It's all over. I haven't even seen him for a month. Poor thing," I sighed gently, reminiscently, trying to slip us into the mood. "I'm afraid he didn't take it very well when I threw him over. As a matter of fact it all happened on the very day that I ran into you at the Dupont—it just—just . . ." And I completely lost track of what I was going to say. Somehow the word 'Dupont' made the whole incident with Larry come flooding back, and I simply couldn't follow any other train of thought. "What were we talking about?" I had to ask. He was waiting for me to go on.

"This man you call Teddy."

"Oh. Well forget it. Anyway, I took your advice, didn't I?"

"My advice?"

"Yes. Stay away from married men, you said. Except as it turns out, he's not married now—although he *was*. He wanted to marry me in fact. It's all very complicated. Look. He just called me up a couple of days ago out of the blue and asked us both to dinner. That's all. Really. I don't know why. I guess he was just being nice." We had arrived.

"I wonder," said Larry suspiciously as we got out of the taxi. That's what kills me. *He* was the suspicious one, not me.

Teddy had told me it was to be a party of six. He had not lied. Six we were. Six exactly. I wonder if I can give you the picture.

The first thing that loomed into view, almost knocking

Teddy down in his rush to get at me, was my loathsome cousin John Roger Gorce. John was a real, earnest, enthusiastic, gee-whiz tail-wagging prig of an American, with the shortest crew-cut and the thickest horn-rims ever to accompany their owner through four ceaselessly interrogating years of Harvard. Behind these spectacles blinked eyes that gawped and stared insensitively at anything not absolutely commonplace to the right side of the five-block area on which he had built his house in Wichita, Kansas.

He was blocking the passageway now, jamming us up against the door.

"Hee-Haw! Hee-Haw!" he bellowed suddenly into my face, his hands flapping by his ears, his nose twitching, his large teeth thrust forward in a really startlingly successful donkey imitation. "Hee-Haw!"

Larry, caught off guard by this bizarre salute, cringed against the door. But I had been tensed for it. It had a very simple, very embarrassing explanation. It was the way John used to make me laugh when I was three and he was eight. Since then it had become his inevitable, unvarying greeting to me whenever I was unlucky enough to get within braying distance. Now he folded his arms and rocked back and forth in satisfaction. He wasn't smiling. He didn't have to *smile* to convey his self-satisfaction. He didn't have to do anything.

"Well, S. J.," he said, addressing me quietly and firmly and almost as an equal, "guess this must be a pretty good surprise for you, what say gal?" He was sort of rubbing his back against the wall as he spoke, making himself more comfortable, savouring his triumph. Drearily I conceded defeat. It was true that he was probably the one and only person in the whole world that I would wish at all times and in all places (and especially then) to avoid, but short of magic this was at the moment impossible. The thing that got me though —the thing that really, really got me was that revolting appellation 'S. J.'. I mean that beat everything, that did. It just showed you; the joke was supposed to be on *him* for Christ's sake. It too had infantile origins. Even as a little boy, John had been so impressed by the J. P.s and P. T.s and

F. D. R.s by which the Big Wheels were designated in newspapers, that he took to initialling his baby cousin, both in his private conversations with her, and in his references to her with others, simply because this made him feel that he actually was hitting it off with some hot-shot—tycoon to tycoon. He confessed this one day to his father, quite matter-of-factly, almost proudly, and Big John, who had always got a lot of simple-minded pleasure from the tiny monster he'd produced, when he was able to stop laughing and pick himself up off the floor, told it at once around the family. In no time it became the family joke. Only John never saw anything funny about it. Nor was he in the least abashed by its constant re-telling. Nor, dammit, did he ever stop initialling me.

"Why John, what on earth are you doing here?" I asked him finally. And actually I was quite curious to know. The last time I'd been trapped by him, I'd been let in on what he really thought of hitherto responsible American Youth high-tailing it out of the States first chance they got, wasting their time bumming around Europe. He thought it was darned *disheartening*. Where were we going to get our key-thinking elite from anyway? He thought *they* ought to be forming the core of our key-thinking elite. He thought *they* should be solving the vital post-war social and economic problems of the Civic Community, not leaving it in the hands of people without the benefit of the fine up-to-date basic training the American University was now offering its students in its contemporary curricula. That was what he thought.

His brow puckered earnestly at my question. "I had a helluva wrestle with my soul, S. J., to see if I *should* take this trip," he confessed frankly, "but I finally decided that the Rag really did need some decent on-the-spot reporting of just how Uncle Sam is letting all his good grey taxpayers' money be spent over here." That was what he'd decided.

Good old John Roger (the Roger was for our mutual uncle, the really rich one), I swear I don't know where he got it all from. His father, except for his over-developed sense of humour, was a terrific guy. He ran a newspaper in St. Louis, and as part of his tireless practical joking (or maybe just to

get young John off his neck), had bought him, upon graduation, a tiny toy newspaper in Wichita to play with. I am sure
its daily editorials kept Big John floor-bound and howling, but
John junior, as is the case with so many of our great men, had
no sense of humour at all, and the Wichita Wrangle, or
whatever it was called, gave him a Mission along with his
folie de grandeur.

"Course," he went on, not giving us an inch more space to
breathe in up there against the door, "I wouldn't have dreamt
of coming if this important Conference weren't getting under
way. I know darned well I haven't given myself very long in
these three weeks to cover it—not anything commensurate
with its importance—but it's all I'm going to be able to spare.
Hell . . ." he let out a sharp little staccato bark to warn
me of the approaching joke, ". . . somebody's got to mind the
store back home." You could see his mind suddenly four
thousand miles away, worrying over some vital, burning
domestic issue—like the contraceptives that had been turning
up recently in the bomb-proof shelters of that five-block
area. . .

"Anyhoo," he shook himself and honoured us again with
his complete presence, "anyhoo, when we went for briefing
last week at a meeting of the Soil Erosion Committee of the
ACFEA. . ."

"The *what*?"

John was always very patient with me.

"The Agricultural Commission for European Aid has been
meeting for the past two weeks right here under your very nose,
for heaven's sake, S. J.," he explained to me, not unkindly,
"and the problems of Kansas as you know being mainly agricultural, naturally my Rag's main interest is going to be
focused on the developments of this project. Anyhoo—at this
particular meeting there was a question I wanted to ask—I
wasn't quite sure of the protocol, so I introduced myself . . ."
(John was always wanting to ask questions and introduce
himself. He couldn't even go to the men's room of a Penn-
sylvania Railroad coach without asking a question and intro-
ducing himself. He was a real man from Mars, that boy, he

even looked like one.) ". . . so I introduced myself to the person sitting on my left. And who should it be but Señor Visconti here." He turned to indicate who he meant, at last acknowledging the presence of someone else in the room. "He's been terribly helpful to me ever since—and darned if he didn't know my baby cousin—so—well, hell, here we are! Say, nobody in America seems to have your correct address . . ." a slight frown clouded his smooth brow at the thought of such inefficiency.

"I moved," I said, pushing him aside (we'd have been there all night if I hadn't), and then, composing myself, I introduced Larry to John; Larry to Teddy; and much to her surprise, Larry to John's wife, who now came drifting towards us.

I think Dody Gorce was *always* greatly surprised at each new discovery of her separate identity. Not one of those wives who have to glance spasmodically at their husbands before speaking; she simply never took her eyes off him at all if she could help it. When politeness demanded she tear herself away to acknowledge an introduction, she wasted no time in returning to her permanent resting-place.

"Mais c'est formidable ces deux cousins, n'est-ce pas? On voit immédiatement la ressemblance!" shrilled a voice behind us and, swinging around in a fury to confront whoever had delivered this malicious slander, I got my first look at the Contessa.

What with one thing and another I was to see quite a lot of this woman, but I'll be damned if I can tell you to this day much about her. For instance, I haven't the slightest idea what her name was or her nationality for that matter. (She could have been German or Austrian or Liechtensteinian for all I knew.) The reason for this was that apart from 'Hello' and 'Goodbye' she never at any time addressed a single other word in my direction, and she wouldn't if I met her now, I'll bet. It was a matter of the strictest principle with her never to talk to a woman younger than herself.

In describing her, on the one hand, and being completely, absolutely, scrupulously, *unnecessarily* fair, one couldn't give her more than forty-two years of age, nor less than a pleasant face, a rosy complexion, and a good though rather full-blown figure. Handsome I suppose her friends would call her. And maybe not only her friends. Her best feature was her butter-blonde hair which she wore short, parted low and softly waving. She knew how to dress. She had on something stark and simple, and made up for it by plastering the rest of herself with plenty of those devastating Ritz jewels. She was a sort of female Teddy—well-cared-for in that mature European way—with a faint, only faint suggestion of outdoors—of going ski-ing, rather than ski-ing : a man's woman; almost a man's man, really, with all her hearty camaraderie. A tough cookie, a real oeuf dur. I remember somebody once very carefully explaining to me about her title, a Holy Roman Empire one, they said, transmitted only through the female line, and I remember thinking then how perfectly this accounted for her Amazonian tactics.

If you want to know what I really thought of her—I thought she was a great, affected, mindless, maudlin, screeching cow. And Christ! was she sure of herself. She took meeting *me* quietly enough (there was a dreadful, *dreadful* moment I never want to think about again when John jogged me and stage-whispered an impressed *"Contessa"* for everybody's benefit), but, boy, she nearly went out of her mind when she came to Larry. The minute Teddy got his *name* out her head flew back and her eyes started from their sockets. You would have thought she'd been waiting all her life for this chance. She wheeled on Teddy, clutching her priceless pearls as if to fling them to the ground in challenge, and every inch of her body stiffened with disbelief. Then the dam burst and she began babbling in some long-forgotten English tongue.

"But I refuse to believe this, Teddy, you frightful rascal. What a leg-pull I must say ! This chap Larry Keevil? Don't be daft. I never heard such nonsense. I shan't listen to another word. No really I shan't."

"Why nonsense?" asked Larry, really bewildered.

"But you are far too young," she murmured, suddenly all soft and wondering. It was like watching an early Dietrich film. "I had heard you were a young chap—everyone *comments* that—but as young as this? Well, *really*. You are a brave one, oh yes you are, bringing us here the English-speaking Theatre in its original! One is frightfully interested in these things—there has always been such a need for it. And such failures. I could tell you—but they lacked vitality just simply. And youth. I see that now. Do you know Jimee Fowler and his bunch? Well, stay clear of them, they are up to no good, I promise. What a row they are kicking up all the time. Such a carry-on, always *tickled pink*. Don't pay them any attention, you must promise me. Oh, I know all about them! Oh yes. I know a-ver-y-thing about them, please understand. Back in '49 it was quite another horse, I assure you. *Such* an attractive little theatre in Montmartre. *Such* personable young men. Oh, I remember them *intimately*. Mr. Schmidt and Mr. Curtis and that terribly nice young man Mr. Bartlett . . ." and lots more of the same—whatever it was.

I flashed a look of amusement at Larry which, to my astonishment, never landed. Quite unselfconsciously—quite unconsciously, you might say, her arm curling into his, the Contessa had manoeuvred him over to a corner where they sat laughing and chatting together, and from that moment on, a sense of helplessness, of being strangled to death by cob-webs, never left me. On the face of it there was nothing to grasp. A silly middle-aged woman was shrilling confidences into my escort's ear, all of which could be heard in the next room and none of which couldn't be shouted from the roof-tops, for that matter. "The South of France *at that time of year*, dear boy?"—a gasp of disbelief, a hand to the breast to still the priceless jewel set quivering by the palpitations of an incredulous heart—"but . . . but . . . it would be *disastrous*. But simply impossible, you know . . . so full of humans and hotels of a-ver-y description. Such a hullabaloo, I can't tell you. And the English. I don't know *what*! A glance at the sun and they become *crazy* people, you know . . .", while the rest of us, as on a spit, were being slowly roasted to death with boredom by Cousin John. There was nothing, one might say, that couldn't have happened before or that wouldn't happen again. Nothing to upset me as much as it did. And yet there was this awful feeling of impending doom that I couldn't shake off—of ruthless, inscrutable and hostile forces at work. And it was only much later on that I realized that if John's conversation hadn't been anaesthetizing my brain, I would have caught on much sooner. Even so I doubt if it would have made any difference. I think from the minute I walked through Teddy's door that night my goose was cooked. The cast was assembled and the die was cast.

But to get on.

As I was saying—crushed, confused, dazed, I was certainly not at my best that evening. John, on the other hand, was in top form—by which I mean he was worse than ever.

We had barely seated ourselves at the dinner table, had barely time to grasp what he was up to, when out from his breast pocket flew a *pad and pencil*. These he placed purposefully on the table, and with a brief apology to the others for 'talking shop' turned to Teddy. It was about the Italian government's new agricultural reform programme that he was concerned. Would the Señor mind giving him a re-cap, so he could re-valuate what he was going to re-write? For instance, what was the *first* most important thing about it? And the second? And the third? . . . That was the soup course.

At the fish, the wine reminded him of a funny thing that happened to him the other day at the hotel. It seems that lunching with his wife, he'd suddenly decided to have a little bottle of vino. He meant, dammit, he'd been watching everyone, even the children, having wine with *their* meals every day, hadn't he? Well sir, he ordered some, and Christ, as he'd be the first to admit, he didn't pretend to know one bottle from another over here, so he left it for the waiter to decide. But this waiter—wait'll you hear—this waiter turned out to be a real meatball. You know what happened? This—this *French* waiter mind you, began pouring the vino into *John's* glass first! How about that? Well, he'd stopped him, of course. *Ladies* first, he'd pointed out, and in his limited French he'd chewed out that sad sack plenty—the poor guy had a face *yea* long when he was finished, he felt a little sorry for him, the way he just stood there you could see he didn't *know* any better—but if there was one thing John could *not* stand, dammit, it was impoliteness to women.

I crossed my eyes and sighed heavily. "Oh God", I said into my plate.

A scream of joy pierced the silence. The Contessa had just seen the light. She was now rushing in to enlighten my country cousin.

"But it is the custom!" she exclaimed, all sparkling. "It was for your *taste*, don't you see?"

John leaned forward and awarded her his first smile of the evening. "Not for *my* taste," said the dumb bastard, grinning away fatuously.

The Contessa shrieked.

It wasn't until the meat course, however, that John really became uncorked. You could see that his two weeks in Europe spent talking mostly to his silent, adoring wife had crystallized a lot of ideas that he was just bursting to try out on a larger group. Presidential candidates, Senatorial investigations, juvenile delinquency—he held firm views on all of them, views which needless to say he was entirely willing to share with one and all, and if the thought ever struck him that there might possibly be people at the table who were uninformed or even just plain uninterested in these peculiarly American problems, it never slowed the steady flow nor quelled the mighty roar.

"John is a parlour *white*," I murmured to no one in particular—to no one at *all*, as it turned out. For worse, far worse to me than John's assaults on my ears, the primary sounds so to speak, were the secondary ones: the gigglings, whisperings and chokings of Larry and the Contessa across the table, too intimate to break into, too murmured to penetrate. For a woman with as piercing a shriek as the one the Contessa normally employed for her conversations, her soft register was remarkable. It required every ounce of my agonized concentration to decipher one-tenth of the words. She was apparently inviting Larry to a gas-chamber. "It will be enormous," she whispered. "Oh yes, I intend to kill off *a-ver-y-one*. Hundreds of them. Oh, three or four hundred at least. Do come. In some minutes now I will give you the address."

I caught Larry's eye just then. He flashed me a brilliant traitor's smile; a gash of teeth and two wiggles of his eyebrows. I had to laugh. It was the first time that evening that I hadn't felt like killing myself. Stick with me, I begged him with my eyes. See me through, I love you and I'll make it all up later. I promise. But even as I telegraphed the message, I felt myself losing contact. He'd slipped away from me and gone back to the enemy.

From the sense of great distance that the wine was beginning to produce in me, I thought John looked rather peculiar. He seemed flushed and trembling, and his voice sounded shaky. I tried to concentrate on what he was saying. He had somehow got himself all tangled up in a question of Constitutional Law and was frantically trying to wrestle his way out, struggling and gasping like some half-strangled grey-flannelled Laocoön. So there actually *were* some people crazy enough to want to amend any old Article of the Constitution just to solve a couple of stupid problems, were there? Well by God, *he* wasn't one of them! He'd fight to the last ditch before he'd see them get away with anything like that! The veins were coming out on his forehead and a savage rallying note began to exhilarate his prose. He was standing up now. "I'll go along with the Founding Fathers!" he shouted, suddenly banging his fists on the table, and triumphantly subsided.

There was a small silence after which Teddy made some soothing remarks and the whispering, giggling and choking started up all over again. I just barely caught, "Mon Dieu, mais c'est penible tout ça—un veritable bag-of-wind, n'est-ce pas?" It fell so lightly on the ears it seemed to be hummed, but it was enough for me. Enough was enough for me.

I had been lumped together all this time with my fool cousin, placed 'on his side', so to speak, by accident of blood, nationality and the seating arrangements. It was an error I intended to rectify. It was dessert now, and I was deserting. He was just heading into a fresh topic—admittedly not one which he found as controversial as the last, but equally dull and equally mysterious.

"*Will* you shut up and *eat, for God's sake!*" It was my voice all right and the words were mine, too, only somehow the delivery seemed more forceful than expected. I was pained and shocked by its brutality.

As for John, he just gawped at me "Huh?"

"Eat!" I repeated. "Just . . . *eat!*" I was still badly out of control, almost in tears.

"Oh." Blinking like an owl, he turned and stared bewilderedly down at his plate. Then, like a good child, he picked up his spoon and began shovelling in the food.

In the really *big* silence that followed I had plenty of time to perceive the extent of my failure. It was complete. I was tied far more tightly to John now than before my outburst, the force of which had even loosened his wife from her moorings. The giggling had stopped altogether, and nobody tried any rescue-work.

Larry was the first to speak. He finished his soufflé, wiped his mouth and announced that he was going to leave. He had to be up very early the next day, he said, for a talk with his set-designer. He gave me another of his traitor smiles—roguish and piratical—only this one betraying me.

Hurriedly I pushed back my chair and clumsily rose to my feet. At the same time I heard the Contessa murmuring, "I'll drive you home, dear boy. I have a car outside. . ."

"No it's too much trouble," I mumbled thickly. "We'll find a taxi." With everyone staring at me I stumbled back over my chair.

"Now don't you worry about my little cousin, Contessa. You two just run along. *We'll* look after her," said the good-natured voice at my side. To my horror, John, having made a miraculous recovery, was genially speeding the parting guests. He had his arm on my shoulder. "We're not letting you off as easily as *that*, S. J.," he said, playfully pummelling away at it. "Gosh, I know darned well I've been talking my head off this evening, but I'm going on the listening end as of right now. I've got a million and one questions stored up

79

to fire at you. Woman's angle stuff. Food. Fashions . . ." he looked at me suddenly and lost his train of thought, "Say, what the heck have you been doing with yourself anyway? I very nearly didn't recognize you when you came in. . ."

I didn't struggle. I remember thinking at the time that it was funny my not struggling. I'd had a lot of wine during the dinner and yet I knew this couldn't entirely explain my listlessness. . .

It was the door that did it finally—that door. When Teddy went to show them the way downstairs (those same stairs I had run down so dispiritedly—his threats still ringing in my ears—not a month and a half ago), he left the door ajar. John was probably still talking; I didn't hear him. I couldn't take my eyes away from that door. It seemed to be undergoing some sort of transformation, turning into a person—a personality, rather—a sort of automation butler, wooden and grotesque, with a very strong but not immediately definable attitude towards me. That doorknob . . . it was definitely making a gesture. It was showing me out! The door wants me to go, I thought crazily. And then I pulled myself together. It was typical of my lunacy to ascribe surrealist motives to a door when the only fact to be grasped was that it was *still open*. And the voices, though growing fainter, could *still be heard*. If I wanted so much to go—if everything I wanted in the whole world was on the other side of that door, why didn't I just go? What was stopping me from barrelling past it (I wouldn't even have to touch it), from shouting *Hey, wait for me!* and sliding down the banisters after them? What kept me frozen there in a despair composed equally of impotent rage and a strange reluctance to shatter some exquisite but invisible structure, neither the shape nor purpose of which was apparent to me? In a word, what the hell was going on?

All this time the answer was coming at me slowly through the door. Teddy was in the room now, he was going to shut that door, shut me away from Larry for ever. It'll be hard to shut, I thought in a panic, looking at its lock, one of those very complicated French ones. And then suddenly—Don't let him fumble! Don't let the door bang and fly open and bang and fly open again. Oh, kill it instantly, I found myself praying. I needn't have worried. He was not likely to bungle the final flourish. He put one hand on the brass thingamajig, the other on the doorknob, and with one clean click the door flew shut.

With the same clean click the bomb exploded in the pit of my stomach. It sent cold water oozing through my veins, trickled damply into my wet palms, and finally shot its vital message up to my fuddled brain. At last the villain was unmasked. At last the Wild West caption: "Cousin John ties Sally Jay's hands while the Contessa makes off with Larry" could be credited to its rightful author—not Fate, nor Just-my-Luck, but none other than that fine Italian artist Alfredo Visconti.

It was his feeling for economy I admired most. Obviously a fan of Sartre's "Huis Clos," he had gone to no unnecessary expense or complication to achieve his effects, simply following the Master's formula of collecting together a few carefully selected souls and watching them torture one another . . . or rather, I realized with a start, watching them torture me. Florentine revenge was apparently every bit as effective as Corsican. I looked upon him with a new respect.

"Well now," said Teddy, and no matter how hard he tried, that silly shameful victorious smile *would* come creeping back over his face. "Well, now—shall we all have a brandy?"

John frowned. "Say, we'd better be pushing on, S. J. Come to think of it, it *is* pretty late." Heavy drinking always discouraged him. A frivolity he couldn't possibly control tended to take hold of people then. "I thought maybe we'd go for a nice quiet drive around some park here while you told me all about . . ." he yawned. "Anyway, there's no hurry. I've still got a week left. C'mon men." Dody Gorce rose obediently.

Teddy, on his way to the brandy, stopped dead in his tracks and looked at John. "Oh no, really must you go?" The feebleness of the protest and the relief on his face produced an effect so much less than charming that it made me tingle all over. For Teddy to be uncharming was as unthinkable as for John to be uninquisitive. Then, too, the circumstances of his triumph seemed to demand our detention. Surely he was going to allow himself the luxury of a little gloating, of playing the innocent, of at least seeing how I was taking it.

He looked tired. A sudden vision of how much it must have cost him in wear and tear, in sheer skull-cracking boredom, to cultivate John for the purpose of this evening, illuminated my thoughts. A flow of vindictiveness warmed my body, sending the blood pounding back through my veins. So Hell was other people, was it? Well, Teddy wasn't the only one who could borrow a page from Sartre. He was going to find out just what Hell old John-boy could be. Yessiree, I thought proudly, my cousin John is a two-edged sword; he cuts both ways. I had just remembered something that could be of the utmost importance if used correctly; I had just remembered Teddy's Special Project.

"John, I think you're being really horrible, eating and running like this," I said, "I haven't seen Teddy for ages, so let's have a nightcap at least." I turned eagerly to Teddy. "Gosh, I haven't had a chance to say one single word to you all night, Teddy. Tell me absolutely all about absolutely everything you've been up to—gulp—I mean of course your work—golly, I do hope they're not working you to death. . ." 'As friendly as a puppy', was the phrase I had in mind, but it put him right on guard. The look he gave me, full of suspicion, told me that. I decided not to notice. "No kidding, Teddy, it's just great seeing you again, and what a *mad* coincidence bumping into John at the whatsit."

"The Agricultural Commission for European Aid, Soil Erosion Division," John said quickly. He'd been shifting restlessly from one foot to another, but saying the magic words settled him back in his chair again.

"But *what* a mad coincidence. I mean what on earth were you doing there, Teddy?"

"What do you mean what was he doing there?" John turned to Teddy and laughed. He had no sense of humour but he just couldn't help laughing at other people's stupidity. It was such an unpleasant sound I looked over at Dody. She sat on quiet and contented. She seemed to have some invisible knitting in her lap. "My gosh," John went on, shaking his head at me sadly, "that's just what I can't get over. If the recently graduated college alumna can't turn her trained brain to some intelligent awareness of our responsibilities in World Affairs, we're going to foul up our leadership like England did, as sure as God made little green apples. Read the papers, gal. Find out what it's all about."

"But what on earth *were* you doing there, Teddy?" I asked him for the third time, ignoring John.

"Braziano as usual," he shrugged. Braziano, a colleague, was not one of Teddy's favourites. He was always having to deputize for him. "His stories are getting wilder and wilder. It seems on this particular occasion he was unable to get to the conference on account of being poisoned by a trout at the Relais St. Germain the night before. You know the tank of live fish they have there? Well, there is an expression that you Americans have—'to shoot trout in a tank' . . ."

"Like shooting trout in a barrel," I said.

"Yes—quite. Well, it seems the American he was dining with *did* shoot one—or so Braziano insists—and to quiet the management Braziano ate it. Naturally it poisoned him and naturally he had to stay home the next day."

I later reflected that this was probably the only amusing thing said that evening, but at the time nobody laughed. Teddy was too exasperated, I was afraid of getting us off the track, and John, of course, saw nothing funny about it. Dody shifted her invisible knitting with a little frown of concentration; she seemed to have dropped a stitch.

I turned to John, dizzy with excitement. We were approaching the crux of the matter now. "You see, at Teddy's Embassy the various Cultural Attachés are assigned to Special Projects from time to time. Braziano's, I suppose, is this European Aid thing, so it's really just a fluke you met Teddy at all. Because it isn't Teddy's project. Teddy's project . . ." I suddenly found I wasn't able to say it. I could only pray that John would pick up the cue.

"What is your Special Project, Señor Visconti?" asked John. It came out quite simply with his breath. It was perfect

—casual, perfunctory, polite. I marvelled above all at the naturalness of the delivery. Now all I had to do was switch off, make myself invisible, convince myself of the absolute unimportance of Teddy's reply. I turned quietly and smiled at Dody.

"Well," said Teddy wearily, "for this particular six-month period I'm handling all the Student Conferences." He sighed, feeling sorry for himself. "We have a rash of them breaking out at the Sorbonne, I can't think why. Next week I have five——" I felt a slight pause; was he wondering whether to use this as an excuse for turning us out now? "Five. One every day to attend."

I couldn't believe my ears. *Five*—it was so much better than I'd dared hope. I turned back to them then. The transformation in John was glorious to behold. He was clenched with seriousness rather than glowing with enthusiasm, but there was no doubt that he was transported.

"Dammit man," he said in a voice choked with emotion, "this is marvellous. Gosh, why didn't I know it before? Dody, did you hear what he said? Student Conferences. Say, that's my *real* interest, Visconti. Anyone'll tell you that. The only hope we've *got* is based on the willingness of today's youth to shoulder their responsibilities. And I never even knew these conferences were going on. That just shows what little publicity they get. Well, I'm going to change all that, all right; they're going to get plenty in *my* rag, anyway. Hell, I know you won't mind my tagging along with you this week—I'm going to need the advice of an expert. Now—" pad and pencil were out "—now tell me about Monday's conference. What I mean is, what do you feel is the *first* most important thing about it?"

I said goodbye to them all. I told John I was sorry I wouldn't be able to see them again, but I had a costume-fitting the next morning and I was rehearsing day and night for the next two weeks. I knew it didn't matter what I said. I don't think he even heard me. Student Conferences—Wow!

Teddy saw me out. Through the door, down the stairs, and into a taxi. We exchanged bitter farewells.

# CHAPTER SIX

I AWOKE THE NEXT morning with a series of explosions popping off in my head like flash bulbs. "Sunday!" That was the first one. Then, following close upon it, and each more agonizingly vivid than its predecessor, scenes from last night's debacle re-staged themselves with relentless accuracy for my edification. I was just wincing my way through the terrible moment at the dinner-table where that cool cat of a Contessa managed to kidnap Larry right from under my nose, when it struck me that there was something peculiar about the whole sequence. I played it back and spotted the trouble: from the time the Contessa announced her decision to place her car at Larry's disposal, to the time she waltzed out on his arm, she had addressed not one single word of explanation or apology to Teddy, and this, seeing as how the rat had really knocked himself out on the food and drink, struck me as just the least bit casual. Not that Teddy had minded. That was odd too. In fact they both seemed to take each other rather for granted, those two...

I sat straight up in bed, my arms gripped hard against my knees in concentration. By the revelation of one simple fact, the whole equation had taken on an entirely new dimension: the Contessa was Teddy's mistress. Of course. How stupid of me. It was all so obvious I could only marvel at my denseness. Well then, that meant . . . that meant . . . I was suddenly overcome by a feeling of disgust. What it meant was that Teddy had deliberately trapped his *mistress* into doing his own dirty work. And all this just to get back at me. Much as I disliked the Contessa, I found myself wondering if I shouldn't warn her somehow. But warn her of *what*? What was I getting so worked up about? The vehemence of my moral indignation surprised me. Was I beginning to have standards and principles, and, oh dear, scruples? What were they, and what would I do with them, and how much were they going to get in my way?

In the middle of all this confusion my thoughts swerved and plunged down quite a different alley. I knelt on my bed —the wall-telephone was just above it—and gave the operator Larry's number. When his concierge told me there was no one in his room I could hardly stop myself from telling her to go back and see if his bed had been slept in. But I gave her my name instead, and asked her to have him ring the moment he returned. I had no idea what I would say. I flopped back on the bed and looked at the clock. Nine-thirty. To keep myself from going mad I pretended that he really *was* with the set-designer and that their appointment really had been for some dreadful hour like nine in the morning. After all, why not? Then I abandoned myself to my grief. It was no longer possible for me to ignore the sexual aspect of Larry's abduction. I lay back on the bed groaning and stared at the ceiling.

Sometime in the afternoon the phone rang.

"Il y a un Monsieur Bright qui vous attend tout de suite, Mademoiselle!" My concierge shrilled impatiently in my ear, irritating me about twice as much as she usually did.

The name meant nothing to me. I barked back that there was some mistake and hung up. The phone rang again.

"Hello. Look, this is Jim Breit," said the voice quickly, "Jim Breit—we see each other around here quite a bit—I'm a friend of Judy's and——"

"Oh gosh, of course," I suddenly remembered. "You're the *good* painter."

"The what?"

"Nothing. Sorry. But you want Judy, don't you? She's on the floor above—four—oh—five."

"No, I want you. I've been looking for you all week, you're never in. Judy's in the hospital and she wants to see you."

"Good Lord, what's the matter with her?"

"Well, nothing serious. At least I don't think so. She gets overtired, you know, and she's supposed to go on a long concert tour with her brother soon, so it's really more of a general check-up, she tells me. Can you come out now?"

"Well . . . oh, all right. O.K. Be down in a minute."

I got dressed and went downstairs and we drove off to the American Hospital in Neuilly, practically in silence. I didn't encourage any conversation. To tell the truth I wasn't too happy about making this excursion. I didn't want to go to a hospital and cheer anyone up; I wanted to go off quietly somewhere and die.

Hospital doors open so soundlessly that Judy didn't even hear us enter her room. When I saw her lying there, pale and listless, I became terrified. I gasped and she sat up and looked around. Now that she saw us, she seemed to spring back to life. It was extraordinary really, watching her colour coming back and seeing how completely it transformed her. Reassured, I began babbling away inanely about how busy I'd been with rehearsals, how much of my time they were taking, how of course I'd have come sooner if I'd known, and on and on.

"Oh never mind, never mind," she interrupted, bouncing up and down on the bed in her excitement. "Tell me everything that's happened. It's a whole week. *Millions* of things must have happened. Tell me about them all." She pulled me down beside her, almost panting with anticipation.

I looked away for a moment. I was always a little embarrassed by her outbursts of curiosity. I found it difficult to believe she really followed my life with the same breathless anticipation as I did; that her interest in everyone and everything was as genuine as it was passionate. But it was genuine all right. I found out later just how genuine it was.

In any case I obviously don't need much encouraging to talk about myself, and before I knew it out came the story of last evening. And the funny thing was I don't know whether it was the time, or the place, or just me, but now the whole thing seemed really more comic than tragic. I found I was almost enjoying myself. Also I was working up a brilliant imitation of the Contessa's fractured English.

"But I know her," squealed Judy suddenly, bouncing up and down on her bed again. "I know her, I *know* the one you mean! Listen, Sally Jay, let me tell you about it. It was the strangest thing. I think she must be mad or something. All her friends are, anyway. Do you know she had us over to lunch, my brother and I, without even knowing our names? Someone had taken her to one of Paul's recitals and she came gushing back-stage, spouting that funny English like you do, and invited us to lunch. She said she knew someone terribly important who would be terribly interested in Paul's career, and she said for us just to write down our names and address like good children and give them to her chauffeur because she was hopeless at such things and she said for Paul to prepare a short programme and that she'd send the car and then she gushed out again. . .

"Have you ever seen her house? Well, it's enormous. Full of lots of scary dogs that look as if they ought to be tied up or they'll tear you to bits, and some of the strangest pieces of sculpture I've ever seen. She was waiting in the hallway when we arrived and gushed all over us again, but you could tell she still didn't know our names. Nobody was introduced. There were about three or four other guests and she hustled us all into the dining-room. She sat Paul next to an absolutely gorgeously elegant middle-aged man, so I guessed that he was the one she wanted him to meet. You could see he took to Paul immediately and after hearing him play he was just in raptures. He gave him his card, and said he wanted to have a long, serious talk with him the next day, and he invited him down to his château for the week-end, where he said he was going to put his special Bechstein Grand at Paul's disposal, and see to it that no one disturbed him from practising to his heart's content, and then he suddenly laughed, he had this strange excited, high-pitched laugh, more of a giggle really, and he rumpled Paul's hair and said he'd just realised he didn't even know our names. When we told him he closed his eyes and murmured—Pablo Galache—sort of softly. It turned out he was Spanish, too. He asked us how we happened to have a Spanish name, so we told him about Mummy and Daddy and their elopement, and all and my gosh you can't *imagine* the change that came over him! I think he must have gone crazy. He looked like he was going to choke. 'José Alvarez de Galache?' he whispered. His voice was so husky you could hardly hear him. We were surprised at him knowing our father's name. 'He was one of my oldest friends,' he said, 'I knew him all his life.' Then he leaned forward and began glaring at Paul—I honestly thought he was going to hit him—but he did something just as strange—he took his card back. What do you think of that? Then he sort of pulled himself together, and stood up, and bowed to me, and wished Paul success, and said he hoped we could all meet again under different circumstances—whatever *that* meant. I mean we just sat there with our mouths open. Then he gave the Contessa an absolutely deadly look and hissed something at her about being careful in the future to whom she introduced him, and flounced out.

"I watched him walk down the hallway, and when he noticed his card still in his hand, he tore it into tiny pieces and flung it on the floor. Can you imagine that? I wonder what came over him? You'd think being such an old friend of Daddy's he would have reacted in just the opposite . . . What's the matter, Sally Jay?"

I was off on my old space kick again, aimlessly prowling around the room. "Nothing . . . nothing . . ." I answered vaguely. What was now crystal-clear was that there had never been any question of Teddy having to *trap* the Contessa into doing his dirty work; she would have done any kind of dirty work he wished. I felt a little sick. "They are corrupt—corrupt," I kept saying to myself, over and over again, as I paced around the room. It was the first time I'd ever used that word about people I actually *knew*, and again the idea that I could take a moral stand—or rather, that I couldn't avoid taking one—filled me with the same confusion it had that morning. And now they've got their mitts on Larry, I thought.

Oh Lord. If I don't stop thinking about those two, I decided, they're going to put me right off sex for good.

"Ouf!" In my travels around the room I had tripped over Jim, whom I had completely forgotten was even there.

"Hey, what's this?" I looked at the scrap of paper on which he was scribbling. It was a sketch of Judy and myself. We looked like a couple of wild women, yapping away together on her bed; it only needed those little balloons filled with exclamation marks popping out of our mouths to complete it. I had to laugh.

"Have you been listening to us all this time?"

He grinned and looked at it too. "It would have been difficult not to."

"Well, what do *you* make of all this?"

"Not too much." He was putting the finishing touches to his work. "You girls. You really know some birds, don't you?" He chuckled mildly.

I was amazed. I wouldn't have expected Judy to see the point of her story, but a man . . . I stared at him. He wasn't a man, of course. He was just a child, really.

When we left the hospital, Jim asked me if I'd like to go out with him that evening. I made a quick guess about him, I guessed he was a damn nice kid—only a kid, of course, but at that moment he seemed infinitely preferable to the grown-ups I knew. He had these light blue eyes, and a light laugh; there was something light and attractive in everything about him, something definitely unsinister. I'd had enough excitement for the week-end. Jim was just what was needed; someone I could have a few drinks with, some food, laugh, talk, and end the evening without finding myself involved in some ghastly situation I couldn't understand, much less deal with. I accepted his invitation.

We were driving along towards Saint-Germain. Jim asked me if I wanted to stop off and have a drink there. Would I *rather* have a drink there, was the way he put it. I saw what he was getting at, of course. The subtle distinction between the cafés of Saint-Germain at l'heure bleue, and his own preferred watering-hole, the Select in Montparnasse, was not lost on me. Saint-Germain is only five minutes away from Montparnasse, and they are both everything that is meant by 'bohemian' and 'left-bank', but they are not interchangeable. Ho-ho. Far from.

The floating Saint-Germainian—and by that I mean the type of expatriate we were likely to run into, not the rooted French Intellectual who is too protectively coloured to be winkled out—was cleaner, shrewder, smarter, more fashionable, more successful, more knowing; in brief more on the make, then his Montparnassian contemporary. As one of the advertising boys enthusiastically put it, six months in the quartier was worth it just for climbing; you could really get somewhere. There was more than a whiff of the Market Place hovering over the Boulevard, and some spectacularly successful examples of the same. Avant-garde magazines springing up in this area tended to be clever excuses for the smooth, level-headed young men who ran them (who were determined to make good in other walks of life later on) to hunt for literary lions as their contributors and social lions as their patrons. The Ancient, that grand old man of the Montparnasse set, was always careful to meet his agent or publisher up there, well away from 'home', for the business drink that would settle his financial problems in the coming year.

What Jim was trying to find out by his question was if I was *that* sort of person. I decided for the time being that I wasn't. I said I'd much rather go to the Select if he didn't mind. He smiled and we drove off in that direction.

What the Montparnassians actually *were* like—as opposed to what they weren't *as like as*—is not too easy to describe. On the whole they were a disreputable bunch of revellers, working on the assumption that every day was their birthday or some such equally weak assumption, and their virtues were largely negative.

For purposes of over-simplification I'd say they were the Select around six o'clock in the evening. If I can only do it justice. Shall I close my eyes so that it comes rushing back to me in all its pungent beauty? Actually it is the smell of the place that comes rushing back first, seizing me by the nostrils :

fresh, damp and rich, a most appetizing mixture of apples and smoke, perfume and garlic, hot chocolate and wet rubber, mixed in with a smell, as the Contessa might put it, full of humans of every description. The interior of the café, a room of goodish size, was designed to satisfy every possible café desire. The counter, with its long brass foot-rail for bar-drinkers, was always propped up, even at this time of evening, by an exceedingly pickled Englishman in the company of his exceedingly sober dog. Along the walls ran a banquette upholstered in very old red plush, ideal for eavesdropping, or reading the evening papers, while the tables, generally occu-pied by large rowdy groups such as the Hard Core, were placed in the centre of the room, thus allowing breathing-space for the other customers. At one point the room took a sudden L turn, and the six or seven booths built into this partition isolated the serious lovers and chess-players from the rest of us. A beautiful, twilight neon tubing shed its mellow glow on the dim, dirty mosaic-tiled floor and flickered over the rainbow-hued coiffures of the women, as many-coloured as the coats they sat in, which were made of the skins of some raffish, exotic creatures, totally unknown out-side the city limits. On the banquettes a lot of American spinsters sat together, talking clearly and precisely of their travels, or else read and smoked alone while having steel pots of un-American tea. It always made me sad to see that there were so many unmarried women in the world—sadder still to realize that they were largely unseen because there were so few public places they dared brave without a sense of strain.

Out on the terrasse chauffée, hordes of French—sometimes as many as eight or nine together—arranged themselves com-fortably around small tables, talked a lot and drank a very little. The French more than anyone—the French *alone*—have mastered the fine art of sweating out a drink. I've seen them time and again in that café, hat, coat, gloves and scarves to the eyebrows, sitting in attitudes of imminent departure—and sitting there all night, the same stemmed glass before them. The Americans and Scandinavians (and there were quite a number of Scandinavians—this café seemed to run to Swedish mountaineers, Danish Princes, and Finnish remittance men) dressed for the Select as for a ski-hut. Bradley Slater had been coming in every morning for two years in a checkered wool-shirt, G.I. pants and ski-boots, copies of *Time* Magazine and the *Herald-Tribune* tucked under his arm. Here he would sit quite happily until lunchtime, immersed in his reading, getting through a fresh *Herald-Tribune* each day because it was a daily, but conscientiously devoting the full seven days to each issue of *Time* as that after all was a weekly. After lunch he retired to his hotel to rest, rising refreshed from his afternoon nap to have a leisurely bath and shave, and showing up spruce and sparkling for his five-thirty re-appearance at the Select, where he remained until closing-time.

The waiters at the Select comported themselves with that slightly theatrical mixture of charm, complicity and contempt that one would expect from servants in Hell. All you had to do was sit there at the beginning of an evening, feeling pristine and crisp, combed and scented, and order your very first drink (it could be something as innocent as a lemonade), for them to indicate by the slightest flicker of their merry eyes that they were aware as you that you were taking the fatal step down the road to ruin. By merely clattering up the used cups and saucers on to their trays, flicking their napkins over the table, the better to clear the stage for disaster, and repeating your order precisely as given, they could predict for you the whole miracle that was going to take place four hours later when you—the now transformed, tousled, shiny, vague-eyed you—would emerge, talking the most utter balderdash, spilling beans of shattering truths or equally shattering lies, singing with friends, fighting with strangers, promising favours, promising love, scrambling into bed and clambering out again . . . all this they could predict for you as relentlessly as any Delphic Oracle, while at the same time it all struck them as so irresistibly funny they couldn't help chuckling.

Whether you looked upon the Ancient as a crusty old poet-philosopher or simply as a dirty old man with a heart as big as a stone, you had to admit, by God, that he actually got along with these waiters. Maybe because it was true that they helped him with all the hard words in his translations of Virginia Woolf into French, or maybe because he was in league with the Devil as well, but the fact remained that he bullied them incessantly and they indulged his every whim.

When we came in that night he was already there at his table. A large formidable figure with his grey hair en brosse and his left hand with its two missing fingers, souvenirs of some well-recalled brawl in Marseilles, clamped like a hook around his glass of beer, the Ancient always began a table. It was his one dignity. He would come into the Select and sit down, and the table would start growing around him with friends and acquaintances. Even though he knew all the people there already, he never joined a table. When he arrived they moved over to him and that was that. So it was always *his* table. There was quite a large group around him that evening; many of the Hard Core and, to get really technical—all the Inner Hard Core. This consisted of an intellectual publisher (always accompanied by an ever-new ever-green secretary), a lazy, devastatingly handsome Yale boy who raced cars and said mostly nothing but Zop, zop; his buddy, also a car-racer, but of the charming, soft-voiced, gentle-mannered, international swindler type, who, it was rumoured, stole cars as well as raced them and was a dangerous man with a bridge hand; Beard Boring and Beard Bubbly; and curiously enough, this youngster Jim. That was the inner circle. As I said before, there were lots of others who clustered around the Ancient, but somehow they weren't held in the same esteem; they had nothing to do with the *ton* of the group; they were just so much dressing for him to lecture to, and cadge drinks from and insult.

As we came up to the table I discovered to my surprise and annoyance Bill Blauer, one of cousin John's room-mates at Harvard, sitting there. John's friends were like John. They had to be. I slank into a chair as far away from his as possible, trying to keep hidden behind one of the Beards, hoping Bill wouldn't recognize me in my new hair. He did, of course, hailing me happily down the length of the table and informing me excitedly that he'd just run into cousin John that morning, of all things.

"A Guggenheim to end all Guggenheims," the Beard (Bubbly as it turned out) growled to me with a despairing slap of hand to brow.

I could see that Bill, who as a matter of fact was a Rhodes Scholar at Oxford, was making himself right at home in our little village, sitting there with this awful *expectant* air of a Rotarian in Wonderland playing over his handsome welcoming features, just the sort of expression, in fact, that you'd *expect* from a young man in Paris between terms and determined to live it up. It was really funny to see how his well-here-I-am-let's-see-what-this-little-old-burg-and-its-natives-has-to-offer attitude was quickly caught by the natives and just as quickly resented.

He thought it was great, just great, bumping into me like that, and disregarding the fact that I had not walked in unaccompanied, invited me to go on the town with him.

"I have a date already," I said.

"Oh, that's all right, bring him along." He made the invitation general. "We'll all go along," he said humorously.

We all ignored this, but the Ancient, after considering him for a moment or two, rose abruptly and announced that he was going to the Dôme. Obediently the waiters came running to his side. He paid and left, and following his example, we all trailed after him.

Bill Blauer, too, though I pretended not to notice.

"Sit down, you bastard, sit down!" shouted the Ancient. It was his greeting to a lanky sweat-shirted Abstractionist, who instantly complied. "See that Frog tart giving you the eye? I could tell you something about her, son, I'd decline the invitation if I were you; I'd duck. You have to watch out for these primitive types," he grinned satanically, satisfied at the success this was having with the two Sweet Briar Exchange students who, until then, had been bravely trying to appear smooth, even though we all knew they had to be in by twelve. The more the Ancient had to drink, the fouler he got. That was the rule and this was only the beginning.

"Zop, zop."

"Listen, Jim, about this new magazine we're getting under way : first of all I want to make it quite clear, see, that we're not having anything to do with all this effete chi-chi they're trying to unload on us now." A would-be Editor disdainfully brandished two small Paris-American magazines he'd just been sold. "I mean ours is going to be really experimental, in the true sense of the word, for Christ's sake. These other bastards must be walking in their sleep or something. Look at this—" he flipped through the pages scornfully. "A reprint of an early Spender poem and a lousy Ugo Betti translation—Ugo Betti, for crying out loud. Listen, you just go ahead and design us a couple of covers, we'll pick the one we like the best, slap it on the first issue and you see if you don't thank us till your dying day even if you don't get a red sou for it. Boy, is it going to be a big prestige deal. We'll work it up to a circulation of millions in New York alone. There hasn't been a *decent* literary magazine since—what the hell was his name? You know, that husband of—what's her name . . . ?"

"I'm going to start a Left Bank Magazine and call it *Anything Gauche*."

"Very funny, ha-ha."

"Zop, zop."

"Listen you bums, this is no fly-by-night proposition. I tell you we're all ready to roll. We're getting the financing under control this very minute. Yeah, you heard me. And we didn't have to go to any nympho Society bag for it either. Wanna know how we did it? Come on, guess how."

"I don't know."

"Well guess, dammit. What does Paris need most?"

"I don't know."

This made the Editor furious. "Think, man, think. Here you are, you and a couple of hundred other hungry bastards like you, sitting around this bistro, knocking it back. So what happens? Maybe a little later you'll try to scrounge up a few lousy potato chips or some such crap, but what would you really go for in a big way if they had it around, easy to get at. In machines? Come on, what?"

"A couple of shrunken heads."

"Popcorn, you fools, popcorn!" he bellowed triumphantly. "I'll put it to you this way : just think how many cafés there are in this vast sewer we call Paris. Then think how many people there are drinking at this very moment, who want a little delicious sustenance to keep them going. Now just roll those numbers around in your mind awhile and you'll get some idea of the business our popcorn machines are going to do. We grow the corn right here in France, pop it, install the machines and walk away with the profits. I tell you the whole thing's just beautiful. And here's the genius who figured the whole thing out." He waved in the direction of the weedy Abstractionist, who came to life at these words, acknowledged them with a modest smile of achievement, and began a scientific discourse on the planting of the crop.

"But how are you going to make France popcorn-conscious? The French won't know whether to eat it or rub it in their hair." This was me.

"All in good time. All in good time," said the Editor soothingly. "We've already started our publicity campaign in a small way. Did you happen to notice the shocking-pink van outside? Well that's ours. Ray" (that was the Abstractionist) "will paint the popcorn sign on tomorrow. And last week when the news of this venture slipped out prematurely —*naturally* we were powerless to prevent it—there immediately appeared in the correspondence columns of the *Herald-Tribune* two letters, one for and one against. 'This nefarious attempt of the Coca Cola Empire to extend its frontier by blasting further commercial inroads into French Cultural Tradition!' The phrase is our learned colleague's here," (Beard Bubbly) "who incidentally wrote them both. Also, we were gratified to notice that the cause célèbre has already spilled over to the correspondence columns of *France-Soir* today, and who knows, if this keeps up a real letter may soon be written on the subject."

I was beginning to get interested in all this. I mean it made a lot of sense to me. I adore popcorn, anyway. I was going to find out more about the magazine when all of a sudden, out of the corner of my eye, I saw Larry. Or thought I did. Just one of those things. I went all weak and woozy. I leapt from my chair and rushed off in his direction, a big, fat, stupid grin all over my face. It wasn't Larry, of course, or anything like; it was one of those gruesome tricks the subconscious plays, but I was halfway across the room before I realized my mistake. Ordinarily, I wouldn't have given it another thought; ordinarily, it would rank with one of the very minor social blunders in my life, but in this case, as luck would have it, the person I mistook for Larry, sitting there in the midst of a bunch of Sinisters, turned out to be one of those drug-store-cowboy-motorcycle types, just past their first juvenile delinquency, only Mediterranean, and the look he gave me back made me want to kick him where it hurt.

I retreated to my table as quickly as possible, but now that I'd started to think about Larry I couldn't stop. I felt restless and unconcentrated. I was anxious to get going when the exodus started. Or—I don't know—maybe I started it. We were a restless mob that night. We were looking for a mood. We went in four cars: Jim's Renault, the pink popcorn van, the Ancient's two-seater motorcycle, and a big open Stutz Bearcat that Zop-zop's buddy had found for Dave Beckenfield. Four cars in search of a mood.

It was a beautiful night; warm and clear and quick. I seemed to get warmer and quicker as it went on; I seemed to be melting as I burned faster, like a candle.

First we went to the Coq Rouge for the Cabaret, and then we went to the Vieux Colombier for the Dixieland, but we didn't stay very long at either.

Then we went up to Montmartre and hung around there for a while and ate some bright red frankfurters with sauerkraut, 'les yanquis,' that were being sold on the sidewalks. I was starving and they tasted heavenly. I ate five.

Bill Blauer was still with us. I pretended not to notice.

Then we went back to Montparnasse. The spiral was starting. We went to the Canne à Sucre, and the O.K., and the Villa Villa, and that cloudy one next door, where we could almost see the nude show from where we stood at the bar, and that was where we started dancing. In spite of all my efforts to evade him, Bill Blaah had been inching closer towards me all evening. Now he asked me to dance. I had to say yes, but I was going out of my mind, I hated him so. I hated him for being so goddam insensitive—he must have known I didn't want to be with him, I'd made no bones about it. I hated him for looking upon Paris as a picnic ground and us as a bunch of monkeys on a string. "Say, do you do this *every* night?" he asked me brightly as we whirled around. Maybe we did and maybe we didn't, but I hated his idea that we *planned* it. These things just happen.

The next two things that happened, though, were entirely planned and entirely related. First, I accepted the invitation of that Mediterranean, the one who I'd mistaken earlier on for Larry, and who I'd been noticing as Blaah was dragging me around the floor—'Crazy Eyes' as we came to think of him—to dance, and second, we finally shook Blaah.

I organized it. I knew it would outrage and discourage him for good to see me going off with an apache type, so I made damn sure that Crazy Eyes asked me, and yet I hated *him* too. For opposite reasons.

I hated Blaah because he was trying to get into our world; and I hated Crazy Eyes because I didn't want to get into his. I mean I was afraid of him. His jiving was out-of-this-world —but it stuck out a mile that he'd hit your head against a stone fireplace if he felt like it. I'm a real phoney, one of those half-baked hothouse plants we're growing nowadays, instead of the honest-to-God two-fisted women we should be, and, neurotic that I am, I shrink like mad from the criminal type. If anyone comes at me with a club, I duck, brother, I duck. And then I run. So I was a little nervous about having this cat think I was leading him on. The outdoors is fraught with danger.

Anyway, we danced a whole set, and at the end of it, to

99

my great relief, he let me go. He gave me those crazy eyes again, but I decided they came with the face.

Then we went on to the Hôtel Etats-Unis, where we usually ended up. The Etats-Unis was run (to use too strong a word) by a group of Resistance Poles, and it was here that at least one American had torn up his passport in the heat of an evening to become a Citizen of the World. The atmosphere since then had remained full of anarchistic sparks. I loved it.

The impromptu jazz bands that found themselves there together at night ranged from professional to inadequate, and went on as long as there was a leg to stand on. Good or bad, they were always danced to by a pretty, abandoned, but not very accomplished young dancer who made up in pep what she lacked in poise. No matter what the music did, she did the same wild mono-dance. I say 'mono' because it looked as if there was supposed to be some other people to it—a man, or a corps de ballet, or something. Also she couldn't seem to decide whether she wanted to be a dancer or whore.

"Je vais partir pour l'Amérique," she would confide to us earnestly, breathless from her recent exertions on the dance floor. "Une amie de Martha Graham m'a vue danser ici, et elle m'a dit que ce soit tout arrangé. Malheureusement, il me manque d'argent jusqu'à present . . . et . . ." sloefully her eyes would wander off to rest on Zop-zop, undisputedly the big success with the girls in the quartier, and he would return the look coolly and enigmatically.

"I may be twenty years too late, but at least I know it, you twerps," said Dave Beckenfield, who always got surly when he felt his beloved Stutz Bearcat under attack. Dave, a Ful-bright, was also, as he never let us forget, an ex-newspaper-man and a lot older and wiser than all of us. In fact, so strongly did he feel that it was his special mission to inform the Hard Core that whatever they were doing, they were doing it a couple of decades too late, that he never let them out of his sight. Everywhere they went, he went, spraying the area first with his disillusion : it was twenty years too late for Paris, twenty years too late for Spain. . .

But for me, who this time last year, like those poor Smith

and Sweet Briar fish had to be 'in' before midnight, but could now stay 'out' forever, it didn't feel twenty years too late at all. It felt great, just great: I wanted to shout for joy and crow with glee.

Much later on. . .

"Now don't give me a hard time." It was Beard Boring. "Just answer me my question. Are you a Catholic, a *real* Catholic, or not? Because if you're not, bud, if you're just trying to get a rise out of me, so help me, I'll poke you in the jaw."

"What the hell's the matter with you, I said I *was*, didn't I?"

"O.K., O.K., so I'll believe you. O.K. So just let me tell you a thing or two about that darling church of yours, and I speak from experience because——"

"Mais tais-toi donc. Je veux écouter la musique. Ah, c'est pas drôle ça. Vas-y. Tu commences à m'emmerder un peu." It was the mono-dancer quarrelling with Crazy Eyes, who'd just turned up.

The boys in the corner, very d'après Hemingway, one of them even named Cohen, had just returned from Spain with Beckenfield, where they were almost tossed into jail for throwing cushions in the ring during a *good* bullfight. They were holding a small audience of friends spellbound with one of them the bull and the rest executing a series of passes around him.

"The mystique is pretty—well, fairly—well, comparatively—sophisticated, in that the good people—I say the *good* people but you know what I mean—aren't sentimentalized—they come off just as badly as the bad people." Doric Steegmeyer, Resident Bore of the Hôtel Etats-Unis, was holding forth on the latest gangster film. Around him, enthralled, sat his wife, his fellow-intellectuals, Beard Bubbly and Lee Harrison (an actor in our company), and the Englishman-and-dog combination from the Select, who had wandered in starry-eyed from the night.

"It's just that the mystique of brutality runs right through—well, it doesn't run, but it's there. It's like that G.I. we knew who went AWOL in the war—" he turned slowly to the Englishman. "AWOL, A, W, O, L," he repeated clearly for his benefit. "Do you have it? I mean of course you have it, but do you say AWOL. A, W, O, L—you don't mind my asking?"

The Englishman nodded vigorously, managing to mingle total agreement with total astonishment, and though neither was exactly what was called for, they had to do, as he was obviously beyond speech. Doric's wife said "Yes, darling, he was AWOL," quickly, to get him back on the track, but Doric, who had been hoping here for a chance to discuss the basic differences between American and British Army terminology, gazed around him, completely thrown.

"The film," whispered his wife.

"Oh yeah, this film. Well, it's like I say, it's very—well, it's *competent*, it's professional, it doesn't make any real comment, it's—well, not *clever* so much as *adroit*. I don't mean it's unedifying, it's just not uplifting. Not that there's anything unattractive in not being uplifting, but, well, you know what I mean . . . it's . . . um, it's . . . *cursory*."

At my side Beard Bubbly breathed fervently at the sheer beauty of it all. That was another thing about the Hard Core, though maybe not the nicest. They went all out for satire. They not only suffered fools, they suffered them gladly. And I mean they sought them out; they tracked them down. Only they had to be really big ones. They were as irresistibly drawn to the real nuts, as the Saint-Germainians to the real operators. Bill Blauer, for instance, they had immediately rejected as being not far enough out, but my cousin John—now *he* would have truly thrilled them. I kind of saw what they meant in a way. Sometimes the only thing in the world that *doesn't* bore me, is listening to bores. Sometimes.

Leé Harrison was the actor I liked best in our company. I mean I liked *him*, not his acting, which could be dreadful. When he had been told by enough people that he looked just like Alec Guinness, he went off to Europe to wait until he was old enough to play all of Mr. Guinness' rôles. The question was whether age or starvation would overtake him first. For three perilous years on the Left Bank he had eked out what to anyone else would have been a wretched and intolerably chancy existence: bits of dubbing, broadcasting, and filming were interspersed with long stretches of absolutely nothing. I have never known *anyone* with less money and less visible means of getting hold of it. He had slept around everywhere, from the floors of friends' studios, to the Metro. There were days when he had literally no money at all, and after a string of such days he would go to the blood bank and sell his blood. More often than not he spent this money on tickets to the ballet. He was into all of us for at least a thousand francs apiece. To me he seemed like some Special Mordant. A bitter, blithe and unconsciously pathetic version of a jeun Cocteau from Greenwich Village. The thing about him, though, was that he thought he was in theatre for Art, whereas he was really in it for laughs. He was especially good at snuffling out the Big Bores, whom he tracked down like a pig after truffles. Doric, in fact, was one of his discoveries. Now, however, he was tiring of Doric. He went over to the next table, bummed a cigarette off Big Ben Nelson, the ex-ice-hockey player, and I could hear him starting on his vituperative account of a certain road production of "A Streetcar Named Desire", his last job in the States. Big Ben listened kindly to the intemperate judgments passed on these unknown, defenceless actors, sucking on a cube of sugar, his big paw curled around his lait chaud. Big Ben could afford to be benign; only three weeks ago he had solved his own acute economic problem neatly by sleeping with his landlady on Saturday nights.

"Advance passionately towards me," I said to Jim suddenly.

"What?"

"Engage me in violent conversation."

"What'll I say?"

"Don't you dance?"

"No. Why?"

"I think Crazy Eyes is about to come this way. I noticed he's just had an enormous bagarre with the dancing girl and he's zigging his eyes in my direction."

"I thought you liked him."

"Are you insane? It was just to get rid of Bill Blauer. Incidentally why didn't *you* get him off me—Bill, I mean? You should have, you know. Technically I was 'with' you, wasn't I?"

"I thought you liked him too."

"Oh *please*. Cut it out."

"Well I did. Anyway I was sort of grateful for his help. I didn't think I could keep a girl of your sophisticated tastes amused all evening single-handed."

"You're kidding me——"

"Sally Jay, if you only knew what a sheltered life I've led," he said, and looked me straight in the eye.

"Haven't we all!" I was on the point of replying with feeling, but I saw Crazy Eyes looking our way again, so I put my face very close to Jim's and cooed huskily. "Tell me all about it."

"Well, I spent a year and a half at Dartmouth down in the cellar of the fraternity-house, painting," said Jim, taking my proximity calmly enough. "The monotony upstairs drove me crazy. It was bridge or football or townies. Look, I'll tell you why I asked you out if you really want to know. When I was sketching you at the hospital I suddenly saw that I could use you as my model. . ."

"Aw, shucks!"

"Wait a minute—the Ancient is getting out an Art Edition of his poems and he wants me to do four engravings. Four kinds of love : you know, sacred, profane—that sort of stuff. Well, I saw when I was sketching you today that I could probably use you for all four of them. I mean I got the idea of using only one model, and using you at the same time, see. Different aspects of you."

"Using me," I said incredulously. I was flattered to death.

"Oh it's just a matter of proportions. By classic standards, you see, your body is all out of proportion, but somehow it adds up. It's full of surprises; the line would be continually exciting." He took out his pencil and began sketching on the paper table-cloth. "Take your shoulders, for instance; they begin by slanting down away from your neck like this, see, and then, unexpectedly, these little sharp bones on each side of the pectoral muscle send them curving up like this, see? That's what I mean. And your arms—they kill me. Very skinny, almost toothpicks, so that when tollowing the line down along inside here, the last thing you expect are the full breasts. Great! Your hips——"

"O.K., O.K. I believe you."

"Will you pose for me? I mean nude, you know."

"Oh? Yes, sure of course. Naturally. Well-um. I'll have to think it over—I'm pretty busy now with rehearsals." Damn this brat, for putting me in a position where it would be just too corny to refuse; where I'd be sure to lose my sophisticated standing by doing so. And damn him also for raising within me yet another moral issue that day.

Crazy Eyes was upon us now, asking me to dance. I mean he reached over for my hand and pulled me out of my chair. I said no but he didn't seem to hear me, so I gathered that the rules were that even if you said no, if you weren't heard, you danced. Jim was no help. He smiled at us both politely.

Crazy Eyes was in quite a different mood from his cool jiving one. He ground his chest into mine and his groin into my groin. I stiffened my spine and tried to dance disapprovingly. Try it. Also he kept whispering in my ear. His accent in French was very strong and I couldn't understand him, so I didn't know if I was justified in getting mad. I tried talking. I tried to explain that the reason I'd gone up to him at the Dôme in the first place was that I'd mistaken him for a friend of mine. "I am a friend of yours," he leered, tutoying me. The music stopped. He tried to kiss me. One of the few things that had impressed me in college was a Southern girl's account of how she avoided being kissed on the doorstep of her house once by wearing a flower in her hair and sticking it in her mouth when she said good night. Only I had no flower. I struggled. I turned and pointed to the mono-dancer, saying coyly, "You mustn't make your friend jealous, must you?" "It is my sister," he replied curtly, and the struggle continued. Looking around (I was twisting my head right, left and sideways, of course), I saw that the group of Sinisters I had noticed with him at the Dôme, had mysteriously reappeared and formed, without actually seeming to, a sort of semi-circle around us, separating us from the tables and my friends. That made up my mind. I screamed, really screamed, for Jim, and in the ugly scene that followed his arrival—all three of us turned out to have several grievances against the other two—we all somehow lost face.

Out in the street in front of the Etats-Unis Dave Beckenfield was bawling out his friends.

"Jesus, have you left these suitcases in the car all *evening*? You're damn lucky they're still here, you jackasses. Hey, don't take that one out, it's mine. Christ, you fools, you ought to know better than to leave our stuff in the back of an open car like this in Paris. You might have told me."

"Where else do you suggest we put the luggage in a Stutz Bearcat? Is there a trunk compartment under the wheels?" asked one of the boys, fed up at last.

"Aw, quit picking on it, will you? Let it be," said Dave, flying as usual to the defence of his beloved. "Hey, I said *leave that suitcase alone*, it's mine. Yeh, leave it. Just leave it." He hopped huffily into his car. "I'm off to the Rotonde. Anyone coming?"

We went along with him, Zop-zop, Jim and I. I don't know why. It was four o'clock in the morning and the night had fallen to pieces around us. I looked in a mirror and rubbed some of the lipstick off my mouth into my cheeks. The effect was still terrible. We sat down at a table at the Rotonde, too tired even to talk. Suddenly Jim galvanized us by leaping to his feet and racing outside. I went over to the window and looked out, expecting to see—I don't know what; a train pulling out or pulling in, at least. I remember feeling very angry at the idea of being subjected to guessing games at this late hour, but mercifully, the tableau that followed was immediately explicit. Crazy Eyes, Jim, and Dave Beckenfield's valise all arrived together, or rather separately, each on the arm of a flic. Crazy Eyes was snarling ferociously and at the same time rubbing his jaw, Jim was grinning an elfin little smile, and the suitcase just looked heavy. This group was closely followed by the Sinisters, who automatically fell into their favourite semi-circular formation.

"Hey, what are you doing with that?" Dave Beckenfield demanded of the police, pointing to his case.

"It is yours?"

"You're goddam right it is. What's up, Jim?"

"I could see from the window this creep"—he pointed to Crazy Eyes—"trying to steal Beckenfield's suitcase. He pulled a knife on me and I hit him, and then his friends tried to jump me." The Sinisters closed in, trying to understand what Jim was saying to us so they could object, and in no time at all the air was thick with accusations. The flics finally took over. They wanted to know if Dave was going to charge Crazy Eyes with attempted theft.

"Of course," he said without a moment's hesitation.

So at five o'clock in the morning, dawn lighting our path, we were all carted off to the prefecture in the Paddy Wagon, or whatever it's called in French; the Corsicans (as they turned out to be) keeping up their spirits by heaping hot coals of curses upon us by the headful. The big surprise when we got there and told our story to the Chief was that he didn't particularly believe us. And when Crazy Eyes advanced his fairy-tale version of what had happened—how he'd simply stumbled across a suitcase lying right in the middle of the sidewalk, only to be assaulted by this American ruffian who had earlier and without any provocation tried to pick a fight with him at the Etats-Unis, it was unfortunate that the Sinisters who backed him up could technically be described as witnesses. As for the knife that Jim referred to—naturally, it couldn't be found.

We were told that the magistrate would arrive in the morning. Everyone was to come back at nine. Everyone except Jim and Crazy Eyes. They were being detained. This was a shock to all of us, and for a moment no one spoke.

Finally Dave stepped forward and said in a surprisingly quiet and reasonable voice, "Will you be needing me as well, officer?"

"It is your suitcase is it not? Are you not accusing this man?"

"There may have been some misunderstanding officer," said Dave thoughtfully. "Maybe the suitcase *was* left out on the sidewalk—some of my friends took theirs. . ."

"But that was in front of the Etats-Unis, not the Rotonde, don't you remember?" I corrected him quickly.

"Well, how do I know what happened? I didn't see anything, did I?"

I always expect people to behave much better than I do. When they actually behave worse, I am frankly incredulous.

"But of course it was outside the Etats-Unis," I explained to him patiently. "I remember it distinctly. I remember because we'd just finished tangling with——" I went up to the desk of the Head Flic. "This is ridiculous!" I exploded. "Of course that man was trying to steal the bag. I saw the whole thing from the café window. It should be apparent to a moron that he's a congenital liar"—'un menteur sérieux', I said—"and if anyone here can accuse anyone else of assault it's *me*, because he tried to assault me——"

"Very well, mademoiselle. You may tell the magistrate all this in the morning when you appear."

"Don't be crazy, Gorce," said Dave, dragging me away by the arm. "Don't get mixed up in this. Play it cool. Please forgive her, officer, she's just a little over-excited."

"Do you wish to drop the charge?"

"Yeh, yeh. There's been some misunderstanding. We're sorry about the whole thing. Come on, lads."

"I'm afraid" said the Flic-in-charge, "that your friend will have to stay anyway, to answer the counter-charge of assault. Leave the suitcase. It is evidence. You may go."

Dave turned to us and shrugged helplessly, as though he'd done his best to save us, and I looked over at Jim dumbfounded. I could have wept at what I saw—the poor sap—from hero to patsy in just one hour had left him looking dogged and manly, but not a little dazed.

I swung on Dave. "Why you stinker. What made you chicken out?"

"Look, give me credit for knowing a little more about these things than you do. Can't you see these guys are all prejudiced? Haven't you ever heard of anti-Americanism? Go Home Yankee? Just wise up and don't stick your neck out. If you're smart," he said, turning to Jim, "you'll take my advice. Apologize all round, say it was a big mistake, offer to pay some compensation and get out. But quick, understand? *Get away from here and stay away.*"

"But we're in the *right*," said Jim mildly.

"I hope they steal the car next time," I said to Dave. "The whole silly old pile of affected junk."

Dave turned to Zop-zop. "You see my point, don't you? These kids. Maybe *they* can afford to get their names all over the papers, I can't. I'm a Fulbright."

Zop-zop chewed his cud for a while and then made one of his few utterances. "Shame to lose that suitcase," he drawled, "but I guess you'll have to if you're going to take your own advice about getting away from here and staying away. Can't very well ask Jim to bring it back with him afterwards——" his voice trailed away.

We all three of us looked at Dave and then at one another, awaiting the decision. Dave looked at the suitcase and then at the keys to his car that he was jiggling in his hand. He didn't disappoint us. "It's not important, anyway. Just some old clothes" he grumbled finally, and shuffled off.

"I'll take you home," said Zop-zop to me. "Where do you live?"

"It's not worth it for a couple of hours," I said, making up my mind about something. "I'll stay on with Jim. You can start sketching me," I added over his objections.

"Well—take it easy," said Zop-zop. "See you in the morning. Oh here——" and he left us a pack of cards.

I laid out the cards and began playing solitaire. Jim sketched. I thought of Uncle Roger, who was footing the bill: what had I said to him that day eight years ago, when he promised to give me my freedom and asked me what I was going to do with it? I'd said I wanted to stay out late and eat whatever I liked any time I wanted to. And I wanted to meet people I hadn't been introduced to. And I wanted to guess right...

I looked around the Prefecture in the morning light. It was cold; I shivered. The paraffin stove that was supposed to heat the room had gone out and smelled awful. Everyone concerned was asleep; Jim, the Corsicans, even the guard was dozing. Was I fulfilling my childhood dreams? Well, I'd certainly stayed out late and eaten what I liked. And I was meeting people I hadn't been introduced to. That was for sure. In at least two cases—Jim and Crazy Eyes—I had guessed right.

I was now more or less in jail.

Uncle Roger, I thought, you can't say I'm not trying.

# CHAPTER SEVEN

IN THE END it took us all morning and Larry—and mostly Larry—to get us sprung from there. We were heading straight for Contempt of Court charges, Jim and I, when he finally arrived, and if he hadn't by some magic fluke already known Crazy Eyes and managed to exert his strange power over him, got me to shut up (I was being the most contemptuous), found out that Jim was an artist and made him show the magistrate his sketches of me, explaining at the same time that I was a Very Important Actress in his company and that rehearsals were being held up on my account (the magistrate, like most Frenchmen, could apparently do without Americans but not without Art)—if he hadn't done all this, I'd probably still be there yelling my head off.

All of a sudden, in the taxi on the way to the theatre, I collapsed. I put my head on Larry's shoulder and almost before I knew what was happening I had fallen fast asleep.

"Hey, zombie, wake up," I heard him saying softly into my ear when we arrived. I stretched and stared and shook myself. I looked up and saw him smiling down at me.

"Oh Larry!" I moaned. "I know you think I was just being one of your typical tourists but it was all your fault, really."

"My fault?"

In my drowsy-cat stage I knew it was going to be too complicated to explain, but anyway I tried. "You know—that horrible dinner-party yesterday—no Saturday, when you just let yourself get dragged off by that—oh, Larry, how *could* you?"

He just laughed. "Yeah," he said, "I never knew what hit me. . ."

Gently he disentangled himself and helped me out of the

taxi. He took me to a nearby café and fed me three cups of coffee. Then, with the same gentleness, he guided me through the afternoon's rehearsal. Which means he *does* care for me after all, I thought happily, as I sprinted out of theatre that evening. At just that moment I noticed a great beast of a car in robin's egg blue, ug—ug, squatting all over the entrance. I slowed down and looked inside. La Contessa, of course.

We were rehearsing in earnest. I suppose it's an admission of something or other, but it was the first time in my life—my gosh, the last time too, come to think of it—that I had ever felt any esprit de corps. Just as the Hard Core was the first group I wouldn't have minded joining if they'd been a club (which of course they weren't, good night, that was the whole *point* of them), this cast and crew was the first I'd ever felt that we're-all-in-this-together-Harry-England-and-St-George sort of stuff about.

Actually I wasn't seeing the Hard Core at this time. As a matter of fact Larry had forbidden me to, but he needn't have bothered. I'd have avoided them anyway. To have got all tangled up with them at this point might have broken the spell, and I wanted to stay spellbound; I thought we band of brothers were absolutely the cat's pyjamas. I was jealous of our solidarity and looked upon the outside world with the same mixture of indifference and contempt that is probably felt by the inmates of some well-run looney bin.

I soon realized that one of the most important things to find while working in theatre was someone to giggle with. To find someone to giggle with I place just below finding someone to flirt with and just above the ability to knit. Those are the only three things to do while waiting to go on. Oh, crosswords of course, if you can bear them. Anything else breaks the spell.

In Lee Harrison I had found an ideal giggling partner, and when I look back with nostalgia it is largely because of him. To begin with his romantic (there is no other word for it) struggle for existence thrilled me to the bottom of my hitherto all too sheltered core. There's plenty to be said for the theory that giving money to a beggar only encourages poverty; certainly without the small donations that I and others felt obliged to contribute from time to time, the epic battle of Lee versus No Visible Means of Support would have ended long ago. Lee would have had to pull himself together, go home, find a steady job, and we would have been deprived of a pleasure that I for one would have been more than sorry to be deprived of. And it was awful too, in a way, I suppose, that it took so little to keep him going—especially now that he was getting rehearsal pay, which for everyone else was cigarette money. He literally kept himself alive by his own burning sense of humour. He was a kind of monk without an Order.

"Lee, *where did* you sleep last night?" I asked him one day at lunch.

"The staircase of the Etats-Unis. Why?"

"There's a very strange odour about you. Dank, musty. I don't know——" I almost said 'dirty'.

"I used to think that was the smell of Russia, but now I know it is the smell of poverty the world over," guffawed Mrs. Wire good-naturedly. She was our rich Patron of the Arts, on whose money the company was largely operating.

I started to look shocked, but Lee just threw back his head and roared, at the same time helping himself generously to my bread (it was a very cheap restaurant and every item was separate), and sprinkling it liberally with his bottle of Lea and Perrins Sauce. He always carried this bottle around with him. It was one of the familiar bulges in his suit. The trouser-knees were two others, and the elbows two more. The reason for the bottle was partly to prove his anglophilism (it was supplied to him free by some English friends who worked at the British Embassy), partly because the food he ate was of such inferior quality that it couldn't help being improved by the sharp disguising taste of Worcester sauce, and partly, I am sure—in many ways he was the most childish of us all—because he shared a name in common with that distinguished label: the Original and *Genuine* Worcestershire Sauce manufactured at their Factory in Worcester, England.

Lee and I spent most of the lunchtime arguing. It generally began with Saroyan. Lee thought Saroyan was a marshmallow. I thought Saroyan was a writer who had written me a large and lovely part in the little one-act Prison Drama we were doing, and I also thought I was not going to be able to get on stage to do it with a straight face if Lee didn't stop his parodies of the Saroyan Style. He always managed to goad me into a rage where I'd find myself hotly defending Saroyan as a stark realist and demanding to know just what the hell Lee knew about jail *anyway,* since he'd never even seen the inside of one as I had (by then I really believed that Jim and I had spent the night behind bars), and then I'd exclaim triumphantly, "Well I can tell you this play is just how people *do* behave in those circumstances—that's life." "That's not life," he would reply irritably, "that's Saroyan." And somehow this led us directly into our argument over the Method. You know, the Stanislavsky Method; working for realism through improvisations and sense memory, and emotional recall and all that sort of—oh well, never mind, a lot of technical stuff. I was devoted to it. Anyway, if there was anything Lee was more contemptuous of than Saroyan it was the Method. Noël Coward himself couldn't have been more contemptuous. Nevertheless, along about this time, Lee began treating us to his home-made improvisations. The third play we were doing, the one by Shaw, had a butler in it—one of those announcing and handing-things-around butlers—and Lee was it. He would call upon us, those of us not in or connected with the play, at the end of each rehearsal, to guess what the new improvisation was about. "What was I being today?" he would ask.

"I don't know. Some sort of dope-fiend I suppose."

"Your friend Crazy Eyes asking people to dance with him."

Once he was Groucho Marx breathing lecherously into the women's bosoms. Once he played it blind, once lame and once drunk. The game caught on; it had tremendous popularity, and then one day he went too far. It was Katherine Cornell being goosed as she went around with the sandwiches, an improvisation full of tiny leaps into the air and gracious acknowledgements—really one of his best—but both the performance and the audience's reaction finally ripped the scales off Larry's eyes. He gave Lee a bawling out that lasted twenty minutes, then turned on us and ordered us out for the rest of the rehearsals. I crept back into the wings to watch the next one. This butler of Lee's, rigid with impertinence, would have been fired on the spot. "What was *that* supposed to be?" I whispered to him when he came off. "That was me!" he snapped, and strode away.

At the lunch break once, one of the actors asked Larry for a couple of days off to do some filming. "What are they paying you?" he asked and when the actor told him he said: "Go back and ask for twice as much." The actor stalled and Larry became furious. I'd never seen him in such a rage before—not even over Lee. "Are you crazy?" he barked at the actor. "They're robbing you. Go back and ask for twice as much or I won't release you. Never under-sell yourself unless you want everyone else to. How many years did you go to acting school?" "Two." "Well, that was your investment in your profession, now you've got to get your investment back." "Yeah," said the boy, "but acting's something I *like* to do. I just can't get over being paid for doing what I like." "Get over it," was Larry's command, and that was the end of the conversation.

I couldn't believe my ears. It was the first time I'd ever heard Larry mention money. Larry and money. I could write an essay on that. I remembered the conversation I'd had with Teddy that evening at the Ritz, when he asked me what Larry did for money and the thought had sprung so quickly into my mind: Larry needs money. I felt it again, I felt it, I always felt it and I couldn't say why. Certainly not from outward appearances, clothes and so on. But some days, for instance, he might say carelessly to the owner of the café at lunchtime, "I'm not hungry now. I'll just have a peach and peel it for me like a good girl, will you?" and in a second I would be wondering whether it was out of necessity or caprice.

When we all sat around moaning and groaning about how

expensive Paris was—and we did, it was one of our favourite conversations—he simply switched off. You could actually see it boring him. And the few times that we dined alone together, at the end of our meal there was none of the usual leaping up from the chair as though shot through with an arrow, yelling Wow! or similar Indian war whoops, which most of my friends felt de rigueur in heralding the arrival of the bill. I was grateful to him for that, and yet it was impossible to say just why, but it was always a *relief* to find out that he had the money to cover it. Did it mean he was going without breakfast next morning, or what? And it was crazy to feel like this, because sometimes you could see he was just rolling in the stuff.

"Are you a gambler?" I asked him finally.

"There isn't anything you do in life that isn't a gamble, Gorce," he replied.

"But do you gamble?" I insisted.

"In a way. In a way." He looked at me oddly.

It just defeated me. I could guess and guess and guess about Larry and still not get anywhere. It all led down a blind alley.

At first I had him sliced like a pie into thirds: one-third High Living (Soldier of fortune, gambler, womanizer); one-third Low-living (preoccupation with 'real' world, anti-phoney, anti-tourist, anti-lounge lizard, pro-student, pro-worker, on elaborate terms of equality with waiters, etc.); and one-third Serious Artist (all the qualities of a good director plus a positive genius for making people do what he wanted them to). But later on, when he showed me with great reluctance and humility his fiercely-penned poetry, I had to re-slice him into fourths, and the last fourth—I hate to say it (I will though)—was Corn, pure Corn. Maybe it didn't add up. Or maybe it didn't add up to much, but to me the charm of his toughness and devilry and elusiveness was fatal.

To take the first part of him, the womanizer, it seemed like the thing he had about money, to be all mixed up with his pride. The Contessa came around, and not only the Contessa, some pretty fancy women came by, and yet I couldn't figure out what he specifically liked about them. Variety seemed to be the only rule. There was something impersonal in the way he treated them. I could see he didn't love any of them, that he didn't even particularly like them; he—I don't know *what* he them'd.

And then, towards the end of rehearsals, I suddenly stopped being jealous. I could tell by certain things, the way I'd catch him looking at me, the way he'd stopped his maddening pretence that I was an abstract type going through abstract experiences, and make some personal remark to try to find out how important Teddy and Jim were in my life, that he was going to get around to *me* soon. The question was when.

I was wearing a dark red corduroy skirt and a blue-and-white-striped shirt one day. I remember that because he'd kept on looking at me until I asked him what was the matter. He laughed. "You look so—" he closed his eyes a moment and smiled slowly, "—so vital," he said finally, and then "Sorry about that evening at Visconti's. I shouldn't have goofed off like that. Should have stayed on with you. Should have taken you home."

"Yes, you should have."

"Have I lost the chance?"

"I don't know."

"When will you?"

"Um. Opening Night?"

"Right. Opening Night. Don't forget, Gorce."

"Oh, I won't."

Larry and Fame; I was now approaching the two things I wanted most in the world with breakneck speed. The only trouble was that towards the first, my inclination was to rush headlong, full-steam ahead, and from the other—the Ordeal —to hold back forever.


The theatre was ice-cold, and as I slumped and quivered in my slip in the dressing-room trying to keep my hards steady enough to put my eye make-up on, I wondered how on earth I'd gotten there in the first place. It was all supposed to be a joke, wasn't it? It was all supposed to stop long before it actually happened, wasn't it? I wasn't really supposed to get out there in front of a bunch of strangers and make a fool of myself, didn't God know that? I took a deep breath and watched it come out in a frozen puff. That's going to look great on stage, I thought, especially in the love scenes.

"Half an hour." The distant clangour of the Assistant Stage-Manager's voice coming along the upstairs corridors was entirely unnerving. Must she bellow like that? All my esprit de corps slipped quietly away. Every man for himself and swim while the shore's still in sight. What use would I have been to them anyway? I couldn't even remember my lines. I began shaking all over. I just made it to the john before becoming violently sick. The spasms were of such excruciating pain that I thought I was going to die then and there, leaning ignobly over the bowl. Everything had come up and yet I was still wracked with contractions. Entrails next, I told myself.

"Twenty minutes." That voice again. O.K., I thought, this is it. And I waited. Perversely enough nothing happened. I lay on the floor for about five minutes. My cold sweat seemed to have encouraged my circulation, and I felt healthy and in a curious state that I could only describe as 'optimistic'. I began to tingle rather than tremble, and some of my lines came back to me. "We are now entering the old manic phase," I told myself, calmly enough, until I realized I'd said it out aloud. Then I picked myself up off the floor.

When Larry came into my dressing-room to wish me luck I was almost able to match his confidence, except that my words came out all funny. "And good luck too to you too!" I heard myself replying.

"Five minutes," roared the Assistant Stage-Manager. What on earth could I have ever liked about that girl anyway, I wondered. Who hired her in the first place? She obviously didn't know her job, going around scaring people to death like that. I'd speak to Larry about it later.

*"Places, please!"* That did it. At last I understood that this unholy Cassandra who had been announcing the end of the world all evening in that impatient, doom-ridden voice was *doing it on purpose*. Naturally. What could I expect? She wanted to play my parts, of course. I would certainly speak to Larry about this later. I would certainly see to it that this sort of unprofessional behaviour was stopped at once. It was outrageous. Either she went or I did. And then, delighted to discover that I was already thinking like a star, I went down on to the stage. The curtain rose. The lovely, warm lights were glistening on me.

Out in front the unexpected silence surprised and flattered me. I imagined there must be hundreds and thousands and millions of people quiet in the dark out there, waiting with baited breath for me, up on that stage and bathed in coloured lights, to say something. I opened my mouth and—hooray—they were going to *listen*.

I suppose Larry was right. I suppose it was a pretty revolting spectacle to come into a dressing-room after a show and find two of its leading players screaming abuse at each other. Especially since I was back in my slip again and sitting on the floor (I'd had such a bad attack of post-something-or-other nerves, that I couldn't even sit on the chair), while Lee was staring starkly at himself in the mirror. It was all Lee's fault, of course. I loved him passionately and devotedly, but I never wanted to see him again. As I said, he was in this for laughs and he never knew when to stop. I know what I'm talking about. I've giggled along with the best of them but dammit this just wasn't funny. I could have killed him.

"Children, children," said Larry, closing the door quickly behind him. "What's all this?"

I got in first. "I should have known. Oh God. I should have *known*. Sure we have this scene together, sure I know what he's like on stage, but this is *Tennessee Williams*, I kept telling myself and Lee *approves* of Williams so it's going to be all right. So what does he go and do, the bastard? Oh *sure* I've seen him horsing around with the butler part, but that's got nothing to do with it, I kept telling myself. I've got nothing to worry about. It isn't Saroyan, it's *Williams*. . ."

"So what *does* he do?" said Larry.

"Didn't you see? Didn't you see him prancing on to the stage with that *cockroach* on his lapel? He comes on with a *real* cockroach on his bathrobe and it jumps off him and starts *crawling* around the set. I nearly died of fright. I tell you if it had started to fly, play or no play, I would have just curled up and *expired*."

"May I point out that the place is supposed to be crawling with cockroaches," said Lee in his fruitiest voice, ponging every other word, "and that you spend the first twenty minutes of the play complaining to the landlady about them? I was merely trying to inject a little realism to help you along with your reactions. Stanislavsky himself couldn't have done more. I was only trying to be helpful."

"You were not. You were trying to break me up. You'll do anything for a laugh and you know it. Where the hell did you find that cockroach anyway? It must have taken months to ferret it out."

"In the places to which I have access they hardly need ferreting out."

"I'm not going on tomorrow night if you're here."

"Oh well, if you're going to be stuffy——"

"You're damn tootin' I am. I'll report you to Equity and get you kicked out."

"All right, all right, that's enough," said Larry. He turned to Lee. "Go back to your dressing-room, I'll see you later. By the way she's right about Equity, you know. You could be kicked out for that."

"Lee Harrison, if I ever see you again I will kill you. I'll kill you and then I'll kick you," I yelled after him.

Larry picked me up off the floor and shook me until I calmed down. "Aren't you ashamed of yourself carrying on like this, screaming like a fish-wife on the eve of your triumph? I was going to tell you how good you were, but now I won't." And then he burst out laughing. He dropped my shoulders and leaned against the wall for support and laughed and laughed.

"It's the Old Pro in you," he gasped, still laughing. "Hardly able to wait till she's off stage to start bawling out the other actor."

"But I am terrified of insects, especially those that fly."

Larry kissed me on the cheek and sat me down at my dressing-table. "Hurry up and put something on to receive in. Your public is waiting," he said and left me.

When he came back a little while later I noticed for the first time that he was in his dinner-jacket. The black and white was almost unbearably becoming to him. He shone and bristled and it was all I could do to stifle the impulse to stroke the back of his neck. Only then did I realize that I'd completely forgotten about my own clothes. At three o'clock in the afternoon I'd been told to go home and bathe and rest and so forth, but I'd been so nervous I'd just wandered around reciting my lines instead. Now all I had with me was what I'd been wearing then : a navy-blue suit and a crumpled white blouse. I'd been trying to take off my make-up and I felt all creamy behind the ears and in my eyes, which stung and swam from the running mascara. I felt as if I'd fallen into a pot of grease.

"Let's go," said Larry.

"Where to?"

"Well, first of all, the Contessa——"

"Oh, *Larry*."

"Honey, I don't like it any better than you. But what can I do? She's gone and planned this elaborate party without consulting me. Don't worry, we'll cut as soon as possible——"

"But I'm so tired. I don't want to have to wrestle with a horde of strangers. I just want to eat about a hundred million oysters and two tons of caviare and go swimming naked in champagne——"

"I don't know about the swimming, but I'll make damn sure you get enough of everything else you want."

"Oh well. You win. You go ahead and apologize for my clothes, won't you?"

I looked at myself in the mirror in despair. I thought of the evening-dress I might have worn. I combed my hair and thought bitterly about my batting average for dressing inappropriately. Why break a record? I flung a towel over the make-up on the table and left without bothering to straighten it out.

We arrived at the Contessa's in an enormous car of snowy white. It was a sleeping car. That's what I said. The back seat could be made up into a bed at night. It slept two. We talked about it on the way over; I mean *they* talked about it on the way over. We were four. There was me and Larry, the Contessa (who having said hello as I climbed into the car had already used up half her conversation to me for the evening) and the King of Lithuania, or someone like that. Just looking at him filled me with foreboding. How was I going to square up to all *this*, I wondered. The sensation of being so close to another human being with whom I had not one single sensation in common left me speechless. I fell to studying him. It was amazing how different even real things—a gold ring, hair oil, the cut of a coat, could be without being bizarre; the fabric of his shirt was woven of some Martian stuff; even his very skin was of another weave. Not a word was exchanged; there was at least an ocean between us. All this time the Contessa was flirting with Larry 'outrageously', as she might have put it, and with an elephantine delicacy (as she most certainly would not have), about the bed in the car. The King listened brightly and I stared at him fixedly, unable to recognize anything.

I began worrying about the transference of bravery. Only four hours earlier I'd said to myself that if I ever survived the ordeal of the first Entrance I would never be afraid again. Now it looked like far from the first fear cancelling out the next one, it was actually going to multiply it.

I pulled Larry aside before we went into the drawing-room. "Larry, I want to leave. It's too harrowing. I won't know a living soul."

"Oh come now. There's nothing to be frightened of. Probably just a bunch of queens."

"Queens !"

"Queers. Fairies."

"Hey, no kidding, *all* of them?"

"Well, most. Oh sure, all of them. Every last one of them. Come on, Gorce, cheer up. I promise you one thing; you'll eat better food in here than you'll ever be able to order in your life."

We walked into the drawing-room, where everyone was sitting around like a bunch of stuffed owls. Gradually they came to life. About seven of them began exchanging glances with each other, very slowly at first and then with increasing vivacity, until exchanged glances were ricocheting around the room like bullets. I waited for the contractions in my stomach to start and the familiar jangle of nerves. I found I was not only *not* receiving them, but totally unable to produce them. I really *was* too tired. A blessed calm descended upon me and I surveyed the scene like it was something through the wrong end of Uncle Roger's telescope. When I surveyed the buffet, I headed straight for it. Larry was so right. I ate as I had never eaten before. Then I looked around. The International Set, I said to myself wonderingly.

The first to engage me in a duel of wits was an elderly American gentleman of the Southern-fried variety. He wanted to know what part of the States I was from but when I told him I'd been born in St. Louis he became violently distressed. He seemed to take it as a personal affront that I hadn't been born in the heart of the Southland—South Carolina, for example. In fact he got so childishly querulous and wrought up about it that I suddenly realized he was batty. In one glorious non-sequitur, he demanded to know exactly what I had *against* the South.

"Too much woodwork," I answered, just for the hell of it. Why should he get a sensible answer? Unfortunately I had chosen one of those split seconds when the clouds parted and the old boy was having a brief spell of sanity.

"Woodwork?" he asked suspiciously. "What's woodwork

got to do with it? What do you mean, woodwork?" he kept on asking me over and over again—boy, it was his Moment of Truth.

I suddenly realized why I'd said it. He looked just like the Woodwork teacher—Carpentry, they called it—at one of my schools. I remembered his report on me at the end of the term: "Sally Jay has done good woodwork but she should try to be more co-operative and less vindictive. Promoted to Fourth grade."

"I don't know. I read it in a book somewhere, I guess. I've forgotten where," I gibbered.

Luckily the clouds had already rolled back again. He shook his hoary locks and muttered something about not understanding why the young folks were permitted to go gallivantin' around the Lord knew where nowadays without their mothers.

I said didn't he think I was a little old to be trailing mother around with me and he said No, by golly, he did not, and I got irritated and said that maybe *he* ought to be with his mother, and then I realized that my God he was. Not far from us was an enormous mountain, about five hundred tons of insipid grandeur, covered in black velvet and topped by a fleece of white hair. One look at the two profiles was enough to convince me that they were out of the same cookie-cutter. It was mothah, all right.

I backed away from him into a cluster consisting of a very famous musical-comedy actor called Rollo, a skinny old woman covered in ornaments and got up rather like a hysterical Christmas tree, and a superbly dressed, superbly indolent, superbly at home young man who was beginning, I noticed, superbly to get on Rollo's nerves. In an evening of 'firsts' I may as well mention that it was also the first Australian I had ever met.

"I think she behaved disgracefully," complained the Australian. "I said it to her back and I'll say it to her face."

"I don't know which is which," snapped Rollo. "A woman of intarissable vapidity. Not you, my dear," he turned to me. "My dear, you were delightful. Completely delightful." He said it in a warm famous voice of such passionate sincerity as to be utterly indistinguishable from the real thing, and then added in a slightly lower but equally carrying tone, "But my dear, who *was* that you were supposed to be playing opposite, poor child? And I don't know *what* to call that last set—an Obstacle Course, I think, really, don't you? No, I mean it, you were quite marvellous. One of the seven wonders of the world, wasn't she, everyone?"

The Christmas Tree grudged me a hideous grimace, fixing her beady eye on me like a kind of Ancient Mariness, and then turned upon Rollo with an ogle of the most vehement lechery I have ever seen. Now that I've been around (hey, hey) I am no longer astonished at the lubricity of these old biddies, but at the time I just couldn't get over it.

The party went on. There were these two young Princes. They were about sixteen years old and one was blond and the other dark. They were like a couple of bear cubs. They'd been evacuated to the States during the war and spoke tough American-English instead of English-English; it sounded so funny on top of their Baltic accents. As I was an actress they immediately assumed I must be an intimate of their great friend Aly Khan, and when—to our mutual sorrow—I had to disillusion them, they smoothly switched the conversation over to the possible drugging and drinking habits of several prominent movie stars they had never met.

"Say, *you'd* be swell in the movies," one of them exclaimed after a long interested look at me. It did just flash past my mind then that maybe *they* were the ones who ought to be home with their mothers.

People started leaving. Two men I hadn't even met came up and kissed my hand goodbye; Mother Southern and her son toddled off; more champagne was opened, and the party apparently was really on.

The two young princes took me on a tour of the house. I saw what Judy meant about the strange pieces of sculpture. In all my life I'd never seen anything so spectacularly ugly. It was one of the Contessa's hobbies, I was told—sculpting. The dogs too, the huge ones all over the place, and the litter of puppies in the kitchen were horrible, red-eyed, long-fanged beasts of an indescribable hideosity.

"The Contessa likes to surround herself with ugliness," I said, hoping to get a laugh, but the Yellow Prince agreed most solemnly, adding with a leer, "She has some—um—rah-ther *special* tastes." He said it in English-English. It was not the last time I was to be led down the garden-path and out through the back gate of the private lives of the Set; but it *was* the first time, and it came out of the mouths of babes, and I was really curious.

"Strange tastes like *what*?" I asked eagerly, but was rewarded only with a wise and totally un-American shrug.

"Come along, little ones, we're all going on to Rollo's new discovery," carolled the Contessa, that merry madcap, coming upon us together in the kitchen and delighted at last that age had found its level.

Rollo's new discovery turned out to be a queer club.

One of the things—one of the many, many, *many* things that fascinate me about myself—is how it is possible for me to know something without really knowing it at all. I mean I seemed to have known about queers all my life, I can't remember when I didn't, and I generally can guess who *is*. I mean, it's no traumatic shock for me or anything like that to discover that so-and-so actually is one—and yet, I swear, I was flabbergasted when I saw that club. There was a style of flirting along the bar where some sailors stood waiting to be picked up, that no starlet could hope to emulate. And the droves and *droves*. I had no idea there were so many. I just had no idea.

By now I was beginning to form some generalizations about the International Set (not that I ever even found out if they were the Real Thing, I mean what standards would I have to judge them by anyway?). First of all, though very few seemed to be married at the time, they were all passionately involved with one another. This had a way of making conversation rather difficult. For instance, when one of them began talking to you it was impossible to predict which of the others was going to get sore. And the reason they got sore was that it was assumed that the one talking to you was also making a pass at you, and the reason *that* was assumed was that it was generally true. And the reason it was generally true, was that they had nothing else to talk to me about. Past parties—past and future parties, resorts in and out of season, their own lineages and those of their friends were their only real contributions to a conversation, except for the one that went "I was in America once . . ." and then petered out into a series of place-names, so that by making a play for me I suppose they felt they were keeping their end up. Another thing about them was the way they kept inviting you places; they invited me to a different place on an average of one every five minutes, but I discovered there were two rules governing this: first, it had to be a place you'd never been to, like "What, you've never seen the Blue Grotto? I must take you there on the yacht this summer"; and second, it was understood that each invitation cancelled the previous one— I'll leave you to guess what the very last one always was. It was also a great mistake to assume that in spite of all this boulevardier stuff they were really au fond homosexual—or rather I should say homosexual as we know it.

But to get back to the queer club. As Rollo led us through the long bar into the dark, highly scented night-club room, the atmosphere became electric with competition for him. He was King-Pin all right, though this fact seemed to irritate him rather than otherwise, and we were immediately shown to the choice table (on top of the piano and under the stage platform) in the crowded room.

"Faggotry here reaches almost pyrotechnical heights," Larry whispered to me as a stream of young men ranging from ferociously grotesque to wistfully good-looking filed past to pay their respects to Rollo; some eager as young brides for us to admire their new home, some flirting so excitedly they even flirted with the women in our party by mistake. The ones I spoke to all confessed to being helplessly enraptured with the sailors at the bar, but with the desperate unreality of women admiring one another's clothes that they wouldn't be seen dead in.

There was a strong sea-motif running through it all which surprised me at the time, though I don't know why on earth it should. All the waiters wore striped fishermen's jerseys, the men in uniform were mostly naval officers and sailors, and the decorations, such as they were, consisted mainly of life-belts and coils of rope.

Buford Wellington, a young American, carried the sea motif further by having the face and the walk, or rather the waddle, of a seal, with fins for hands and the suggestion of web feet. He arrived at Rollo's side flapping his flippers into Rollo's face in a way that did nothing to improve the latter's temper.

"Thank God you've come at last. *Such* a difficult time with that French crowd over there. I simply can't make myself understood. Half of them think that I'm a snob——"

"How blind of them," said Rollo.

"——and the other half that I'm an intellectual!"

"How deaf of them."

Boofie Wellington, it seemed, was an old doormat that Rollo allowed in his presence from time to time because he did all the packing. It saved hiring a valet.

"Don't sit down," ordered Rollo as Boofie began to pull up a chair next to me. "I told you, you weren't to come near me until you did something about those disgusting nails."

I looked down at the soft white hands and noticed two or three enormously long fingernails on each of them.

Boofie sulked and sat down anyway. "I only grew them because you promised to take me to Greece. All the aristocracy in Greece wear their nails long, don't they?" he asked the King of Lithuania, or whoever he was, who had fallen into a deep abstraction and didn't answer.

"File them off by tomorrow or I'll have you thrown out of the hotel," said Rollo casually, in a tone that cut through Boofie like a knife through butter.

"Haven't I seen you before?" pleaded Boofie to me, trying to recover. "I wonder who we have in common. Do you know Tanny Pop——"

"Nope."

"I had an awful time in Venice last year," he went on. "I was asked to leave. Some silly political scandal, bounced cheques, and all that sort of thing. So I exiled myself in Ibiza. My dear, don't. I stared at those goats for five months. I got goat-blindness. I had to be carried off to Tonjay to recover. And *then* we found so many Hollenzollens lying around the house we almost couldn't get into it. I was combing them out of my hair all day. I knew it would happen. I told Paul it was a mistake letting them get in, in the first place. By the way, how old do you think I am? I'm thirty-two next month. I look younger, don't I? I was Groton's, St. Paul's, Harvard's and Oxford's only remittance man in Ibiza. Do you know Peter Windsor? I met him on the street the other day and he *still* wants to know why he isn't happy. All that money and still so unhappy. It's that American thing you have about work, I told him. You want to make a great splash in some artistic pond and you haven't the talent to do it, so you don't work. *That's* what's making you unhappy. The puritanical commercial American success drive——"

I'd stopped fighting it by now and was rolling with the punch.

The cabaret had finally started. It was quite desperately bad. It was all so puzzling. It was as though they were deliberately setting out to debase themselves. I saw that Rollo, whose mood had been getting steadily worse, was now drunk as well. A man, more or less dressed as a woman, did a hula dance, the effect of which was impossible to describe. It couldn't strictly be called 'funny' because he was trying so tragically hard, and yet for the life of me, I couldn't get away from the feeling that basically he was meaning to be funny after all—or horrifying—or, oh hell, I don't know.

"It isn't Tulip again—oh no!" groaned Rollo very loudly. "That damn Dutch queen is in every night club I go into——"

"I told you to stop calling him Tulip. His name's Derek and you know it," said his Australian friend, no longer suave but full of menace and very red in the face.

Rollo turned on him, speaking carefully with slow, cold

contempt. "I'll call him Tulip if I like. I think he is a tulip. I think he's a whole *bunch* of tulips. Don't try to get tough with me, Kangaroo. I'll send you right back where you came from and don't think I can't do it." He picked up one of the glasses and deliberately smashed in on the floor.

"Hey, Tulip," he called out, "where'd you get that necklace? Avec ce bijou—là tu a l'air tout à fait lesbien." Everyone laughed.

The hula dancer, Derek, motioned for the music to stop and came down-stage towards us. He was very frightened. "I am sorry you do not care for my dancing, Monsieur Rollo——"

"You're damn right I don't. Get off the stage. How dare you presume to be on it?" And he smashed another glass. The princes roared with laughter. They were enjoying themselves hugely.

"I wonder if we have anyone in common," said Boofie trying me again. "Do you know Cecil——"

"I don't know *any* Cecils."

"She doesn't know any Cecils," he said wonderingly, and looked around the table for someone to share his pity.

"How many Cecils do *you* know?" he asked Larry, and without waiting for a reply started to play what was obviously one of his favourite games. "Let's see, there's Cecil Beaton, Cecil Day Lewis, Cecil Woodham-Smith."

They were all listening to him, idly waiting, after the incident of the smashed glasses, for the next distraction.

"Cecil Rhodes," said someone.

"Oh really—the dead ones don't count."

"David Cecil."

"Groucho Cecil," said Rollo, and made as if to stand up, but the next minute he crumpled abruptly, his head falling to the table, and passed out.

Everybody was enjoying themselves. Everyone but me and the King, who had turned quite black with melancholy.

A jazz trio started playing and one of the princes asked me to dance. Boy, Crazy Eyes had nothing on this kid! Put them in the ring together and I wouldn't know who to place my money on. Served me right of course for even *thinking* these two baby gangsters might be queer.

I returned to the table black and blue, two buttons ripped off my blouse and mad as a wet hen. I confronted Larry. "Goodbye," I said. "Go to hell and take this whole bunch with you. Do you know what I think? I think they should be driven into the sea with *pitchforks*, like a horde of great crab things." I gesticulated wildly, and my handbag swung out and hit something or somebody, and landed on the floor, butter-side down of course, and everything spilled out—lipstick, compact, passport, mirror. It was the Ritz all over again, except the gesture had popped the last button of my blouse as well. I stamped on the mirror in sheer temper. Then I sat down. I didn't know whether to laugh or cry. Everyone, I noticed, was very polite about my outburst, which for them was merely the next item of distraction which they expected to have provided; Larry picked up my bag, put all my things back in it, handed it to me and told me to go to the Ladies Room and have the attendant sew the buttons back on my blouse, and that we'd go on as soon as I got out.

And *then*—oh gosh—I know all this next part by heart— I *should*, I've been over it so many times. And *then* I came out of the john and told Larry I'd lost my passport and he said, "No you haven't, here it is, I found it after you left" and he took it out of his jacket and slapped it against the palm of his hand a couple of times and asked me why on earth I carried it around with me. I said because I didn't know where to put it down. Oh Lord, just *saying* these words even now makes me groan with boredom, when I think how many times they've bounced off dead walls and deaf ears. Anyway, I said I didn't know where to put it down because I was always losing things, even in my hotel room, or they were losing me, rather. It's a gradual thing—I kind of slowly miss them—it's as if they're weaning themselves away from me. I've never known a fountain pen longer than a month and I'm lucky if a lipstick stays with me for three weeks. So, as I said, that was why I carried this passport around with me. Larry said, "O.K., O.K., it's none of my business," took my bag, dropped the passport in, clicked it shut, and handed it back to me. And that, as I was later to say about a hundred thousand million times, was the very last I ever saw of that passport.

"Well, everybody, we're going on."

But everybody, it seemed, was going on with us.

I turned to Larry. "Only if it's somewhere entirely different. And without the Dead-End Kings."

It was different all right. It was a lesbian joint. Again, my first. But—and I can imagine how *this* is going to sound—it seemed, by comparison, terribly innocent, almost wholesome. To begin with, there was a jolly all-woman orchestra and a lot of rather gorgeous, slim, long-legged mannequin-looking girls floating around with urchin hair-cuts, dressed in torero pants. In fact, some of them did actually look like the pictures I'd seen of bull-fighters. And the whole atmosphere was so much lighter and less frantic than the other one that I decided —all chauvinism aside—that women simply do look more attractive trying to imitate men than the other way around. But probably it's just that I'm more used to girls.

We had by now, thanks to Larry, lost the gangster princes. But we had gained Boofie. This meant I'd exchanged the chance of being pummelled to death for the chance of being bored to death by the steady beat, beat of flapping gums, remorselessly forging their way back through old laundry-lists.

It was an evening of firsts. But dancing with girls wasn't one of them. I'd spent four years in college doing that, so I'm afraid I didn't get much depraved joy dancing with what I suppose is called a Professional Woman. She didn't even dance very well—though no worse than some of the girls at school—but dear me *suz*, the heavy-handed raillery that went on and on and *on* amongst the Set about what a dangerous vamp I was getting to be. I mean they kept splitting themselves in half laughing at what they were saying, even though it was getting less and less amusing. They were stimulating themselves to death. Well, I thought, here they are—Café Society—and how do they keep from screaming?

"How do they keep from screaming?" I asked Larry.

"O.K. Let's blow."

But it wasn't as easy as that. First there was a lively scene between him and the Contessa that I had to try not to overhear (I did catch a lulu though—"I weesh you were a hole in the ground!" she hissed at him as we left), and then we had to recover from the huff that the quarrel with the Contessa had put him into.

We stood there in the middle of the street waiting. "Dammit," he said, fuming, "there's a film director she *knows* I want to meet. What got into her anyway? She's never been so unreasonable before."

"It's me," I said. "It's because I had an affair with Teddy."

"What's that got to do with it?"

"She's his mistress."

"What? Oh no, you've got that all wrong. They've known each other all their lives; they're practically brother and sister."

"Have it your own way. But that was the whole purpose of that charming dinner-party he gave for us with cousin John. It was revenge. He set her on *you* to get even with me, and it's just dawned on me she set *herself* on you to get even with *me* for Teddy. Don't you see? Don't try to figure it out. What's the difference anyway? They're just a couple of pimps."

My summing-up must have had a profound effect on him, for he automatically started walking away and then suddenly he let out a shout of laughter. "Gorce," he said, "you're dead right. You're right on the nose. That *is* just what they are. Now that we've got that settled—" I had caught up with him by now "—where shall we go?"

"The Rotonde's near my hotel."

"Good. We can walk there."

He began teasing me about the Lesbian I'd been dancing with. He said he hadn't put *that* in his course for Tourists, and he wanted to know what she'd written on the slip of paper he'd seen her hand me. I said it really was sad in a way—although it was funny, too, of course—all this fuss, and all she'd really wanted out of me was to find out how to get over to the States. That was why she'd given me her name and address. I'd told her I'd ask the Embassy about it and let her know. I mean I was all for it. Why not everybody change countries with everybody else?

Larry went into one of his funny furies. "Oh sure let her use you. Let *everyone* use you. Listen, Gorce, you've got to be tough. Which are you going to be—monster or doormat? It's one or the other. Make up your mind," and he strode off.

I called out that it was something I couldn't decide right off like that, and hurried after him, but all the while I was crumbling inside. This race to keep up with Larry was such an Externalization of the problem, as the Stanislavsky boys would have it. I had no technique for dealing with him : only an overpowering, unnerving, irrational, chemical desire to be with him. Yes, all of that. The fear of losing his physical presence was tying my reflexes into such knots that I was incapable of behaviour as such. When we got to the Rotonde, I sat in a miserable stupid downcast silence. The invisible thread that had been pulling us closer together all that past week was stretched to breaking-point.

"What is the significance of you and the Contessa?" I asked him finally. I could have kicked myself for trying flippancy, but it was the only language I knew.

"The Contessa and I understand each other."

"And we don't?"

"No. We don't."

"Why?" asked the timid doormat.

"Well that's a long story and I'm not going to tell it." A pause. "I'll bet you can't guess what my father was. He was the Golf pro at Farringdale."

"What's that?"

"Exactly. Anyone who *knows* knows that. Anyone who matters. Anyone of distinction, I mean. I learned my manners and my morals there and when dear old Daddy died I sort of became their mascot and I learned a few more things besides. Do you know what those fine old club members were white enough to do for this poor little orphan? They were white enough to take up a collection to send him to the very best schools. Yes sir, Larchmont High never saw my dust again. Now don't you think that was pretty damn white of them? Only naturally it was understood they weren't going to be white enough——" He broke off suddenly with a crafty look. "Oh no you don't," he said. "I'm not sorry about anything. You don't get the story of *my* life, you don't." He grinned, making one of his lightning switches back to the old lady-killer, and reached over for my hand.

"Do you think we ought to get ahold of the Herald-Trib to look at the notice?" I asked, hoping it was the right thing to say.

"It'll be too early yet," he replied tenderly; and then, "Hey, I'll be damned!" He sat up suddenly. "Speak of the devil! Look who's over there will you?" He indicated the bar, where Crazy Eyes and his sister the Mono-dancer stood at the far end over in a corner, and waved at them gaily. Larry's erratic behaviour was beginning to get me down. All this blowing hot and cold was making me dizzy, and apart from everything else the idea that he could *like* those two infuriated me.

"Well for God's sake don't ask them over here," I said.

"Why not?"

"Because I can't stand them, that's why. I spent the night at the prefecture on account of him, you remember, and—oh, why go on? She's nothing but a prostitute and he's just a common thief."

"Oh-h-h. Oh, *well*. Thanks for telling me. That makes all the difference of course. I wouldn't dream of asking them over now that I know *that*. Pimps, prostitutes and thieves. You've got a label for everything, haven't you, Miss Gorce? Why don't you try living in this world for a change?" He rose. "Excuse me for a minute, will you? I'll just go over and say hello."

I wanted to cry; I couldn't think why I wasn't. The unfairness of it all. What had I done, anyway? I sat on, propped up on the table, staring blankly at nothing, like one of those Absinthe Drinkers. I noticed my elbows and arms were caked

with dirt from all the dirty tables I'd been sitting at, and my
hands black from all the dirty people I'd been meeting. I
felt myself kind of slipping away.

Larry, back at my side again, was apologizing for jumping
down my throat. He said he didn't know what had got into
him, probably his delayed First Night reaction, and then he
fell into one of his corny moods and got all wound up about
how if only he had enough money he could tell them all to go
—— themselves and start his *own* theatre, a Balletic Puppet
Theatre like the one run by someone called Dertu Dubecq,
which was the only True Theatre, because it was the
Universal Theatre; theatre everyone could understand. And I
said everyone except me, because people were always telling
me ballet was universal, but I'd never seen a ballet whose
story I was able to follow even when the programme-notes
were in English. And he laughed and said the hell with all
that, how about ordering a bottle of champagne to celebrate
living in *this* world? And I said I'd had so much to drink I
was practically out of it.

It was true: the evening was swimming together into a
great, big, shiny mother-of-pearl oyster-shell floating off to
infinity. . . But time was spreading itself out before me now,
instead of slipping away. . .


It was halfway through the morning, the sun shining into
my hotel-room between spaces in the drawn curtains, and I
was lying naked under the bedclothes feeling that something
had gone horribly, horribly wrong. For one thing, there at
my feet sat Larry, getting dressed not *quickly* exactly, but,
well, *steadily*. For another, although I couldn't remember any
of the details, the whole thought stretched across my mind
was: What a stupid thing to have done. What a stupid thing
to have done. . . But what? *What?* It was no use. Whatever
it was seemed destined to remain buried deep down inside
that bed forever.

I made a colossal effort. I raised myself up and said hello.
"Good morning," said Larry. "How do you feel?"

"Gosh, I——" I stopped. Quite independently of anything I knew about myself, I found I was all hot and faint. My breath was coming in gasps. Larry went right on dressing. The suspense was suffocating.

"What . . . happened?" I finally asked.

There was a pause during which I had to close my eyes. "Don't worry, it's O.K. Nothing," he assured me.

Nothing! I was reeling with shame.

"Was I . . . just . . . too *awful* . . . or something?" I whispered faintly.

"Oh *no*. Oh, *come* now. As a matter of fact we were both pretty drunk you know, and tired, and exhausted and over-wrought. I—um—I didn't mean to take advantage of you. . ."

"Oh, but you *didn't*. I mean please don't——"

"Well, luckily nothing happened, so it's all turned out for the best."

I slid down under the bedclothes and over to my other side. Larry's reluctance—he just didn't *want* me, *that* was the thing —*that* was the final piece in the emotional jigsaw of last night. That was what my feelings of shame and humiliation were all about—oh, brother. . .

"I've got the most *awful* hangover, so that I don't think I shall live unless I have some aspirin," I groaned. "Could you please go over to the shelf by the basin and pour me out a couple of hundred?"

"Sure honey." In a thrice there was such a clatter and clash among the bottles I had to bite back a scream. Eventually he stood over me with a glass of water and two aspirin. I took the pills and fell back, closing my eyes. He finished dressing quickly and I felt him at the bed again, standing over me. I'll just pretend to be asleep, I thought, then he'll go away and I can forget about the whole thing.

He stood there for a long moment. I began breathing evenly. Another age went by: there was an itch on my leg that I simply had to scratch. I tried to combine it with a sort of sleeper's stretch.

"Gorce," he said softly.

Much unnecessary business, waking up slowly, stirring sleepily, blinking eyes, etc.

"Gorce?" A little louder.

"Oh. Are you still here?"

"I'm just leaving——"

"Then *get out*!" I exploded.

"Yes. Yes, I know. Well—thanks for—I mean—oh, you know—I'll see you around, darling—goodbye. . ."


After he left I started to cry. Then I fell asleep again. At two o'clock I woke up, suddenly remembering I'd made a date with Judy's Frenchman, the painter Claude Tonnard.

He took me to his studio, poured me out some perfectly ghastly tea and we looked at his paintings a while. Then, as if it was the only thing left to do, he made love to me.

The studio was dark and cold when I left. I felt experienced without feeling that I, personally, had been through anything. I'd really shocked myself, to tell you the truth. I was a long way from St. Louis. My past was receding a little too rapidly.


I got to the theatre in time for the half-hour call.

There was a knock on my dressing-room door. "Sally Jay?"

"Come in. Oh, it's you." It was Lee.

"Sally Jay, I'm sorry. Never again, I promise."

"I forgive you." We kissed.

"Still love me?"

"Oh, sure—till the next time."

"Where've you been?" asked Lee. "You look as if you've just got out of bed."

"I have. I just got out of the bed of some Frenchman."

"Take it easy, Zelda. Scotty's been dead for years."

"Zop, zop."

"Wonderful notice for you in the Trib. Here—" He put the paper on my table.

"Thanks. I've seen it." I picked it up and read it again. I sighed. "So this is fame. I don't feel it. I don't feel anything.

138

Where're the photographers? Where're the flowers? Oh, here're some." I looked at the card. They were from Teddy. Indefatigable. I dropped it back into the flowers. "What boots it in these miffless times——" I said.

Lee was already in the doorway. "What say?" He came back in.

"I said what boots it?"

"Well, whatever *that* is, it isn't right. You've got it all screwed up."

"You ain't jest clicking your teeth," I replied, and started to put my make-up on. But already I was feeling much better.

# CHAPTER EIGHT

I DIDN'T SEE LARRY for a while. After a show opens it doesn't belong to the director any more, it's the stage manager's baby, and Larry never came around. I wasn't exactly happy, but—hmm, I don't know—but, but, *but* I wasn't absolutely *unhappy* either. I found that I liked acting and that, after those first few terrifying minutes each night before I went on stage, I was really enjoying myself. I even liked always having to be at the same place at the same time. I mean, the question actors most often get asked is how they can bear saying the same things over and over again night after night, but God knows the answer to *that* is, don't we all *anyway*; might as well get paid for it.

So I jogged along. I took up with Hard Core again. And I began posing for Jim. Later on somebody told me that there isn't a girl in the whole world who won't take off her clothes if she's convinced she's doing it for aesthetic reasons, but at the time it seemed to me I had taken one more giant step.

Otherwise things had changed very little in Montparnasse. Judy was out of the hospital and getting ready to accompany her brother on his tour, Dave Beckenfield had slunk off to Germany, and Crazy Eyes and his Mono-dancing sister had apparently changed quarters, or, at any rate, disappeared from ours. I did a bit of dubbing, a bit of radio, and got two offers from film companies, both of which fell through. From time to time I was fawned upon by the odd Stage-door Johnny, but if this was fame, it was keeping itself very quiet. Very quiet indeed.

Gradually it dawned on me that my passport was gone for good. I went through all my handbags, all my pockets, all my drawers. I went under the bed, on top of the wardrobe and back to the boîtes of the Opening Night. Then I went to the Etats-Unis. "I have lost my passport," I told them, "I am a citizen of the world."

"The hell you are," said the Ancient. "You are a prisoner of the world. You'd better get yourself over to the American Embassy first thing in the morning or you're going to be in some real trouble."

The next morning turned out to be the coldest of the year. I had to put on practically all the clothes I owned before daring to go out into it. When I arrived at the Select for my morning coffee I saw Bradley Slater, that compulsive reader, waving me frantically over to his table with an old copy of the *New Yorker*. Word had got around that I was going to the Embassy, and he was eager to accompany me. He hadn't been across the river in weeks—it would make a nice outing for him. By the time I'd finished my coffee I was surprised to find there were so many members of the Hard Core to whom the prospect of Crossing the Seine made a pleasant break in their otherwise strict routine of café-sitting. Both Beards, I remember, went along.

'In rowdy high spirits,' is a good description of that gallant little band arriving at the Embassy in the teeth of a howling gale. It had been an eventful journey. We had lost our way a number of times, had boarded several false buses, had been practically blown and frozen to death, but in the end we had succeeded. The Canteen at Gander in a blizzard could hardly have been a more welcome sight to the rescued pilot and his crew than the Reception Room of the Embassy to us. We stomped about in our boots, exhaling streams of frozen breath, rubbing red hands together and clapping each other on the back. Had cups of hot chocolate been distributed, we would have been pleased but not surprised.

After thawing out a bit we were ready to confront—or rather I should say *affront*, since they all looked shocked—the Passport Section : a large room divided in half by a wooden railing with benches of huddled people on one side, and officials and their typists on the other. It was very, very quiet; even the typewriters seemed to have mutes. I leaned over the railing to the Official Side and told a muted typist that I had lost my passport. She whispered back that the Man in Charge would see me in my turn. I looked over to where she was pointing and smiled at a stern grey-haired man with pince-nez seated behind an enormous desk. He looked away. I went over to the benches and began huddling with my friends and the other huddlers. Judging by the number of them there before us, I was prepared to wait several hours. It was my turn much faster than I expected. Rather astonished, I set off towards the Man in Charge and then quite unaccountably somewhere between approaching his desk and actually getting there, my spirits sank. He was eyeing me steadily through those damn pince-nez. Rabbit to snake, I kept on walking towards him; he kept on eyeing me. What he was seeing so steadily and so whole, I suddenly realized, was probably not calculated to inspire confidence. Proofed against wind and weather, I was a bundle of old clothes topped in old coats and toed in old boots, while, in direct contrast to all this shab, my hair was still that striking shade of pink I was telling you about earlier, and my face a startling white death-mask relieved only by some heavy black work around the eyes—an effect I thought pretty exciting—though I could see it wasn't having that effect on him. It wasn't exciting him, I mean.

"I've lost my passport," I said to him when I felt my knees touching his desk.

The Man in Charge swivelled away from me in his chair and looked at a poster on the wall of happy natives dancing around a village in Switzerland. He seemed lost in thought.

"Where did you lose it?" he finally asked me.

"If I knew it wouldn't be lost, would it?" I replied facetiously.

"I see." He seemed very sorry. "I don't know," he mourned, "if you young people realize in what a serious predicament you put the United States Government with your carelessness."

I tried to cheer him up. "Oh now, it can't be as bad as all that. I mean look—I've reported this—well—practically immediately, so how could anyone else use it, if that's what you're worrying about?"

"Forgive me," old Pince-Nez cut in smoothly. "Forgive me, but we have only your word *when* you lost it, and the same applies as to *how*, doesn't it?" And he gave me a long sad smile that said if he'd heard I'd sold it for a consignment of marijuana, it would in no way be taxing his credulity.

"Sold it!" I exclaimed suddenly. "You think I've sold it, don't you!" I called out to my friends on the benches, "Hey come here, he thinks I've *sold* it!"

Beard Bubbly was the first one over. "But didn't you sell it?" he asked me innocently. "I remember your telling me they get double the price for baby actresses outside American Express these days——" and then of course they all joined in and there was a lot more of the same.

"Shut up," I said, when I saw how old Pince-Nez was taking this. "They're only kidding, of course," I told him exasperatedly, and I tried to explain how after Opening Night, in the general hoopla of celebration, I'd gone to a lot of different places and that I could have lost it at any one of them. The entire Hard Core expedition was clustered around me by now, nodding and shoving and shouting "Yeah, that's true, Gorce, that's so true!" at every opportunity during the narrative, in an effort to strengthen my case.

When I finished the Man in Charge looked at all of us. "I'm glad I've got you all here together to state the official position," he said at last. "It must be brought home to you people that as long as an American passport is at large and unaccounted for your country has been placed in grave peril——" Lost, sold or stolen, it seemed, they could never be sure that at that very moment it wasn't working its way back to the States to do irreparable harm and so on, and so on— and then the blow came—"Therefore the American Embassy in Paris," he said quite calmly, "is not authorized to issue you another regular passport. We can, however, issue you one which will return you directly to the States."

"Not on your sweet life," I said.

"Then I suggest you apply immediately to Washington

for a new one, stating exactly how you happened to discover that it was—hmm—missing, though honestly I can't hold out much hope as to the outcome. However, my secretary, Miss Bowen, will type it out if you like."

"How long will it take Washington to decide?"

"Some time, I'm afraid—six months——"

"Six months! But I want one right now. Suppose I should want to go to some other country?" This was my second encounter in France with the law, and it was not mellowing me any. "I see what I should have done," I snapped, "I should have told you I'd thrown it in the fire. It wouldn't be at large then. I suppose it would have been all right then!"

I regretted the words the moment they flew out of my mouth, and looking at those bright glasses flashing into the silence around us, I knew he was going to make me regret them even more.

"I beg your pardon?" He said it mildly enough, but with a persistence that was forcing me either to repeat my outburst or back down. I backed down.

"Isn't there *any* other sort of passport you can give until Washington issues me a new one?" I pleaded. "Please. I'll be much more careful next time, I promise."

"I have already stated the official position."

"But can't you at least give me something to prove who I am? I mean I don't even have a driving licence or anything like that."

"How long have you been here?"

"About six months."

"You'll have your carte d'identité, then."

"Oh hell, I never got around to getting it."

"Yes. Well I'm afraid there's nothing we can do about *that*," he said, dismissing me.

Rather surprisingly it was Bradley Slater who jumped in. "This is outrageous!" he shouted. "I never heard of such a thing. You can't let Sally Jay wander around without any means of identification." And he banged his fist on the desk to show he knew how to do those things. "She *demands* another passport immediately. You can't stop her. It's her *right* as an American citizen."

I could see by his triumphant smile that old Pince-Nez had us there too. "An American passport is a *privilege*, not a 'right'," he said. "The sooner you people learn that, the better. It may be," he continued, in a frenzy of satisfaction that was at last beginning to crack through his officialdom, "it may be, let us hope, that Washington has at last ceased its weary tolerance of these Left Bank irresponsibles who are forever losing their passports, their money and their minds, and is growing understandably chary of reissuing new ones again for use as shopping-lists and toilet-paper. Good day. Miss Bowen, will you please attend to this young lady? Meanwhile I advise you to leave no stone unturned to recover that passport."

I went to Miss Bowen and stated the facts as gently as I knew how, and as I turned around to leave I looked at those patient huddlers on the benches who had hardly moved, and a horrible irony hit me: they wanted so badly to get into the States; I wanted so badly to stay out.

I sat down that afternoon and thought very, very hard. Then I rang up Larry.

"Larry, listen, I've lost my passport."

"Who *is* this?"

French phone or not that was a blow. "Sally Jay. Sally Jay *Gorce* in case there are two."

"Well, hello. Hello darling. . ."

"What'll I do?"

"Better look for it. How did it happen, anyway?"

"That's just it, I don't know. I've been over it and over it and I figure it must have been sometime Opening Night with the Contessa and her zoo. I mean that was the last time I saw it—you know, when I smashed my mirror at the queer joint."

"Shouldn't have done that, Gorce. Seven years bad luck."

"That's not so funny. There's a jerk at the Embassy who thinks I've *sold* it. Do you think it could possibly have been stolen? The trouble is there are too many suspects. I can't go around accusing everyone."

"How do you mean too many?"

"Well, it might have been that lesbian, for instance. My God, she was dying to get to the States, she even told me so herself. Or Crazy Eyes. I haven't seen him or his sister around lately, so that looks pretty suspicious—though he'd have had to have done it by osmosis, because I didn't go near him that night—at least I don't think I did. Or take Boofie—he's the type who goes in for what's laughingly known as living by his wits, and he's always in trouble with the authorities, or at least he was in Italy anyway. Or those dreadful brats, or the King of Lithuania, or whoever the hell he was, or even the Contessa for all I know. She hates my guts. And then there's a wild possibility it could just be the French painter I went over to see the next afternoon, though I'm dead sure I didn't take that particular handbag. In fact everyone but you."

"Why not me? I'm a little hurt not to be in such distinguished company."

"Well, you were the one who found it and gave it *back* to me."

"By God, so I did."

"What I wanted to ask you was—oh Lord, this is going to be embarrassing—what I wanted to ask you is that although I remember up to the Rotonde and the champagne distinctly that evening, it begins to cloud over a bit after that. I mean where else did we go?"

"Don't you remember?"

"Would I be asking you?"

"Well, let's see. I'm not too clear myself, but it seems to me there were a couple of other bars—some places near your hotel—would that be possible?"

"It would indeed. Oh Christ, this is hopeless. I'll never get to the bottom of it. And that man at the Embassy is so awful."

"Want me to go over there with you? I might be some help. Let's see what I can do."

"No. Some of my friends have tried already and made it worse."

"Start pulling some strings from the outside."

"Yeah, that's it."

"And don't despair. It'll probably turn up. Sorry I haven't been around to see the show, I've been too busy on another project—I've got to know Dertu and his puppets—it's fascinating! But I'm coming around in a couple of days to see how you're all making out. I won't tell you when, so stay on your toes."

"Sure. Well—sorry to have bothered——"

"Bye, Gorce. Take it easy, child." Click.

"Bye." Bang. That was me.

I went to the O.K. and the Villa Villa and the one next door. Nothing. I went to Shugie's. Shugie didn't even remember seeing me that night. Just as well, I thought, I must have been in wonderful shape.

I had thought of Uncle Roger almost from the very beginning. Uncle Roger was the one person I could count on to get the thing straightened out. But unfortunately it was in our agreement that I wasn't to get in touch with him for two years.

So I did something I almost never do; I wrote to my mother and my father. It was a most unusual step for me to take. However, when they got over their surprise at not being surprised to find me in another scrape, they pulled themselves together and rallied their forces and yes, I must admit it, they really did their very level best. Mother, in San Francisco, where she owns and operates a cosmetic firm, began contacting powerful senators (whose letters, postcards and wires to the Paris Embassy were all Kafkaesquely re-routed to that powerful Man in Charge, who flung them back scornfully, assuring me that they would not 'constitute official recognition'); while Daddy, who, after a series of failures in love and finance, got religion, and now edits a Jesuit magazine out in Brooklyn, uncovered for me forgotten Embassy officials in forgotten rooms overlooking the Avenue Gabriel, where I sometimes spent fruitless but pleasant afternoons having tea and looking out at the chestnut-trees.

Then I got busy myself. Almost daily for two months I

bombarded Washington with angry, pleading, and servile letters. I spoke of the career aspect—it was essential for a promising young actress to be able to travel; I spoke of the educational and cultural aspect—it was monstrous for a girl of my age to be prevented from visiting the art-monuments of the world; I even spoke of the patriotic aspect—it was heartbreaking as a citizen of our great country to be denied so important an identification with her beloved land. Nothing doing. They would consider the case in their own sweet time.

# CHAPTER NINE

**B**UT DON'T THINK life was all passports and acting. More
and more there was Jim Breit—though to this day I
cannot understand what on earth he saw in me, except, of
course, my bones, or my surface textures, or whatever else
he happened to be painting at the time. In fact, if he ever
writes his memoirs, I shall probably appear as The Girl on
the Boulevard Montparnasse, or the Floradora Girl, or something like that. I mean he didn't exactly altogether approve
of me. Not that he ever said anything about it. The worst
thing he ever said to me—and that was not until a whole lot
later—was that I was impure. I had to admit that if anyone
ever had the right to say it, he did. For he was pure all right;
as pure as the driven Mobile for which he eventually gave up
representational painting.

"I suppose for a girl of your sophisticated tastes—" was the
way he always started off sentences, teasing me about the gay,
mad, theatrical whirl, or my friendship with Lee Harrison
(whom he found chi-chi and affected), or my tenuous connection with the International Set (the King of Lithuania, who
revealed himself to be only a Roumanian Count, turned up
one night as a Stage-door Johnny and went glooming all over
me at a supper-party). I mean Jim thought I was pretty wild.
Yessuh, deep, deep down—although you would never have
got him to say it in Paris—he thought I was *fast*. He also
disapproved of the colour of my hair. He thought it was just
plain silly.

In a way he was the most abstract person I've ever met.
That sounds wrong, it sounds as if I meant he was a philoso-
pher or absent-minded. 'Plastically sensual', which sounds like
God knows what, would be closer. What I mean is, when he

went to see a film he was so busy looking at the chiaroscuro he never saw the actors, and when he went to my theatre, he came out talking about my elbows.

"Well, how did you like it?" I asked him.

"Wonderful! I really saw your elbows for the first time. Those stage-lights give your body a whole different perspective. I must come back."

Practically every inanimate object his eye fell on gave him pleasure; a rusty tin can that had been run over by a car, a hole in a cake of kitchen soap worn smooth by his constantly cleaning paint brushes in it, or the wildly coloured woollen blanket thrown over his divan.

He was a country boy. That was it. Actually he came from Wilmington, Delaware; but he was a country boy, nevertheless. I'm sure there are some people, some basic country types, who bring the whole countryside into wherever they're living as easily as some city types do the same thing the other way around. At least he could. And in Paris; the Paris that I had hitherto seen alternately as the rich man's plaything, the craftsman's tool, the artist's anguish, and the world's largest champagne factory, he managed to turn into a country village. His studio, unpromisingly wedged into the heart of the Boulevard Raspail, somehow became his farmhouse; the Select his General Store; and the dear old Ancient, the Crackerbarrel Sage.

I spent deep, peaceful afternoons there in that farmhouse-studio, posing for him throughout the long, cold winter with the rain outside and the fragrant warmth of glowing wood-fires burning and mixing into exhilarating smells of turpentine, canvas, and oil paints. Gradually it began to seem rather an anti-climax just to get back into all my clothes after lying around with them off for so long, and I found I was staying longer and longer in my dressing-gown after the painting session was over, while the light faded, the firelight flickered, and we sat drinking white wine.

"Oh God. You're so beautiful." He said it in such an absolutely heartfelt way that I knew he was no longer being abstract. He leaned forward and for the first time I felt his breath on me. He smelled like new-mown hay. I kept my eyes level with his and waited ... when his face came too close for me to see it clearly I closed them and let him kiss me. "Let's go ... let's go ..." he whispered.

The trouble was of course that what Jim really, *ideally* needed at that point was some nice, simple, outdoor, bohemian girl; brown-haired and with rain in it. As I said, I don't know *what* he saw in me, but then I don't know what on earth I saw in him either, for that matter. It seemed incredible that I, who had spent all this time in Paris, adrift, so to speak, in an uncharted ocean of raging passions, should be knocked over by so small a wave. And yet he was, I suppose, my first real relationship.

The disagreement we always had—quarrel would be too strong a word—was about my refusing to go and live with him, move in with him under his roof. There'd always seemed to me something so dirty-sweatered and dirndl-skirted about living with a man you're not married to. I mean it was too intensely domestic for one thing; the next thing you knew you were darning socks and cooking. And to be quite honest there were some phone calls I wouldn't have wanted to take with him in the room and some that frankly, I couldn't.

But Jim was a bundle of virtues. He was sweet, he was sensitive, he was intelligent; he was humorous and solid; he was simple and straightforward. He was good around the house, he *liked* to fix doorknobs and electric switches, and he knew all about his car. He was polite and he was stable (paradoxically I was most attracted to his stability—it intrigued me as much as anything), he was—let's see, have I left anything out? ... Gaiety. Nope. He wasn't gay. But what he was most deadly earnest about was his art. He was constantly trying to 'purify' it. And Judy was right. He *was* a good painter. I felt it personally from being around his paintings so much. Most paintings just disappear off the wall for me after a while, but these were paintings you wanted to have. And a lot of art-dealers felt that way about it too. He exhibited rarely—at the Salon d'Automne and a few others, but he wouldn't sell anything yet; he felt he wasn't ready.

"What's the matter?" he asked me one night after the theatre.

"Nothing."

"Yes there is."

"I want to go to the Ritz," I said, already uneasy at the suggestion.

There was panic in his voice. "Why? What do you want to do that for?"

"Because I feel the need to sin. Quelle façon de parler."

"To *sin*?"

"Oh God." How to explain? "I don't mean it like that. I mean . . . oh. . . Luxe . . . satins and silks . . . leopardskins and peacocks' tongues. Silk—that's what I want rubbing against me. I feel so woollen all the time."

A pause for the struggle with his soul, and then reluctantly "O.K., I'll take you there——"

"No," I said sadly. "No, it's no good. It wouldn't be any fun. You couldn't afford it. I only like spending rich people's money."

We went on eating in silence.

"I've got to tell you something," he said finally. "I haven't been honest with you. I *am* rich. In fact, my father is *very* rich. One of the richest men in Delaware. . ."

This was so much like something out of the Student Prince that I started to laugh, but when I looked at his grief-stricken face I had to stop.

"Du Pont?" I asked gently.

He nodded miserably.

"The *President*?"

He smiled wanly. "No, it's not that bad. I mean he's on the Board. I'm . . . running away from it. I'm trying to live it down."

I looked at his chequered wool-shirt (one of three), his muddy shoes with flapping soles, and his Army ducks, and nothing could stop the twinge of annoyance snaking around my stomach. How typical, I thought irritably. But of course it all made sense now, it all fitted in; his unwillingness to sell his paintings yet, and his determination to live like everyone else on the Left Bank. What worried and depressed him more than anything, he confided in me, quite seriously, was that when he'd told his family of his decision to go abroad and paint, having two other sons they hadn't taken it too badly. He would have felt much safer being cut off without a penny. And I suppose there *was* some kind of rough logic in his assumption that to begin being an artist, you had to live like most artists begin living.

At any rate I felt sorry for him and I said "Never mind, I don't care about the Ritz. Really I don't. Let's go to the Select."

Gosh he was funny about his money. All very rich people are, I suppose. Suspicious, afraid of being used, afraid they're not being loved for themselves and all that. But Jim was funny in his own special way. For instance, while he would gladly have bought me six dozen dry martinis in a row at one of the Left Bank cafés, the Deux Magots, let's say (and they would have cost exactly what they did at the Crillon), or a trip around the world on a tramp steamer, or every bit of equipment needed for a ski trip or under-water fishing, I could never have got out of him a single fur, or a single jewel, or a jar of fresh caviare.

You couldn't blame him in a way; he just wasn't the type, I mean he was small and mild and serious and utterly unlike all the grandeur and pomp and splendour that attaches itself to great wealth. He stretched his own canvases and he drank beer and his car was a baby Renault. But it wasn't out of meanness. I mean he paid for all the meals that we had together and willingly 'loaned' me money at the end of each month when I went broke, which I seemed to be doing more and more. And for a very curious reason. Before Judy left, she'd told me about the sales that all the big French fashion-houses have during the winter, and she gave me cards to all of them. So there I was secretly going around buying glamorous, slinky French models like crazy, and all they did was just droop about in my wardrobe.

Winter rained itself into Spring. Those plays I was in finally ran out of audiences and the theatre closed down. Now that Jim and I were seen around more and more in public, it became obvious to the Hard Core that we were 'going together'. They approved. Not that they were ever, of course, so crude as to betray it by word or gesture; but they approved. They approved of both of us; and they approved of people whom they approved of choosing their lovers from other people they approved of within the circle. White of 'em.

As a stamp of *their* approval, other young couples began having us to dinner. It was just at the time (and it may still be, for all I know), when the Aubergine, or Fried Egg-Plant school of cooking was getting such a grip on beginners' cuisines, and I remember very few dinners without that harmless but insipid vegetable staring up at me from the main dish, often quite unadorned except for a sliver of melted cheese on top.

Still, I might not be so testy about those meals today if I could have just got around to *eating* them. But the amount of jumping up and down required on the part of both hosts and guests to get the meal assembled and in eating order kept my stomach in a constant turmoil. It had rather the same effect on the conversation, which settled down only after the last dish had been cleared away and we women were busy at the sink washing up. For the female guest, the washing-up was then followed by a sort of Homage to the Household Gods, rites which involved unqualified and highly vocal admiration of everything in sight. After that we were allowed to listen to the menfolk for a while and after that it was bedtime.

Jim always enjoyed these dinners immensely. He loved arguing Art Theory, and never more so than with Ray de Wald, the Popcorn King Abstractionist, who was something of a nut.

"We must have the de Walds to dinner *here* next time," said Jim to me one afternoon after we'd spent a week-end in their windswept hut just off the coast of Brittany.

"Why can't we take them out?"

"It's not the same."

"What about the cooking?"

"What do you mean what about the cooking?"

"I mean I can't cook."

"You can't cook . . . why, good Lord, Sally Jay, I thought every girl knew how to cook." He looked at me, his little Floradora Girl, and gave me a wry sort of some-women-are-made-for-only-one-thing smile. Then he shook his head hopelessly.

"Marion de Wald cooks," he said grimly. "She does all the cooking and looks after two kids as well."

I tried to remember one minute that whole week-end when Marion and I weren't either feeding people, or clearing up from doing it, or preparing to do it again. And presumably she never stopped doing it. But I couldn't quite see why just because she did, I should. I mean, here was I practically fresh out of the egg, everything was so new to me, and here was everybody telling me to stop *drifting*, and start living in this world; telling me to start cooking, and sewing, and cleaning, and I don't know what. Taking care of my grandchildren.

I sat in the studio lost in thought, watching the evening get darker and darker and colder and colder, unable to move. Finally I roused myself and went to look for Jim. I found him wandering aimlessly around the kitchen, peering every now and again into one of the empty cupboards, hoping as if by some miracle to find that particular one filled.

"What is it, Jim?" He looked so forlorn.

"I've . . . I've already *invited* them to dinner on Thursday."

I took a deep breath.

"O.K." I said. "Which is the stove and how do you light it?"

Shopping for food in Paris, as I soon discovered—but not soon enough—called into play words I'd never even heard before, much less used; a dish-towel, a bottle-opener, a can of anything, a pound of anything—all the weights and measures, I hadn't any idea how to ask for them. It was so different from the simple "Colgates, s'il vous plaît," or "Est-ce que vous avez d'autre espèce de savon aujourd'hui?" that I was used to.

Any moron can cook a steak, I kept saying to myself, as I went about my work in the kitchen early Thursday evening. I was not only going to give them something to get their teeth into, but I was going to serve it to them all by myself.

Everybody was terribly kind and co-operative at dinner and it took all four of us ceaselessly moiling and toiling from kitchen to studio and back again to organize and consume a simple meal of soup, steak and onions, peas and potatoes and salad. And even then the process was simplified by my just leaving the loaf of bread, just simply forgetting it and leaving it at the bottom of the shopping-bag. Coffee was Nescafé, and at the end I said to Marion as I was about to drop, "Let's for heaven's sake leave the dishes, the woman who comes in can do them tomorrow."

Marion took a few tentative turns around the place, trying to say "Oh how lovely, where did you get this?" every once in a while, but as I never knew where (not having asked Jim), and as, in any case, there were so few things to admire —no dear little rugs freshly ripped off their looms at Antwerp, or new chafing-dishes from Vallauris for future egg-plants— the tour wasn't much of a success.

We were suddenly all four of us together in the talking-room with nothing to talk about. The presence of women so early in the Discussion Period seemed to constrain Ray, and this was odd, because he'd talked freely and for hours on end to me at various cafés. He began prowling around the room. He picked up a wire coat-hanger and some string and a couple of paint-brushes and a shoe, and started making them into a Mobile, and Jim joined in.

I went home early. I had to go out to the Studio Grandcourt the next morning to do some dubbing. I did quite a bit of dubbing for this studio and now that American companies were making more and more pictures in France, hiring French bit-players and then discovering they couldn't understand their English, it was quite a lucrative set-up. The people were pleasant. In fact I was something of a heroine to the boys in the Control Room. The Paris winter and all the shouting I'd done on stage had lowered my voice to a husky growl which went over big with them, accustomed as they were to having their eardrums pierced by the shrill French ingénue whose voice, even under normal circumstances, is about an octave higher than an American's.

When I got there that morning the first thing I saw was the familiar back of Someone standing by the mike running over his lines. As I came in he turned around. It was Larry. I tested myself for symptoms (actually, they're the same for me in all my subjunctive states of doubt, fear, and strong emotion : dizziness and shortness of breath); they were still with us. He smiled. It was no insane demonstration of delight but it sufficed; the symptoms increased.

"Come over here, Gorce," he said without moving. "Get a load of this script. We've got a big love-scene together."

At the vin blanc break around eleven o'clock he said to me, "There's a great big Canadian around the Left Bank who's nuts about you. No kidding. He saw you at the theatre and he's been following you around ever since. He's dying to meet you. How about it? He says you smiled at him once."

"I smiled at him?" I sighed wearily. "I must have been smiling in my sleep. I really don't want to know anyone else, Larry. I'm mixed up enough as it is. What does he look like? I've never noticed him."

"Tall. Rugged. Very handsome."

"Oh."

Our eyes met for a split second and set off a tiny spark. That's what killed me about Larry. He could get inside you so quickly when he liked. We were going to be conspirators again, I felt. Conspirators? Again? Over what?

"Nope. Sorry. Not interested." I was firm.

The next day, out at the Studio again, Larry said : "You were standing right next to him at the Etats-Unis last night."

"Who?"

"Bax, Sawyer Baxter—the Canadian."

"This is beginning to give me the creeps. Why didn't he talk to me?"

"He's shy. He won't till he's introduced."

"Well, I'm too busy."

I went over to Jim's that night, determined to cook him a good meal and what's more, enjoy doing it.

I made lamb chops and soup and peas and potatoes and a salad.

It was the same rat-race as before, except that I remembered the bread this time.

Afterwards we sat around in the studio. It was a hot night made stuffier by all the cooking. It didn't seem so much of a farmhouse any more, without a log fire burning in the fireplace. I flung open the windows. Spring was ravishing around town, bursting and budding and blooming. It was one of those nights when the air is blood-temperature and it's impossible to tell where you leave off and it begins. I was filled with that restlessness of vague desires. It was like the evening I stood at my window before going to the Ritz to break it off with Teddy. I wanted to go swimming. I wanted to go down to the beach and go swimming.

"Let's go out," I said to Jim. "Somewhere. Anywhere."

"Do we have to? We went out last night, didn't we? I've only just started to get this Mobile balanced."

I sat down and tried to read, but I couldn't. After ten pages I was in a state of cold fury. Read! I didn't want to read, it was just a substitute for living. Time was running out. I'd been in Paris for almost a year now; I wanted to get moving. The disaster of my passport made me so angry I slammed the book shut. I'd give Washington one more month to come through with an answer, and then I'd get my father to tell Uncle Roger about it. Then I'd go.

Go where?

I looked at Jim, unaware of my treacherous thoughts, absorbed in the new Mobile which he was going to hang from the ceiling over his bed. His face showed his perfect contentment. Wasn't *this* life as everybody else lived it? What more did I want? To anyone coming in from the outside and seeing us there like that, wouldn't we have seemed perfectly O.K.? Absolutely apple-pie American? Unless, of course, they'd eaten the meal.

I put down the book. "I'm a little tired, Jim," I said. "I think I'll go on home."

He looked up, hurt, and I could have bitten my tongue off. It was the word 'home' that did it. He wanted me to think of there, the studio, as being our home.


It was seven o'clock in the morning and I'd just been awakened by loud knocking at my hotel-room door. I was frightened out of my wits; I thought it was the French police checking up on the cartes d'identité.

It was Larry, happy and excited.

"Come to the Côte d'Argent!"

"Wha-at?"

"How would you like to go to the Basque coast around Biarritz with us next week for a couple of months? Expenses paid."

"Us?"

"Me. And Bax and Missy. Just the four of us." Missy— Melinda May Carter—was an outsize blonde Southern belle of voluptuous proportions from New Orleans. She was studying at the Sorbonne.

"No," I said. "Go away."

"What can you lose?"

I thought of Jim. "Everything," I said.

Larry sat down heavily on a chair full of my underwear and put his head in his hands. "Please," he said. "You've got to come. You'll be spoiling three people's good time if you don't."

"What's it all about?"

"We've been up all night talking about it. There's a house we can rent dirt cheap just outside Biarritz—St. Jean de Luz——"

"Not the same one that——" but I stopped. I'd suddenly thought of his old girl friend Lila, and also that I wasn't supposed to have heard that conversation between them that night outside the Dôme.

"The same one that what?"

"Nothing."

"No *what*?"

"Well, the Contessa——" I lied.

"That old bag. Christ no, that's all over. Listen, Sally Jay, I think I'm in love. For the first time. I know it, in fact— I'll just *die* if I can't take Missy away with me." I'd never seen him like that before. I mean it was heart-breaking in a way.

"Who's stopping you?"

"You are. It's Bax's party. He's got the car and he's going to pay the rent and his heart is set on you. He won't go without you."

"Don't *you* have any money?" There. I'd asked it.

"I invested it all in sending Dertu Dubecq's Puppet Theatre on an American tour. It flopped, of course. Couldn't even get the theatre critics over there interested enough to go and see him. They all sent their second string or those ballet birds. Peasants! What the hell. It was a gamble. Let's get back to the house-party. It's the chance of a lifetime, isn't it? You've *got* to come. Missy won't go without you either. She doesn't think it's a good idea to be the only girl in the house. I see her point. She likes you *terrifically*, by the way. But anyway the whole point is that Bax has got his heart set on you. You just don't know what you do to that boy."

"Without even *meeting* me? Tiens, tiens. I've never had such a dazzling effect on anybody, even in my own mind."

"Do you want to meet him now? I'll call him up right away." Larry made a dash for the phone.

I stopped him. "No," I said. "No, I don't want to meet him until we start down there. If I'm going to do this thing at all I'm going to do it right."

I had no idea what I'd said until Larry had; Larry and I both suddenly realized it together. I don't know which of us was more surprised.

One of the piquant factors in this interview was that it was taking place with me in my pyjamas and Larry fully dressed. This was putting me at a decided disadvantage. In fact I felt quite shy. I didn't want to slink down under the covers—it would be emphasizing the 'in bed' part of the scene too much; on the other hand, every time I sat up, I was reminded that there were several buttons missing from my pyjamas. My mind went searching desperately for my dressing-gown, but when the possibilities narrowed themselves to the hook which held a raincoat and a sweater as well, or the chair on which Larry was sitting, and I realized that one of the missing buttons was the one that held my pyjama pants together, I gave up.

"Please get out and let me get dressed," I said, wondering how I was going to back down now.

"You're coming!" he shouted. "You're coming! You're coming. I knew you would, you darling!"

"No I'm not," I said desperately. "No I *can't*, Larry. What'll I tell Jim? You're ruining my life," I wailed desperately.

"You'll never regret this, Gorce, *please*. Just for a couple of weeks. If you don't like it you can turn right around and come back. I'll drive you to the station myself."

"Oh all right, *all right*. Only get out now and let me get dressed."

"You'll come then? Promise? Word of honour?"

I took a deep breath. "Yes."

"Gorce," he said solemnly, standing over me, "I'll do anything in the world for you. Anything. Just ask me."

"Let me get dressed," I mumbled.

"Meet you at the Dôme in half an hour. I'll have Missy there and we can start planning. You won't regret this."

It was only after he left and I started getting dressed that I realized with a thud of amazement that he'd seen me with a lot less on than a pair of pyjamas. "I must be losing my *mind*," I said aloud in my surprise at the unexpected turn of events.

I began combing my hair. I made a wise and soulful little moue at myself in the mirror. "Oh Jim," I murmured softly into it, "you poor, poor fool. It's just your luck to get mixed up with a heartless bitch like me." I leaned closer to the glass, clouding it with my breath, and made an imprint on it with my mouth. I stood back, letting my eyes fill with tears. Then I picked up my eyebrow pencil and pencilled my eyebrows into dark wings.

Then I gave myself one last challenging look and ran downstairs out and over to the Dôme to meet Larry and my change of fate.


I told Jim about it one night while he was painting me. He went right on painting.

"I suppose I can't stop you," he said.

"No."

"Why are you going?"

"I don't know." Why was I going? For curiosity? For adventureship or friendship? For the sun or for the moon? "It's just the way I am. Flighty. It's only for a couple of weeks, anyway," I added, trying to soften the blow.

He didn't stop painting.

"What *do* you want?" he asked me finally.

My sense of bewilderment increased. "Oh . . . how do I know?"

"Do you want to . . . marry me?"

"Oh, Jim, I just don't *know*. What about you?"

He put down his brushes and looked me straight in the face. "Yes. I'd marry you. I'd marry you to keep you." He said it very slowly.

"Oh, Jim, I'm sorry."


Later on, in his arms, I said sadly, "Who will you paint after I'm gone?"

"I don't think I'll paint people any more," he said calmly. He gazed up at the Mobile swinging slowly over our heads. "Human beings are so impure, aren't they? Look at that mobile. I've never painted anything that's given me as much

162

pleasure. Look at the lines. Pure and simple and clean and perfectly balanced."

"Will you stay in Paris this summer?"

"I don't know. My art-teacher from college is going to be in Florence. I may join him."

"I think Judy'll be there sometime this summer with her brother. Say hello to her for me if you see them, will you?"

"I will. . ."

"Well . . . I suppose I ought to start packing. . ."

"Goodbye, then."

I suddenly felt myself in real pain. "I love you, Jim. I really do. Isn't that funny?"

# PART TWO

"They shoot rapids, don't they?"
—CYRIL CONNOLLY

# CHAPTER ONE

May ~~10~~—sorry 5th, 1955.
Sunday.

DOWN HERE A week—no, wait a minute, not even a whole week, now that I look at the date. Only five days. Holy cow, things must take much shorter to happen (or not to happen) than I think.

Rain sans cesse. Time heavy on the hands and even worse on the tempers.

Que diable allais-je faire dans cette galère?

Larry passes the time writing corny poetry or painting even cornier pictures. Missy sulks in her room and eats fruit all day. Can't get near it any more for the cherry stones and plum pips. She's getting so languid, she's just going to melt away in rivulets. The South has brought out the Southern in her. Bax chops wood, or starts to chop wood, or has just come from chopping wood. Never without an axe. So yesterday when it was my turn to do the shopping, I went to the local bookshop and bought this enormous Diary and that's what *I'm* going to do to keep myself from going mad.

The trip down was hell. I mean *hell*. Can't think about it without feeling double-crossed. Things went wrong from the very beginning; from the very first crack of dawn that we started out in, with the rain, and this leaky, tricky old second-hand Citroen breaking down regularly and everyone else quarrelling about which route to take and it slowly coming through to me that in the dazzle of Larry's enthusiasm the whole set-up had been *grossly* misrepresented. Of course I probably helped things along by getting Canada all mixed up with Texas—oil-wells and all that—but still, it made me furious to realize that while it was perfectly true that old

Canadian Bax *was* footing the bills, the bills were going to have to be mighty modest; the flow of dough was not going to be limitless, nor the spree luxurious. Hated myself for feeling that way but felt that way. Just couldn't help it. Anyway I was getting car-sick.

Now that I've thought about it a bit, I realize that even under ideal circumstances (if there is such a thing in travelling) I do not travel very well. For someone who likes to get around as much as I do, I really travel quite badly. Planes frighten me, boats bore me, trains make me dirty, cars make me car-sick. And practically nothing can equal the critical dismay with which I first greet the sight of new places.

Hated France when I first got over here. Got on the train at Le Havre, and looked out of the window and thought it looked so exactly like America, I wanted to cry. The scenery flying past, the hills and barns and cows, were just the sort of things you keep coming across through a train window in the States. The Untrained Eye, I told myself, training it enough to see that all the signs were written in French, at the same time letting the untrained nose get its first exotic whiff of garlic from my travelling-companions, and the untrained stomach its first attack of French dysentery. But still, these were the only differences. I asked myself finally what exactly did I expect France to look like? No answer.

I hate plans. Hate even listening to people telling me about theirs. Plans spoil suspense, I say. Don't believe in looking where I'm going. But that first day, trapped in the train speeding towards the complete unknown, it did just strike me as the teeniest weeniest bit careless that for all my insatiable longings and dreamings and pinings to get here, I knew nothing more concrete about my beloved France than what was painted on the screen in my nursery: children playing with hoops in the Bois de Boulogne.

And if the French countryside failed to impress me, boy, my first glimpse of Paris failed even more easily. Succeeded, I mean. Succeeded in not impressing me. I found an American Express man at the Gare and asked him to give me the name of a hotel and he directed me to one called the Hôtel Lord

Palmerston. Lord Palmerston! Real French. Real French comme ambiance aussi. It's probably the only perfect replica of a Victorian mausoleum still standing in Paris. There were a couple of busts of Victoria and Albert in the lobby, and it was full of dusty red plush and ancient frock-coated hotel retainers whose ambition was, if not actually to displease you, at least to depress you. Chamber-pots everywhere and brass beds that sank and rocked when you lay down on them and floors that sloped away sharply when you tried walking on them. Just what I needed after six days on a boat and one on a train : pitching beds and lurching floors. Deathly ill for first fifty-two hours. Finally had my life saved by un petit médecin du pays working wonders with magic vials of brown fluid.

So I recovered and lived to see the Champs-Elysées.

And the rest is history. But the moral is I should have been prepared. I probably could have been prepared but for this terrible, tragic flaw in my character.

So here I am at it again. Poor old Gorce, c'est toujours la même histoire.

On the other hand, if I always knew what I was going to do, would I do it? Would I have left Paris and Jim like that to go goofing off in a broken-down Citroen in the company of two lovers and a stranger, Michelins in hand, all eyes to the front trying to guess at the next good cheap restaurant and the next good cheap room? And believe me, at sixty miles an hour, they're plenty hard to guess at.

I suppose I was kind of disagreeable on the trip down. I complained steadily. At first I tried to stop myself and then I didn't try to stop myself. And then I couldn't. Of course I was encouraged by the others. Since it was only by my consenting to come along in the first place that we were there at all, they naturally felt I ought to be the honoured guest. And by God, honoured guest I was determined to be. The sweeter they got the more difficult I became. I took it out on Larry especially. Once, after we'd spent hours trying to disentangle ourselves from some large industrial town, entirely on account of his faulty map-reading, I let loose on him such a volley of abuse that he just kind of sat there with a stunned smile on his face, not knowing what hit him. I almost felt sorry for him.

About Bax. If there's one thing that hasn't been misrepresented about this trip, it's Bax's good looks. He does look exactly as described. He *is* a rugged, handsome Canadian. A great big broad-shouldered ruffly black-haired crinkly brown-eyed Canadian. Clean-cut. The great Outdoor Boy.

I think he just hasn't got the imagination to look any different. He's what they call a Natural Leader. You can see him as a kid becoming the Chief of his Camp Fire Group or some such because everybody thought he looked as if he should.

We treat each other like a couple of minor United Nations officials, Bax and I. Very protocol, very wary.

We ran into a snag our very first night out. It was early evening, and we were just coming up to some mournful little town, one of Nature's Airports—Dax, or Digne, or something (we'd argued so much about the route I've forgotten which) —when we were stopped by the police. The next section of the main road was being closed down for re-tarring.

"Great," I said to Larry, quick as a flash. "Just great. Christ."

Larry parked the car on the side of the road and went into town to see what was going on. When he returned he was terribly excited : "Say, the whole town's turned out en fête to watch them fix the road. I've never seen anything like it. Man, you can have your Pamplona Ferias and your Bordeaux Vendanges. This is it ! How many people do you know can say they've seen an honest-to-God local *Tar* Festival?"

This was supposed to cheer me up. I said it was an experience I would gladly forego, but he made us get out of the car and have a drink at a café on one side of the street, so we could see what he was talking about.

We asked the waiter how long he thought it would be before the road was open. He said about four hours. Too late to try to hit the next town. So then we asked him if he knew of a good cheap hotel there, and he said all the hotels on *our* side of the street were full up. The only one left was on the other side.

So we were stuck.

We were all dead tired, our hair stiff with dust, our bodies aching from the inactivity of a long day's drive. Missy and I went to wash up in one of those outhouse-chickenhouses and nearly fainted dead away from the smell.

Then we had a really lousy meal at the café and sat around and watched and waited. The town really seemed to go mad over the tarring. They were all there all right, lined up on both sides of the street—priests, peasants, police, the works. It was mad.

What with one thing and another it was about one o'clock du matin before the road was crossable and the crowd had finally dispersed and the town settled back into its Dignity (or Daxiness) and we were finally able to fall into the hotel whose dank and dismal beds we'd been so desperately awaiting.

Anyway, next day over the mountains, through the valleys and down to the sea. Bayonne, Biarritz, Bidart, Guétary, et nous voilà à St. Jean.

It's a perfect villa. A heavenly villa, a bougainvillæa villa on top of a hill, with boxwood hedges and stone jars full of geranium plants and terraced gardens growing wild in the back. Roses and gladioli and morning glories. And zinnias and cannas and an indescribably blue flower called plumbago. Pine trees and oleanders and mimosa. Bird-baths. And stone steps leading down to the sea.

"O.K., Gorce, start grousing about this," said Larry as we drove up the driveway. "It's still raining," I pointed out. Which was true.

We left our bags in the car and went inside to explore. It's a large airy villa with the calm fresh feeling of summer-houses. It has stone floors and long French windows. We wandered through, opening doors and peering out of windows, trying to decide which bedrooms each of us wanted.

Mine has a balcony and looks out on to the sea. Every

night I stand there watching the lights along the shore glisten and twinkle in the rain.

"It's cold," I said, when we met downstairs again in the large living-room. "Let's have a drink to warm up." There was another reason why I wanted one. My own private celebration. A few minutes before, alone in my bedroom, it had burst upon me that for the first time in my life I was in a house—actually in a whole house—without a single grown-up! I felt I could have walked on air. On water I mean. I couldn't possibly have explained to the others what it was all about, this exaggerated sense of liberty. Frequently, walking down the streets in Paris alone, I've suddenly come upon myself in a store window grinning foolishly away at the thought that no one in the world knew where I was at just that moment.

But Bax said no, we couldn't have a drink just then; there wasn't time and there wasn't anything in the house either. Said we could have some wine at lunch if we liked. Said he'd been making a list of the things we needed. Asked who wanted to go shopping with him then. He was very fair about it all, true-blue leader that he is. Said he didn't want to seem to be pushing us around, but didn't we think that the smoothest way to get things organized was for us to go on a rotating schedule of chores? Two of us doing the shopping, two the cooking, and two the cleaning, was the way he saw it. But there was no hurry, he said. We could talk it over at lunch.

This was the last straw.

"You mean we haven't even got a cook or a housekeeper around the place?" I moaned, the joy of freedom promptly evaporating. "I'll go shopping with you, Bax," I said grimly. "I've got a telegram to send."

Larry muttered, "Spare us," under his breath, and they all three exchanged glances.

I saw that I'd gone too far.

"Bax and I are getting the provisions, they'll be too heavy for you girls today," said Larry decisively. "You can do the lunch. Get yourselves unpacked while we're away. *Un*packed," he added, looking at me. "And none of your tricks, Gorce."

172

They went out and got the supplies. And we unpacked. And Bax chopped wood and built us a fire. And then we had lunch. And after that we started teaching Missy how to play bridge.

That night, when we were ready to go to bed, we all borrowed warm sweaters from Bax and filled the clay hot-water-bottles we'd found in the kitchen and took them to bed with us, where we slept under the rugs of our bedroom floors.

One thing about the four of us: you never know who's going down next. The morning after we arrived, for instance, I came waltzing in to breakfast determined to be a good sport and make the best of it, rain and all, and who should be deep in the sulks but Missy. So now it was up to us three—the new us three—to pull *her* out of them.

When we were doing the washing-up together that evening I finally asked her point-blank what was eating her.

So then she asked me point-blank if I'd ever been to bed with a man. I blinked and said what did she want to know for and had *she*?

She said no.

This surprised me. She looked like such a voluptuous sexpot, with her blonde hair falling all over her face, and her slow, melting movements. She kicked off her shoes and sat on a kitchen-stool wiggling her toes, sucking on a plum, and staring at the floor in an embarrassed kind of way. You could see she wasn't lying.

I asked her again why she wanted to know about me and she said she wanted my advice. She said she didn't know what to do about Larry.

I asked her how she felt about him.

She said she thought he was real nice. She said she thought she was really in love with him, but she wondered if he wouldn't lose respect for her if she gave in to him. I said, what made her think *that*? And she said her mother.

I said if I were her I'd jump in first and decide whether he was losing respect for me or not afterwards, but she said she knew her mother would jes' *die* if she ever found out. She said Southern mothers were very strict with their children and made them go to church every Sunday at home.

So I asked her what her mother thought she was doing right now, and she said oh, that house parties were different. They were perfectly all right. She'd been on dozens of them in the South. Only Southern boys *understood* Southern girls. They understood you could do everything *but*.

So then I said, well, if she had all these qualms about it maybe she'd better not, and she said but the trouble was she *wanted* to.

What a world, I thought. Nothing but sex as far as the eye can see.

My own feelings were getting pretty mixed-up.

I love Larry, I really do. I love him no matter what. But all this was nothing to do with me. You can tell from seeing them together that nothing's going to stop what's supposed to happen from happening. Besides, he's already told me that he's in love with her, so I've more or less got used to it.

However, *one* of the things I thought was, that if they did start to have a real affair, maybe I'd be able to get over him.

On the other hand, there are plenty of reasons why I hope they don't. One of them is Bax.

I don't like the way he's looking at me.

I'd made it quite clear to Larry when I said I'd come along, that Bax wasn't to get any ideas about me. And Larry had said, no, absolutely not, he'd straightened him out first thing. But I still don't like the way Bax is looking at me. And the atmosphere around those two, Larry and Missy, is so heavily charged with sex *now*, I can imagine what it'll be like *afterwards*—and I mean for me and Bax as well.

The Lovers keep having little showdowns, followed by periods of heavy necking, followed by more showdowns, and so on. And then Larry goes off to his lousy poetry and painting, and Missy goes off to her room to suck on her plums, and Bax goes off to his wood to start chopping it, and that's what's been going on here for the past five days in the rain.

Rain.

Missy is trying to make a Southern gentleman out of Larry. She won't get out of the car unless he opens it for her, and she won't get into it unless he does, and we all stand around in the rain waiting for him to make up his mind. The doors of the car have got stuck with the damp and it's like trying to get in and out of a safe, anyway.

Then she says would he mind running upstairs and getting her coat for her, and he says, yes, he would mind very much, and then we all have to wait around again until he thinks better of it and goes up and gets it.

Then she says just a second, if we're going into town she has to comb her hair, and she wanders upstairs in slow motion and stays there for about an hour combing it. Or putting on lipstick. Or just looking at herself in the mirror.

Then we go out to this cheap restaurant that we've found in town and Larry gets even with her by flirting with the waitresses in a way that would cause a sailor from Marseilles to blush, and Missy just gets more and more plantation, and magnolia, and Southern belle. Then we all go back and play bridge.

Missy won't play with Larry any more. She's jes' not used to being spoken to like that, merely because she forgot what trumps wuh. So I play with her, and Larry plays with Bax, and as bridge has an insidious way of getting under your skin by the time the evening's over we're lined up solidly against each other; boys against girls.

Even Bax has begun to crack under the strain, and lets go with a few sharp retorts from time to time. But so far, poor jerk, he's always at the opposite end, trying to pull one or the other of us out of our frantic gloom.

Today was something of a miracle, I suppose.

It began unpromisingly enough with the usual steady rain

and bickering around the breakfast table, but suddenly, by lunchtime, it became apparent that Larry and Missy were getting along for a change. They were in one of their sexy moods, which lasted right through the meal and afterwards as they lay around the living-room kissing each other and holding hands all over the place.

Bax went off to chop wood, and I went upstairs to my room and picked up the oblong rug off the floor and flung myself on the bed and took a nap.

I dreamt vividly of Jim.

Woke up at seven feeling rotten; rotten in the stomach and in the throat. Heavy, leaden, out of tune. Looked out of the balcony window at the lights in the harbour.

Raining gently.

If it doesn't stop I shall go mad.

We ask the people in the shops every day when they think the rainy season will be over. They shrug. Now they're getting quite excitable when we ask them. What can they do about it anyway?

There was another bridge game this evening. But obviously something *has* happened. Missy and Larry played together.

May 9th.
Thursday.

Have been watching our house-*chat* for some days now, a real phoney if I ever saw one. Noticed him hanging around the garden the first couple of days we got here making sure we were staying on. Then one morning—he must have waited hours for us to get up—he came barrelling over to the back door just as Bax and I got to the kitchen, wriggled in through the screen door and deposited a token mouse at our feet. Bax threw the mouse away and the *chat* went right back and retrieved it. A much-used mouse. We threw it in the garbage-pail and gave the *chat* some milk. He seemed to like it just so-so. All right, nothing to go mad over—all right for a start you know, but not really what he was accustomed to from the house. I don't know how he managed to convey his fairly complicated chain of reactions, but he did. Let us know he was strictly a filet mignon and strawberries scraps *chat*. We did the best we could for him and he finally went away. Next morning he was back again without the mouse, but I think he's got it back anyway. The mouse seems to have disappeared from the garbage-pail—not that I've examined it too closely.

So like it or not we now have this house-*chat* all over the place making it clear in no uncertain terms what he likes and doesn't. He rewards our cooking efforts by hanging around *inside* the house—we can't keep him out, he knows the place so much better than we do, probably owns it—making exaggeratedly hammy and wholly unconvincing but totally *unnerving* leaps into the air to indicate 'mousing'. There aren't any mice here except for his. But then I don't think he's really a *cat* either.

He was gone yesterday.

I think he leaps out of bed in the morning, zips himself into his old fur cat-coat, gets the mouse out from the box under his bed and goes to work in the area.

If he comes into my room I shall scream.

Saw something funny today that I got a big kick out of. I mean it made me laugh and laugh.

The *chat* was looking longingly at this stupid little sparrow perched on one of the stone jars and he finally made a melodramatic lunge at it and this idiot bird flew himself smack into a telephone wire. I mean he must have been flying for years, he ought to know his way around the air by now.

Hate birds. Hate cats too. Wish every bird would meet every cat and then every cat meet every dog. Don't like dogs much, either.

May 11th.
Saturday.

Still raining.

Larry and Missy just don't appear any more, except occasionally for meals.

Here is the story of Bax's life: he was born in Canada. He was raised in Canada. He went to Toronto University and has never been out of Canada before. He doesn't know what he wants to do, but would like it to be something artistic.

May 12th.
Sunday.

Bax loves everything in Europe, he says, because it's so old. Look at those walls, look at that door, he keeps saying when we drive around the old village. He's crazy about their texture. He keeps taking pictures with his new Rolleiflex in the pouring rain. Perhaps, he says, he'll become a photographer.

Larry is painting Missy now. Looks about like what you'd expect it to. This Master of all Arts kick he's on isn't coming off at all.

Jim now. . .

Started to write to Jim the other day. Couldn't think of anything to say so I tore it up. But I think maybe I do really love him. If I still love him as much in a couple of days I'm going to phone him and tell him I'm coming back to Paris.

May 13th.
Monday.

Rain.
Breaking-point.

May 17th.
Friday.

On Monday the 13th, thirteen days after our arrival, at exactly 9 p.m. (the grandfather clock in the hall had just struck), I was staring wildly at the carcass of a chicken we'd eaten for dinner and I suddenly went berserk.

I picked up the carcass and threw it across the room at the cat (hit him too), and then I bit the top off a pear and flung it against a wall like a hand-grenade, and then I kicked over

Larry's easel. I noticed them all standing well back watching me uneasily, more in sorrow than in anger sort of thing, and this annoyed me so much that I broke a couple of plates as well. Then I started to laugh. So then they all got really worried and Larry shoved me down into a chair, pinning my arms tightly to my sides, and asked me what the hell was the matter.

I said I wanted to get the hell out of there and he said they all did and that we'd get out just as soon as it stopped raining and I said, "And *then* what are we going to do?" And he said we were going to do exactly what everybody else did on vacation—go down to the beach and swim and sun-bathe and take it easy and I looked at each of them and said, "Is that *all* you want to do?"

Larry : Yes.

Missy : Yes.

Bax : Yes.

Me : No ! ! !

So they all asked me what *did* I want to do, and I said I didn't know—gaiety, laughter, song-and-dance, shoes in the air. And they asked me what that meant and I said, "Oh, just have a *good time*." And they said how, and I said I didn't know exactly but brother, not like this.

So then Larry said, "Christ, the trouble with you, Gorce, is that you've got no inner peace." So I said, *he* was a fine one to talk. I said it was all right for him to have inner peace, in the circumstances, but what about me? I could go drown myself for all he cared. And then I lost my temper and said that he'd got me into this and he was damn well going to get me out of it. So then he turned wearily to Bax and said, "O.K. Take her to Biarritz. Give her the bright lights." And Bax said quickly sure, sure, he'd be glad to, anything, anything, and I felt like such a fool, but anyway I went upstairs and got out of my jeans and put on a dress.

Then Bax and I drove over to Biarritz; and we almost didn't get into the Casino because I hadn't got a passport. We finally signed a paper both swearing that I was over twenty-one and they let us through.

I'd never gambled before.

Christ, it's boring. I don't know what I thought it would be like, but I thought it would at least be more convivial. I mean you just sit there putting down chips and nobody speaks to anybody else. I played roulette because that was the only one I could understand. I lost all the time. Bax, standing around making all kinds of disapproving noises, only had the effect of egging me on to further disasters. So now I've lost my whole allowance for this month and will have to ask Bax for money every time I want to buy something, even if it's only something cheap like sun-tan oil.

Yes! Sun-tan oil! That's what I said. Because—miracle of miracles—the sun has finally come out.

I can't help feeling that it's entirely due to *me* that our luck has broken. I mean the whole episode at the Casino had such a discouraging effect on Bax that he just wanted to slouch on back to the villa as quickly as possible. But now that I'd really *really* hit rock-bottom I found myself full of bounce.

So I talked him into taking me to a night club and we found this divinely sympathique little cave, all barrels and dripping candlewax, called the Club de Caveau. It was practically empty when we came in, and the proprietor, a gnarled little Englishman who's lived in France so long he speaks Cockney with a French accent, was terribly sweet to us. Asked us who we were and what we were doing down there, and so on. Promised us that the rain would stop the next day (it did). Said it was off season, of course, so nothing much was going on for the time being, except for a couple of American battleships anchored off the coast for manoeuvres, and an Anglo-American-Franco-Spanish company, who was setting up to shoot a film about a Bullfighter right near us in a little village. He said the Co-ordinating Director and the Art Director came into the club every night along about this time and as I was an actress, he'd sort of see that I got to meet them if I liked. I almost fell off the bar-stool for joy.

Sure enough, dead on schedule, who should come rolling into

the place but the Art Director (Italian) and the Co-ordinating Director (Hungarian) of this Anglo-American-Franco-Spanish film company. Gosh, they were nice. The Co-ordinating Director especially—Stefan Something-or-other—is a great charmboat in a twinkling, grey-haired, pink and paunchy way. I just, love sexy fat men. I really do. They make me feel so—oh gosh I don't know—so feminine. Anyway, he's a real jazzy kid, this Stefan. Full of beans. And we hit it off right away. Almost before we'd manoeuvred ourselves into position, he said he was sure there'd be something in the film for both Bax and me. Bax said firmly that I was the one that acted, not him, but Stefan wouldn't hear of it. He said naw, we were *both* to come down to the village in exactly ten days time to meet the Casting Director, and he'd have it all sewn up for us. Made us promise we would. He uses this mock-American accent, makes fun of himself and everyone the whole time, but I know he means it about the movie. Anyway, I'm going to show up. "I'm crazy about these two kids here. A couple of real sweet youngsters," he confided to the proprietor through his cigar. Then he bought us a few rounds of drinks. I felt great, just great. On top of the world.

All at once we had an invasion of the American Navy. Then things really started moving. They were in terrific form. The little French jazz band started playing (they turned out to be not half-bad, really très zazou) and as I was practically the only girl there, I danced with all the sailors.

If anyone had put it to me an hour before that I would suddenly find myself in the midst of a bunch of exquisitely mannered seamen whose whole purpose in life was to request the pleasure of my company for the next dance, or see to it that I was constantly supplied with cigarettes and lights and ash-trays and pretty compliments, I would have been frankly incredulous (only I wouldn't have used that phrase). But the boys, before coming ashore that day, had apparently been given one of the stiffest chewings-out in their naval careers about behaviour becoming to the uniform and a long list of do's and don'ts relating to their treatment of civilians, with the result that I might have been at one of those gracious Southern Balls Missy's always going on about, with all those well-brought-up Southu'n genne'lmen in full chivalric flower. Which just shows you.

Isn't it funny, I had so *definitely* planned to write Jim when I got back that night. In fact the letter had been forming itself in my mind the whole way out to Biarritz. But when we did get back it was five o'clock in the morning and I just flopped into bed. And when I woke up the next afternoon the sun was out and I'd forgotten every word of it.

Now we eat breakfast every day in our bathing suits on the patio, the early morning air pungent with aromatic smells of food and flowers, and the coffee tasting of the sun.

I sit on for hours afterwards staring idly at the snails clinging to knife-blade leaves growing in our garden. Sometimes I pick them off. They make a sucking noise and there's a small round wet spot where they sat. Are they eating the leaves or just balancing on them? Everything shimmers and hums around me—the sun and the sand and the sea—a pale sky high above and gravel crunching under foot—breezes blowing butterflies.

The sun burns through the iron garden-chairs and insects fall into my coffee-cup and try to crawl out. I get dizzy and close my eyes and open them again on the rest of the garden —mimosa and large tousled magenta roses with bright red buds, orange gladioli, a pine tree dead as if strangled by the morning glory vines climbing up it, its long tan needles blowing in the soft warm wind like hair.

Eventually the sun gets too hot and burns the ground under my feet. Then I put on my sandals and go down the stone steps into the sea.

We take sandwiches with us for lunch and spend the rest of the day at the beach. The cat is furious because we're never around to feed him any more. He'll probably bring us that mouse again.

Received a sweet letter from Jim today. Must write him soon. Must, must, must.

Boy, we met a *real* nut on the beach today. A skinny young American with a fierce black moustache called Hugo McCarthy. He'd just left the South of France a couple of days ago, where he'd been kicked out of Somerset Maugham's villa in Cap Ferrat for the third time. Every time he thought about it he became absolutely doubled up with rage, his whole body trembling under the impact of his emotions.

"Where does he come off giving me the bum's rush?" he steamed. "Who the hell does he think he is anyway? He needs me, boy, I don't need him! *I'm* the colourful eccentric all these characters write about. Hey, do you know I'm in three books already? Met an Englishman called Tynan in Spain a while ago and he put me in his bullfight book, and a couple of Americans I ran into last year ski-ing at Klosters—wouldn't be fair to tell you their names until I hear how it comes out, but they're very well known—anyway they're *still* fighting about which one's going to get to have me in his."

"But Somerset Maugham doesn't write novels any more, does he?" I asked.

"That's just it! Of course he doesn't. Ran out of ideas. Ran out of characters. That's where I could help him. Look, don't get me wrong. I'm not asking for money. I'm no bum. I'll sing for my supper. Let 'em all get rich on me, who cares? All I ask in return is a little hospitality. I'm not completely broke. I'm doing O.K. I'm waiting round here for Irwin Shaw. He's due to arrive any day now. Any of you writing a book?" he asked hopefully.

We said we weren't. I asked him what he thought Maugham had against him.

He became even more aggrieved. "That's just it. Nothing. Not a goddam thing. Hadn't even seen me! Wouldn't see me. Always sent someone out to say he wasn't in. Goddammit, I *knew* he was there. I know where they all are," he added gloomily.

"What about Françoise Sagan?"

"Been in Paris for the past two months," he replied promptly. He brooded for a moment. "Anyway, I don't think she writes my type of novel. Do you think she could use me?"

"Why not?"

"Yeah. Well maybe. I'll wait and see if she turns up here this summer."

He flung himself on the sand beside us and asked us where we all came from, and we asked him where he was from and he said New York, originally. He'd been away five years. "Don't get me wrong, though, I'm no remittance man," he said. "I'd go back again like a shot except I'm afraid to, if you want to know the truth. You know what I'm afraid of? I'm afraid of getting killed back there. I'm not kidding. I mean really killed. Shot. Mugged. Beat up. You've no idea what it's like now. You're walking down the street minding your own business and the next thing you know someone's come up from behind and slugged you. Taken your wallet. Even if you don't have a thing in it they give you a going-over just for the hell of it. Ask my mother. She lives there. She's got the whole apartment wired for sound. Has to call the police every time she wants to open the window. I'm not kidding. I don't want to go back to that, no thanks." He turned suddenly to Bax. "You finished with that sandwich, Bud?"

"I've got an idea," I said. "What about trying the movies? There's a film . . ." but Larry shot me a warning look and I shut up.

"Movies? What movie?" asked Hugo. He'd been lying two away from me on the beach next to Missy, but he sprang up when he heard this and landed with a bound at my side, kicking sand all over my face.

"Sally Jay's got hold of some rumour that they're shooting a film here sometime this summer. She's kind of stage-struck," Larry explained to him, with a deprecating smile, while I tried to get the sand out of my mouth.

"Yeah? Yeah? Where is this outfit?"

"Over in San Sebastian, we hear."

He thought it over a minute. "I may hitch on down tomorrow."

"No hurry," said Larry. "We heard they won't be ready for at least a month. You know how long it takes these things to get set up."

We finally parted, promising to meet him again the next day, same time same place.

Tonight at supper I asked Larry what the big idea was of giving poor old McCarthy the double-cross about the film company. I said except for his moustaches I thought he wasn't at all bad-looking. So Larry sighed and shook his head and gave me one of his when-are-you-going-to-wise-up looks, and started off as though he were speaking to a two-year-old, with it's like this see, and I'll explain slowly, and so forth. He said if I'm really serious about getting a part in the film tomorrow (*am* I!), the easiest way to louse it up would be to turn up with a hundred other people climbing on our backs trying to horn in. Then Bax said if that was the case he'd be perfectly willing to let Hugo go in his place, but Larry said no, definitely not. He wanted Bax to go as planned. We'll all of us go, he said. But we'll go just by ourselves.

"What do you mean all of us?" asked Missy, deeply offended. She said she had no intention of becoming a Movie Star. She said her mother would jes' *die* if she ever saw her daughter on the screen in front of all those people in a public movie house, and Larry raised his eyebrows and said her mother had a lot to learn about her little daughter, he wondered what she'd do if she ever saw her in action behind a certain screen in some *private* house, and far from climbing on her high horse as I'd expected, Missy giggled and said, "Hush yo' face," and then smiled dreamily into his eyes and got all silky and proud like a well-fed lioness, and they went into another of their prolonged necking bouts. This sloppy stuff is really getting revolting. I can't look at it any more. Makes me want to urp. But finally Larry came up for air long enough to reach over the dinner-table, rumple my hair, and assure me that he was going to take an active interest in my career. "Just put yourself in my hands, Gorce," he said. "I'm planning the strategy."

Thank God for that, I thought.

"We'll all turn in early tonight," he said. "We have to be up at eight, looking our best."

But Missy got stubborn and dug in and refused to come.

"O.K.," said Larry. "You keep McCarthy occupied on the beach tomorrow. Tell him we've gone to Biarritz to look at the Virgin on the Rock or something."

Missy pouted, and said that sounded right *mean* to her. She said she thought the poor boy looked mighty peaked. And Larry said never mind, that we'd do him a lot more good getting somewhere ourselves first. Larry is really brilliant about this sort of thing. I see exactly what he means.

I've been thinking a lot about the film. I mean it really would be the most terrific break if I got discovered down here, wouldn't it. Like Audrey Hepburn.

I've been wondering what sort of parts there are that I'd be right for. At the Club de Caveau that night I asked Stefan why they were shooting a picture about a Bullfighter in a French fishing-village, and he told me not to worry my pretty little head about it. I got the feeling he didn't know either. But that's the whole point. Will they want me to be French or Spanish or English? French I hope. I think I look more French than anything else right now.

My hair has turned a very strange colour. The sun's been working on its original pink dye and it's a kind of greenish yellow. But I don't think it looks too bad, though. I have a gorgeous sun-tan (I adore watching myself change colour) and I've noticed that all the girls on the beach have had approximately the same thing happening to their hair.

But it would have to be *modern* French. I mean suppose it's a costume picture? French girls in period movies would tend to have black hair, I feel. Or maybe they're all going to be Spanish, because of the Bullfighter. I bought some carbon paper at the bookshop this evening and I can't decide whether to rub it on my hair and become a brunette or just leave the old straw as it is. I wonder what the sun does to carbon-papered hair. I'd better not try.

Got *another* letter from Jim today. It's awful. He says he misses me terribly, more than he ever imagined he would, and that it's so unbearably lonely in his studio he's going off to Florence. I don't want to think about it. I don't want to feel his pain. I must write to him. I must, must must. I'll write tomorrow. I'll have something to tell him then and anyway I'm too tired now. The sun makes me so sleepy.

Up early tomorrow, glug, glug. Gosh, I'm getting so nervous and excited I bet I don't sleep a wink anyway.

May 23rd.
Thursday.

We very nearly didn't get to the village at all this morning. The Citroen had one of its coughing fits and we had to roll it all the way down the hill before it started. The offices of the Anglo-American-Franco-Spanish film company, I think it's called Cherwell or maybe Starwell Productions, are in a broken-down warehouse on the wharf. Stefan came beaming down on us almost as soon as we got there, and Larry said, watching him approach, "Who does he think he's kidding?" He was a sight all right. He looked like a Hollywood director out of *New Yorker* cartoon; full-flowing foulard, red shirt and beret, the works except for riding boots and a megaphone. He was in high spirits, very pleased with himself, absolutely delighted to see us. We admired the colour of his shirt and scarf and he admired the colour of my arms, pinching them a couple of times, and before we knew it we were ushered into the Casting Director's office, where the keen-eyed quivering-nosed smooth-haired Englishman (I almost said terrier) looked up from behind his desk and said through his teeth, "C'm in, chaps, c'm in. Nice of you to drop in. Always helps to run into people who speak the same lingo, eh?" Only he had to repeat the last sentence several times before we understood him.

Then Stefan said, "Well, what do you think of my youngsters?" and Larry shoved Bax and me forward, and the

Casting Director looked at us awhile and said, "Remarkable, absolutely remarkable. Let me take their particulars."

"And who is the other gentleman?" he asked finally.

Larry stepped forward. "Larry Keevil's my name," he said suavely. "This is my client. I handle Miss Gorce."

I waited for them to laugh us out of the room, but they didn't turn a hair. They acted as if it was the most natural thing in the world for an unknown actress to show up out of the blue, agent in hand.

"And Mr. Baxter, Mr. Keevil? You handle him as well?" Larry said he did.

"Well the position is——" began the Casting Director, but he got no further. Stefan, who had been talking on the intercom, suddenly turned and said dramatically, "He's here! They arrived an hour ago and he's outside the office now." The Casting Director sprang into action, whipped the papers off his desk and said, "Show him in, old boy, show him in immediatlih."

The door opened and in came a beautiful little brown boy in a pale gaberdine suit two sizes too big, almost completely hidden by several other larger Spaniards. They were all smoking cigars. The Bullfighter. I knew it immediately. I tried not to stare but I couldn't take my eyes off him. Stefan asked us to wait outside until they were finished and we filed out of the office, and as I passed, one of them—I *think* it was the kid himself, took the cigar out of his mouth and said "Wappa," something like that, and then another one said, "Mwee wappa," at least that's what it sounded like.

We sat around outside for about fifteen minutes, and then the door flew open and Stefan poked his head out, winked at me, and called Larry in. Then another fifteen minutes passed, the door opened again, and I heard the Casting Director saying to Larry, "Well, if she wants to do it, we're delighted," and Larry answer, "Of course she will. Just let me handle it." Then they came out and the Casting Director said, "Good-bye, Miss Gorce, Mr. Baxter. Good of you to drop in. We'll be seeing a lot more of you, I expect," and the door closed again.

"Will I do what?" I asked Larry excitedly.

"Shut up. Wait till we get out."

We found a café near the wharf and sat down. "I'll buy us a drink," said Larry, "we need it."

"What happened, what happened? Don't sit there like that. Come on, tell us, for God's sake!"

Larry had tilted his chair back from the table and was balancing back and forth looking at us both, shaking his head in wonder. "Whew!" he said, "Wait'll you get a load of this. I've had a lot of shocks in my life but this caps it." Then his chair came forward with a bang and he leaned over and started playing with his St. Raphael while we breathed all over him with impatience.

Finally he turned to Bax.

"They are crazy about you, boy," he said simply. "Really crazy. They think you are a find. They want to test you for a big part, and if you shape up right they talk of putting you under contract."

Bax was calm; almost despondent. "Is that all? No thanks," he said in a bored sort of way.

"No thanks? It's the chance of a lifetime!"

"Look," said Bax, "I only came down today because you thought it would help Sally Jay if I did. I don't know why, but ever since I can remember I've been followed down the street by talent scouts wanting to discover me. I've been all through this before. I even resigned from the Mask and Wig Society at college, and I'm crazy about the theatre, because every time I wanted to do something artistic like designing scenery or getting on the board that chose the plays someone tried to talk me into acting. Or some Director or Producer or agent would come to give us a lecture and take me aside afterwards and ask me if I wanted to go into the movies. They always picked me out. I don't know why. I look just like everybody else. But get this straight, Larry, I don't want to be another Rock Hudson or another Gregory Peck or another anybody under contract to anyone. And I don't like horses. And that's final."

Those were the most words I'd ever heard Bax say at a

time. Practically a speech. I'd been studying him fiercely, trying to figure out just what it was about him they wanted so much. I mean Larry's handsome, too, with his carroty hair and full, sensuous mouth. At least I think so. And much more exciting-looking, flashing and quicksilver and expressive. And Bax—as he himself said—looks just like everybody else. I finally saw what they meant, though. There is in Bax all the sturdy ruggedness, the woodsy woodenness and strict regularity of feature of a certain type of Hollywood Hero.

I was thoroughly disillusioned. It was a rude awakening on two counts. First to discover that all of Stefan's joviality had really been designed to get a hold of Bax, and secondly to face the fact that I'd lived twenty-one years without being discovered once. It was obviously the sort of thing that started happening to you young. I mean if I hadn't been discovered up till then, how would I ever be?

We sat around the table for a while, in silence.

"Will I do what?" I said to Larry suddenly.

He looked at me blankly. "What are you talking about?"

"I heard the Casting Director say something to you about, 'Well, if she wants to do it.' Do what? Sweep floors I suppose," I snorted.

"Not quite as bad as that, Gorce." He patted my hand. "I gave him this big build-up about you, see, and there are a couple of small parts going, small but *good*, I understand, and the Casting Director says there might be a possibility that they'll use you for one of them, I mean if you want to do it. Don't worry about the money, I'll squeeze them plenty for it."

"Stick with Larry and you'll be wearing diamonds," I said glumly to Bax.

"Cheer up, Gorce. Behave yourself and I'll tell you something nice. You know who the key figure is around here? It's that little guy the Bullfighter, who by the way is one of the top bullfighters today. He's got his own money in this deal and he's going to have plenty to say about what's what. You made a great hit with him, Gorce. He wants us to have dinner with him Monday night. He's leaving now. He's got a fight in San Sebastian on Sunday, but when he gets back he wants us to have dinner with him. What do you think of that?" He let it sink in for a minute, and then said, "Play your cards right *there* and you can probably have any part you want. Stick with *him*, kid, he's the one with the diamonds."

This didn't go over too well with Bax, but it did cheer me up considerably. I mean, gosh, a *real* bullfighter! In fact I got so excited about the whole idea I practically had them talked into driving down to San Sebastian to see the fight, except that Bax pointed out that it's in Spain and I don't have a passport.

That settles it; pact or no pact I'm writing to Uncle Roger for help as soon as I finish this entry. No more horsing around.

We sat at the café until lunchtime. A couple, two English people, sat down at the table next to ours just in time to see the Bullfighter and all his pals get into a shiny lavender Cadillac and drive off in a blaze of flashing chrome. The woman, a large Junoesque creature with a sensationally unhappy expression on her face, had slapped on an enormous pair of sunglasses as he came out and had been studying him intently. Suddenly she turned to her companion. "Well, there's another dream gone down the drain—he must be every bit as high as my waist," she announced sullenly. "He really looks such a boring little man, doesn't he, so utterly clueless in those revolting American clothes, I can't *think* why we're going to do this picture. Basil wants us all to go down to San Sebastian to watch him on Sunday but I don't think I'll bother. This morning's plane journey has finished me off nicely, thank you very much. The man next to me never stopped yammering. I suppose it simply doesn't occur to some people that one *might* be trying to recover from the night before." She took a large gulp of her drink. "I'd quite like to see the bullfight though, wouldn't you? I do adore cruelty. Everybody back home's too dreary, going on and on about the horses. Papa's forbidden me across the threshold if I go to one. Can you believe it? That's an added incentive." She finished her drink. "I hope at least that I get a chance to hear some decent Spanish spoken. Everyone I meet in London seems to be talking the most disgusting Catalan; it's quite hopeless. Not that I place much faith in what our brave little torero is going to sound like. He's probably Andalusian, or worse still Basque. Wouldn't that be the end? Just my eternal rotten luck! Oh do look, here comes the reconnaissance party."

Stefan and the Casting Director, who turned out to be the Basil of her tirade, Basil Plinn-Jones, were coming towards the café. So then we were all introduced. Her name is Angela and she was described as the Plinn-Jones' Girl Friday. And the man, the one on the listening end, was the Assistant Director, Robin something.

"I thought you might be Americans," she said when we joined tables. "I do hope you didn't mind my remark about his suit, but he looked too ridiculous, didn't he?" She turned frankly to Bax. "It would be quite another story on you," she stated baldly, her eyes measuring him for size.

We all had lunch together; a rather uncomfortable lunch. I was getting a slight déjà vu about it all. It seemed to me you could plunk them all down in the middle of the Contessa's crowd and not miss one.

I didn't think anyone was enjoying themselves much, but when we started to leave Stefan asked us to have supper with them tonight at a restaurant in Ascain which is on top of one of the mountains, and Larry, curse him, said yes.

I suppose he knows what he's doing.

Must stop now and get that letter off to Uncle Roger.

May 24th.
Friday.

Last night was one of *those* evenings. I wouldn't know what to call it. Eventful in an uneventful way. Boring; but interesting. Nothing much happening on the surface and everybody seething and stewing underneath—changing character all over the place.

We are caught in the middle of some mysterious

psychological shuffle now, our loyalties shifting and sliding back and forth like ships in a storm.

First of all there was Bax's revolt. He never does much talking, most of the time he's just listening, but yesterday all the way back to our villa and for the rest of the afternoon there was a different quality to his silence: he was *thinking*. And when the time came for us to start out for Ascain he turned up in a dirty old sweat-shirt and announced calmly that he wasn't going with us. He said he thought he had made it clear that he didn't want to be in the movie and he didn't like the people, so what was the point anyway?

So then Larry hit the ceiling and said he *had* to come along, that he'd spoil everything if he didn't.

At this point Missy went over to Bax's side. She told Larry to stop bullying him and leave the poor boy alone. She said why should he come if he didn't want to? She said she didn't much want to come either, they all sounded terrible. She said what difference did it make if Bax came or not, as long as he wasn't going to be in the old movie anyway.

Larry said desperately, "Help me, Gorce, make him see the light." And I said what could *I* do, and Larry said didn't I see that Bax was our strongest link, our only selling-point, and Missy wanted to know what Larry was getting so excited about; he certainly wasn't going to take ten per cent. of our salaries, was he? And Larry looked at her as if she was a worm and asked if it ever occurred to her that he might want to direct a film sometime and that being around these people would enable him to learn something about how it all works.

I couldn't help noticing how quickly Larry's inner-peace-down-to-the-beach-and-take-it-easy philosophy was wearing off, but that's Larry all over. He's just like me. His curiosity gets the best of him every time.

Then he spoke to Bax very seriously and said that he wouldn't ask him to do anything he didn't want to do, but didn't Bax understand that they had their eye on him and him alone and that if he dropped out so early on, it could easily mess up our chances. "And I mean Sally Jay's chances," he added.

"Oh hush all this fuss! Sally Jay doesn't care whether she's in the stupid old film or not, do you?" Missy was getting indignant.

"Yes I do," I said. Suddenly I knew I did. I really did, even if it meant just a small part. Suddenly I knew I couldn't get through the summer just sitting there watching Missy and Larry together. Or lazing around not learning anything, not accomplishing anything, not seeing anything new.

I went over to the armchair where Bax was sitting and knelt at his feet and said, "Please come along tonight. For my sake." And Larry, right behind me, said "Just play along with them for a little while, won't you? It can't hurt you and it can hurt us. Even if you pass the test, who says you've got to take the part? And what if you do take the part? Experience is experience, and it's everything in life, boy. What else have you got to do this summer?"

So Bax finally gave in. He said, "O.K. I'll go, I'm sorry to be like this, it's only . . ." but he didn't finish the sentence. He smiled wistfully at me and got up and we all went down to the car.

On the way out I took his hand. "What's the matter?"

He shook his head. "I don't know. I just feel I'm getting deeper and deeper in."

So we arrived in Ascain a rather divided group.

The whole evening was like that. Everyone at cross-purposes. It never really got off the ground. There were great spaces when the whole thing seemed like an awful waste of time. Stefan was worried and distrait. The special kind of fishing vessel which the Italian Art Director had gone to such trouble to find had loosed its moorings and gone drifting out with the tide, probably lost forever. Even the sight of Missy didn't perk him up, and his squeezings and pinchings were half-hearted to the point of absent-mindedness. The English themselves were divided in spirit. Plinn-Jones was a conscientious host but stiffly aloof and ill at ease and over-conscious of his position. Robin, the Assistant Director, young, ruddy and blue-blazered, with darting black eyes and a fixed avid grin, was drinking heavily and roaring to go in all directions. And Angela—well, Angela was just Angela, and I ain't never seen the likes. Whoever called the English reticent must have had his ears full of golf balls. Our Girl Friday's duties included, as we learned from her own mouth not ten minutes after we dined, being part-time mistress of Plinn-Jones. Only she doesn't think much of him, she told Bax and me with an enormous sniff. She doesn't think much of any men. In fact she hates them all. And after hearing the story of Angela's love life I think I see why.

Apparently just as she had decided that her ex-husband—after such various pranks as trying to push her off a mountain-slope ski-ing, taking pot-shots at her grouse-shooting, and just plain holding her under water—didn't much *care* for her, he went and stole the family silver, which subsequently re-appeared at the next dinner party she attended, where, to further humiliate her, he had dressed up as a waiter. As she put it, the time had come to give *him* the push. However, getting rid of him proved another matter.

How this was accomplished we never learned, because suddenly Robin, the Assistant Director, who up till then had been assuring Larry earnestly that there was no point whatever in asking him about his job since he hadn't the faintest idea what it was about (no gentleman ever did), decided to set us all straight about himself. First he made sure we got his name right. "It's Halkens not Heakins. Good God, Heakins is *Irish*. I'm Norse. I could hardly be mistaken for an Irishman with this nose, could I?" he said, grinning eagerly and inviting us to study the old Norse beak, which was long and thin and pointed downwards.

Then we heard all about Daddy (grand old character) and how he used to terrify all the children as they sat around the huge table in the Dining Hall, while he bellowed at them to recite the capitals of the European countries.

Then we got again how bad he was at his job (in the old days, as his father always said, one didn't have to be *doing* things all the time, it was enough to be a gentleman).

Then we got his deep sentimental attachment to the Ballet. "Give me Swan Lake, Swan Lake, *Swan Lake* every time!"

Then we got his outdoor prowess. "I walk *everywhere*."

And then we got his school tie.

That was my fault. I was staring at him, fascinated, thinking what a curious set of credentials to present and wondering if he wasn't just drunk, when my eyes happened to light on the weird knotted mass around his neck. It was the smallest tie I'd ever seen on a grown man, about two inches long: a miniature tie, perfectly formed. It might have been his youngest brother's, except that it was black with age. Under the soup stains I could just make out a striped pattern of some badly matched colours. It looked like a trophy, so I asked him about it. It was his old school tie, he said, smirking modestly. Stonehenge, I think he said. The smiling modesty changed to smiling impatience when we didn't react.

He was becoming truculent under that smile. If you happened to mention that you didn't think the beach at Ciboure looked very good for bathing, he would say, "Oh you Americans. You're spoiled, that's the trouble with you. Try bathing *anywhere* on my salary!"

Then he would say, "You're children, that's what you are, *children*, with your ridiculous idealism! And you're supposed to be running the world now. Well, the best of luck to you, that's all I can say."

It wasn't, though.

A moment later he leaned towards me with that same grin that was beginning to make him look insane and said, "Begging your pardon and no offence meant I'm sure, but admit now, *admit* you don't know how to begin organizing a World Federation!"

By now I'd had enough of this jolly old Viking. "Maybe not," I said, rising, "but I know how to end a conversation." And I went to the john.

A hoot of laughter followed me, and when I returned, there was Angela, still in stitches, carefully explaining to each and everyone just what *he* had said to me, and what *I* had said to him, hugely enjoying Robin's discomfiture. "Well done.

Oh, masterly," she crowed at me. "It's made my evening."

It was unmade for her a few seconds later, when they let off some fireworks, and Angela, whose nerves are understandably jumpy about such noises, leapt ten feet in the air every time one went off.

That made Robin's evening.

So, then we drove to another mountain-top, a place called Béhobie. It's really one of the most beautiful old villages I've ever seen, and under most circumstances I would have been moved to tears, but as I say, it was one of those evenings.

Bax's spirits, however, soared like an eagle at the sight of all that texture on the old walls and doors and steep winding streets, and by the time we'd found a picturesque little bar in which to have a night-cap he was his old affable, co-operative, smiling self. It was nice to have him back. It made me realize that he was probably the only genuinely nice person in the whole group. Amongst us all he stands out like a good deed in a bad world, as they say.

Missy was bored and sulky and sleepy. No one was paying any attention to her, not even Larry, who was trying so hard to put himself across with the Directors it hurt.

Angela was flinging back her night-caps fast and furiously.

"Ouch!" she shrieked, suddenly executing another one of her leaps. "Goddammit, don't do that!" Stefan, in a fit of abstraction, had absent-mindedly pinched her.

"What is it?" he asked, surprised. I don't think he even realized what he'd done.

"You pinched me," said Angela contemptuously. She turned to Bax. "I do hate being pinched so much, it's not *true*, don't you agree? One doesn't mind being slapped or punched, I quite enjoy it as a matter of fact. But pinching, ugh! It's so *piddling*." All at once she became very coy, opening her eyes wide and saying in the voice of an excited child, "I adore violence. I think the spectacle of two strong men pounding each other around the ring is the most picturesque and alluring thing in the world. Do you box? I hope so, you'd be magnificent."

She's a handful, that babe. Bax just goggled at her. She

really baffles him. He can't figure out if she's kidding or what. I thought I'd better come to his rescue. Besides, I don't trust old Angela.

"Let's dance," I whispered to Bax. The bartender had put on some dreamy French records and I love dancing with Bax. He's much taller than I am but it doesn't seem to make any difference. He sort of folds himself around me and we dance so well together I don't talk at all.

We went out on the terrace and looked down at the lights of towns far, far below, and he kissed me.

At first I couldn't seem to keep my mind on it, but then I thought of what a picturesque and alluring spectacle we must be making, locked in each others arms high on a mountain-top in the moonlight, and how furious Angela would be if she could see us, and how I might be kissing a future famous *movie star*, and it just worked wonders. I'm a real celebrity-hound.

Just before the party broke up, Plinn-Jones gave us the name of the hotel that the Bullfighter was staying at and told us to be there by 6.30 the following Monday. "Till then," he called out as the four of us climbed into the old Citroen for the long drive home. It passed in unbroken silence, each of us heavy with his own thoughts.

I'll bet the only thing we were unanimously agreed upon was to stay out of their way till then.

# CHAPTER TWO

MANUELO SANCHEZ, 'EL WHEERO' (that may not be spelt right; it's the first time I've tried) was waiting for us in the lobby of his vast hotel. The first thing that struck me about him, sitting there so gravely in the middle of his Quadrille, was the air of tragic solemnity surrounding him. The second thing was how he gleamed. He was the cleanest person I've ever seen. He had the cleanest ears and the cleanest hairline and his teeth matched his shirt in whiteness. His skin was burnished brown and his hair water-black.

We all shook hands, Bax, Larry and I, Wheero and his gang, and the next thing I knew I was in the chair beside him, an enormous Cadillac brochure across my knees from which I was supposed to choose the one I liked best. There must have been about five hundred cars. They all had names like horses. I finally chose Sand and Sable. El Wheero looked at it for a minute and then flipped over to the one he preferred. He asked me what I liked better about mine and I said "It's bigger." We laughed.

From that moment on everything changed. His tragedy vanished and my nervousness with it. He began laughing at me and I began laughing at him laughing at me and it went on like that until we reached the stage where practically everything is unbearably funny, especially if it isn't.

"Me gusto mucho los Chestairs!" he announced, triumphantly producing a pack of American cigarettes and offering me one. We sobbed with glee. Then, as if that wasn't funny enough he added, "Me gusto mucho whiskey." That destroyed us.

It occurred to me vaguely that he was being quite unlike my preconceived idea of a bullfighter, but I couldn't even remember what that was. I know I'd been worried about the language barrier. I hadn't dreamt it would be so easy to get over. He had a vocabulary of about eighty English words and I had a Spanish vocabulary of none. But we got along like a house on fire.

Dinner was a riot. We threw pellets of bread across the table at each other and made airplanes out of the menus and sent them sailing around the dining-room. Then we had a really great idea. We were going to put a pat of butter on the end of a knife and use the knife as a catapult to see if the butter would stick to the ceiling. But Larry stopped us, so we flipped water at each other with our spoons instead.

Bax and Larry thought we'd gone crazy. I don't know what the Quadrille thought, except it was clear that anything old Wheero wanted to do was O.K. with them. They were all twice his age, but if he'd been the King of the Underworld, they couldn't have been more under his thumb. Unwritten law of the Bullring.

We drove off to Béhobie in the lavender Cadillac with the hood down, Wheero and I sitting on top, our feet on the back seat, waving to the cars that passed and nearly falling off at every corner.

We found the little bar we'd been to the other night and started playing some more games. We took the labels off beer-bottles and put them on everybody's wallets, sticky side up, and threw them at the ceiling so that the labels stuck there and the wallets came clattering down all over the drinks on the table.

El Wheero suddenly asked me if I liked ice and I said yes and he took a piece out of his whisky-glass and dropped it down the front of my dress.

So I gave him a hot-foot.

Then I had to try to teach him how to do it on one of his Quadrille, a gnarled monkey-faced old man of infinite patience who held his foot politely in position while Wheero kept putting the match in his shoe the wrong way round.

Then we sang that song about the Sinking of the Ship Titanic (Wheero had learned it from students in Mexico) and after that we started dancing. Then I told him how I'd run away from school when I was thirteen to become a bullfighter and he said he'd loan me one of his bullfighter's costumes so I could have a picture taken of me wearing it. We measured each other to see if we were near enough the same size for it to fit me and were laughing so hard we had to sit down.

Suddenly, from nowhere, Stefan and Les Anglais appeared.

They sailed over to our table in formation, so to speak, spearheaded by Angela, undulating like the prow of a ship, pouring in and out of her dress, which was showing a great deal of arms and breasts, Rubensesquely pink from her few days in the sun. Her expression was prouder and angrier and more disconsolate than ever.

It was quite a sight, come to think of it, though nothing compared to the sight of the Spaniards reacting to it.

She started a chain of emotion, beginning with Wheero and going around the Quadrille in ever-increasing circles of intensity, that made the air positively ring with cries of Wappa! and Wappissima! (when I was able to hold the monkey man's attention long enough I made him write it down for me and he spelled out ¡guapa! on the tablecloth). Anyway the air was ringing with cries of ¡guapa! and ¡guapissima! for quite some time

Boy, they were really galvanized. Inflamed. Stirred to the roots.

And what's even harder to believe—and hardest of all to admit—is that from that second on, I became invisible.

Angela spoke Spanish, which was a help, but that had nothing to do with it. They just went for her, that's all. Every inch of her. They couldn't believe their luck. They poked and prodded and patted her; they filled her with champagne; they nudged each other, shaking their heads in wonder. The few words they addressed to anyone else were merely to thank us for their great good fortune.

Angela herself was less pleased than surprised. "I simply don't understand it. Christ, what a racket they're making," she said to me in what could hardly be called an aside. And, sniffing contemptuously three times, she re-inclined her head towards El Wheero, pouring out his heart in rapid Spanish to her other ear.

"It's *too* funny," she said to me after a while, again in her normal tones, which are a lot louder than most. "He keeps breathing 'que barbaridad' passionately all over me. Don't you just adore 'que barbaridad'? Imagine hoping to flatter one by calling one an *outrage*!"

I maintained a dignified silence.

From then on she kept me well briefed with the progress of his infatuation.

"He's invited me to dine with him every night this week. . ."

"He's invited me to the next bullfight. He says he'll dedicate a bull to me. . ."

"He's just asked me to the Feria at Malaga. . ."

"He's just asked me down to his bull-ranch outside Seville. Goodness! He'll expect me to meet his mother next. . ."

"He says I'll adore Spain. Apparently everyone in Spain is mad about large women. That's something, anyway. Still, rather you than me. Now for God's sake don't desert me!" she said, suddenly clutching at my arm.

The Spaniards, unable to control themselves any longer, were determined to bear her off to some other Spaniards who owned a night club in Biarritz.

Angela and I got into the lavender Cadillac with them. The rest followed on.

It was a long drive. Even in the car they all kept trying to talk to her at once. I let the language flow around me, understanding nothing. The top was still down, the night was still warm, and as I looked up at the endless stars I tried to tell myself that my life wasn't completely over; that there were other things in the world besides a small, faithless bullfighter. There was nature, for instance. There were the snails in our garden in the sunshine. I tried to think of some other nice things, but I couldn't. There would be other bullfighters, I said to myself. But I want *this* one, I replied. I was just making up my mind to learn Spanish as quickly as possible when I realized with a jolt that one part of my brain was following along their conversation exactly as if it were in English.

To Angela: "Marida?"

Angela: "Divorciada."

"Y los chicos?"

"Ningunos."

What happened next is astonishing. Although I can't remember ever really hearing Spanish before last night, in the highly technical discussion of Birth Control that followed, I caught every word. I mean it. Every single word. Angela, who was still shouting bulletins at me, started to bring me up to date, but I told her not to bother. ¡Boy! I really surprised myself. Then they got on to another subject and I was lost again.

"He's got a point there, you know," Angela roared suddenly.

"Who? Where?" I'd completely switched off.

"The one in the corner. *You* know. The one who isn't a *complete* idiot."

I winced with my whole body.

"What's the matter?" she asked. "Have I done anything wrong? Do tell me, I've *such* an inferiority complex about offending people."

"Stop talking about them like that," I whispered fiercely. "They do understand English, you know."

Angela looked at me as if I'd suggested they were the boys behind the Oxford Dictionary. "They're Spaniards," she said, dismissing the whole fantasy. "Of course they can't understand. Incidentally their Spanish is quite good for gypsies. I suppose they *are* gypsies, aren't they?"

I just groaned.

We arrived at the night club and Angela created her usual Spanish riot—too pointless and painful to describe—all over again.

Then the Flamencos came over to our table and started singing at us.

"Good gracious," said Angela, "they're singing about me."

"What are they singing about you?" I asked between clenched teeth.

"Well . . . it's something about the beautiful Angela has come all the way to France and we hope she enjoys herself and stays a long time and. . . Oh really, it's too ridiculous—they're hopeless, aren't they? I say, do look at that one! Hasn't he got the sexiest bottom you've ever seen? But still not one of them looks *anything* as good as your friend Bix, do they?"

"Bax," I spat at her. "*Ax, ax, ax,*" I added insanely.

Stefan was baffled. "I don't understand it. I simply don't understand it," he kept saying in amazement, over and over again.

"They like *fat* women, that's all," I snapped.

He was thunderstruck. "But of course. Of course they do!" He hit his forehead with his fist. "I'd forgotten all about that. Well, Angela can coach him in English then. Sorry it lets you out, but it saves us money, eh Basil?"

"I say, steady on," murmured Plinn-Jones.

"What's that? What do you mean?" I asked indignantly. "I don't want to coach him in English!"

Stefan looked quickly at Larry, who frowned back.

"Just a minute," I said slowly. "Who said anything about teaching him English?" It was coming back to me now. Larry at the door of the office and Plinn-Jones saying to him, "Well, if she wants to do it we're delighted," and Larry answering, "Of course she will. Just let me handle it."

I rose. "Bax, I'm going. Will you take me home please?"

"I say, steady on," murmured Plinn-Jones.

"Don't desert me now," commanded Angela, tugging at me hard. "I've absolutely exhausted my Spanish and I'm getting so cross I could scream. Why are they all being so piggy? Why are they making such a disgusting fuss over me with you right here under their noses with your lovely naturally blonde hair—" (it was greenish-orange that day) "—and petite figure——"

I, too, had come to the end of my tether. "Horses for courses," I replied, and pulled away.

"Well, don't bite my head off," she sniffed. "I can't do anything about it can I?"

I got into the Citroen, Larry and Bax following. Larry was driving.

"O.K., Keevil, suppose you tell me what the hell all that was about?"

He shrugged. "The Bullfighter liked you. They wanted someone to help him with his English. You wanted a part. It follows."

"Oh sure, everything follows," I said bitterly. I was filled with disgust. I saw us for what we really were: beggars and toadies and false pretenders. "That may be your way of doing things, but it sure as hell isn't mine. Don't mix me up in your schemes. Look Larry, *just stop pimping for me*, will you!"

There was a shocked silence. I looked at his face. It had turned green under the yellow arc lights. That meant he was dead white.

"Easy, Gorce, easy," he warned me quietly.

Bax put his hand on my shoulder and said miserably, "Apologize to him, Sally Jay. I'm sure he was only trying to help you."

I felt bad but I wouldn't back down. I'd had too terrible a time that night. "Don't help me," I said over and over again. "Just don't anyone help me." And I curled up into a corner to lick my wounds.

# CHAPTER THREE

June 14th.
Friday.

WELL, WE'RE MOVIE Extras now, Larry, Missy and I. That's where all that sharp operating landed us.

Not Bax, of course. Bax is different. He's the fair-haired boy, having passed his screen test (which consisted mostly of having him jump off the recaptured fishing vessel and swim around the ocean for a while—it's an outdoor picture) with flying colours. They've given him the part of the best friend of the hero, who, in turn, is the best friend of the Bullfighter, which, you'd think, would make Bax a bit removed from the central action. But it doesn't. He saves their lives on practically every other page of the script.

It is a period picture, after all. I'm not sure what period, though, and I still can't figure out what a bullfighter is doing in it at all. I suppose he *is* a Period Bullfighter.

The reason Missy is an Extra is because she didn't want to be left alone all day, and the reason Larry is, is because he still thinks he can pick up some pointers on how to make a film, and the reason *I* am is—God knows. Because this is really for the dogs, this is. We get 1,800 francs a day, rock-bottom minimum, and have to be down on the Quai, ready in make-up and costumes, by seven o'clock every morning. And we can't goof off; we've been signed on for three weeks. I'm afraid I shall be looking back on this whole episode as yet another example of what my total and abysmal ignorance always gets me into.

When we realized that all we were going to get were jobs as Extras, it seemed pointless to keep the film secret from McCarthy, so the day before we started working, we took him along to the warehouse to meet the Casting Director. Wheero happened to be there at the time and their eyes happened to fall upon one another, and they went into a Recognition Scene—Mac and the Wheer—that was worthy of Euripides. Apparently they'd known each other back in Mac's Spanish Period when he was running around posing for the Englishman's book. And so, Angela's nerves having proved unequal to the strain (". . . unfortunately that sexy little villa to which he's retired to prepare himself for his taxing little rôle is jammed tightly between Route Nationale Dix and the French Railway, making it quite the *noisiest*, not to say *shakiest* house I've ever been in. It was really the effect on one's intestines as much as anything else . . ."), who do you think is teaching my darling Wheero zee Engleesh? None other than that picturesque and alluring old lunatic Hugo McCarthy. For this he gets twice as much money as we do and three times as much social prestige. We are the lowest of the low; the untouchables. Not that we see much of them any more.

El Wheero works in the afternoon in the Studio along with Bax and the other principals, and when they do come down to the waterfront they stay on the boat—except for Bax, who keeps diving in. We work mornings only, from seven till one, because the film is in technicolor and the sun registers differently on celluloid in the morning and in the afternoon. Or something.

The fact is, we don't see much of *anything* any more, dammit.

That includes the cameras. They're too far away.

We stagger blindly out of bed every morning, go down to one of the warehouses, and put on our mouldy old costumes.

I seem to be some kind of tart, judging by my Hogarthian tatters. I needn't have worried about my hair, either. It's all hidden under a hideous cap. But the French girls working on the picture *kill* me. It's never too early for them to begin flirting. From the minute they get into a chair to be made up by the make-up men, the eyes start flashing, the hips rolling, the lips inviting, and you suddenly realize that whereas before you always thought of a film set as peopled with people, it is, in fact, peopled with *men*.

As I say, we can't see the cameras and I'm beginning to think the cameras can't see us. Not us, personally. At least the American Director, a tough old monster, can't. He picks up his megaphone and shouts at Stefan "O.K., get those bastards moving, will ya!" and Stefan, way down amongst us, all tricked out in his Directing Outfit, beret, red shirt and scarf, picks up his megaphone and calls out "Allez, allez, avancez mes enfants! Mais allez-y! Soyez gentils. . ."

What we are doing is, we are in the market place, see? Among a lot of stalls, see? We are supposed to be buying—or selling—they haven't told us which—and just generally foule-ing around. The second morning we arrived starving to death and realized there was nothing actually edible on all those stalls. Not an orange. Just a lot of stinking fish and a gigantic octopus some real fishermen had caught the night before.

In the beginning, while I, eager beaver that I am, was practically buying and selling in the *water* in an effort to get near the fishing vessel (that's where the cameras are) Missy was backing away from it as fast as possible. She eventually found herself on one of the balconies of a row of houses facing the waterfront. There she struck up an acquaintance with a very nice woman, a painter, who owns the house to which the balcony is attached and who happened to be looking out the window at the time. She invited Missy in for croissants and coffee. When I heard about this I promptly lost my ambition, and now I join Missy in her coffee-break. This lasts quite a long time each day (the woman likes to show us her work), so I shouldn't be at all surprised if we've missed several shots altogether.

It all goes at such a snail's pace. A maximum of two shots a morning, with a minimum of three takes to each. Poor Larry is exhausted. He is in the foreground, tying up the boat.

We are luckier than most, having our balcony hideout. All the other Extras, local French and mostly old men, have taken to wandering into the bistros that dot the waterfront as soon as they're opened. By eleven o'clock yesterday the foule had thinned out so much, they had to comb all the bars and rout them out. Now there is talk of posting spies at strategic points.

Bax has started working in earnest. Not just in and out of the water, but around the Studio too. I promised to help him with his lines, but there's no need to. He never has more than one, or at the most, three a day.

It's a funny thing about Bax. At first I felt terrifically guilty about him. I mean it seemed that of all of us he'd got the rawest end of the deal. He'd been tricked into both taking the test and taking the part under the assumption that he might be helping us out. And now he's stuck with it. But, as the days go by, the thing I've been noticing is that he doesn't seem to mind at all. Of course I wouldn't expect a Canadian ex-diving champ to mind any of that water stuff, but he enjoys the Studio part equally well. He's become great pals with the French Still-Cameraman, who also has a Rolleiflex and gives him all sorts of pointers on how to use it. He was terribly impressed to hear that Cartier-Bresson had started his photographic career in films. He doesn't even mind the eternal waiting around. "It's not so bad," he says, "kind of peaceful." And it gives him a chance to study the lighting set-up. He doesn't much like gadding about all night and he doesn't much mind getting up in the morning. In short he has the perfect temperament.

Larry minds terribly not being In Charge, and Missy obviously minds terribly what it's doing to their love-life. She's gone back to the old Plantation stance, and started that business of sulking around her room again with a bowl of fruit, and last night, for no reason at all, she went out with Mac. I am so punchy trying to arrange my life around the seven-to-one schedule, that I don't know whether I'm coming or going. I find that it leaves me two possibilities for the rest of the day—either to go to sleep in the afternoon and then be raring to go all night and dead again in the morning, or to try staying awake, puttering around, in the afternoon, and get my second wind *anyway* by evening, so that I don't get any sleep at all. I've lost practically all my sun-tan and my mind wanders so I hardly know what I'm thinking. . . I can't finish this, I've forgotten what I was about to say . . . something about Jim. . .

Oh yes. I wonder if he's got to Florence yet. I wrote to him but I haven't heard.

June 21st.
Friday.

Spent the first half of the week waving hello (or good-bye) to the fishing vessel. They didn't say which; they just said wave. Missy and I still in and out of our friend's balcony.

Spent the last half of the week in a Tavern sequence. They actually took the cameras off the boat and got us all inside one of the bistros and shot the scenes there. It was a rare sight. The French Extras were drunk every day.

June 25th.
Tuesday.

We have taken to the hills without explanation. Mules and things. Something about stolen treasure. I may be wrong. Also they've issued us with new costumes. Spanish, I think.

Bax and I have been kissing each other occasionally and holding hands. He hasn't forced the issue yet, but I suppose I'm leading him on. I feel I should draw the line soon. I'd like to, only I don't know how. To tell the truth I've never drawn it.

June 27th.
Thursday. 3.00 a.m.

Have been crying steadily ever since two o'clock this afternoon when I came back and found Jim's letter waiting for me.

I sat down and replied to it immediately, tears splashing all over the pages and my hands trembling. I sealed it and sent it without even re-reading it. It'll probably make me curl up and die in a couple of days but I can't help that.

Here is a mystery: it's a phoney letter all right but there's nothing phoney about my grief. This *has* been the worst day of my life. So far.

Jim is getting married. He's marrying Judy in one week's time.

He wrote me all about it. They ran into each other his very first day in Florence and he knew at once that he'd loved her all the time. ". . . She doesn't know about us—about you and me—and I didn't think I ought to mention it." *Mention* it! That killed me. I'm no more to him than that—a *mention*.

What the hell is the matter with me anyway? Why have I written that *monstrously* awful letter begging him not to go through with it, swearing black and blue I've never loved anyone but him, that I only came down here in the first place to test us?

I mean—*lies*. Nothing but lies.

And yet I *know* I wouldn't get that letter out of the mailbox even if I could. Nor will I write him another cancelling the first. My grief is too real, and my tears, and my pain. Someone quite independent of myself has taken control; I can only obey. It's no good saying over and over again, "But you didn't want him . . . you didn't want him. . ." It's worse than no good. I mean it makes the whole thing worse, because now I *do* want him.

I can see him so clearly. Yesterday I might have said I've forgotten what he looks like; today I'm cursed with total recall. His light-blue eyes filled with tenderness and his mouth curled into a quiet smile; how many times have I looked up from his pillow to find him gazing down at me in that certain way?

The hardest thing to accept is that I could have been so wrong about him, that I could have guessed so wrong. The whole time I've been down here he's been in the back of my mind as the one person in the world I could count on. I was the unfaithful one. Those two letters he wrote me—I keep reading and re-reading them—they *are* sincere, I don't care what's happened, I *know* they are. Well then, how to explain his change of heart in so short a space? The Jim I knew was incapable of erratic behaviour.

Have we all gone mad or something? On top of everything else, what I'm really afraid of is that he *may* reconsider. What on earth would I do then? I don't really want to marry him. Do I?

And I like Judy so much. I like her better than any girl I've ever met. And I know they are right for each other. They are The Innocents. And me—I suppose I'm the Sophisticate. Anyway, that's what Jim thinks. "A girl of your sophisticated tastes . . ." he used to say to me all the time. It's so unfair. How I hate that word. It means shallow and superficial and God knows there's no one in the world who's more a slave to her passions than I am. Complicated, or rather what the French mean by 'compliqué' would be closer. Les Compliqués : Los Complicados : that's the only club I'll ever belong to—though not by choice. I may not have been born into it, but I became a member at a very early age. A life-member.

So why cry? Why carry on like this?

When did all those nightmares begin? My mind keeps going back to that Christmas vacation, sophomore year, when I had an English paper to write and spent most of my time in the Public Library. People kept mistaking me for a librarian. They kept coming up to me and asking me for books and things. I thought it was maybe because I didn't wear hats and at first I was merely annoyed. Then I became frightened. I somehow became obsessed with the idea that the reason they kept mistaking me for a librarian was because that's what I really was meant to be, and instinctively they knew it. It was sheer fantasy, of course. I mean they probably asked dozens of other people as well and I just didn't notice. But it started to prey upon my mind. Then I began having this nightmare. Actually I have it so often I've even given it a name. It's called the Dreaded Librarian Dream.

It's all very vague. It takes place in sort of a vast hall, in the centre of which sits a girl behind a desk, or rather a circular counter, which completely surrounds her. It's funny about that desk: I've seen it somewhere before, I know I have, although it's quite unlike any desk I've ever seen in a library. Anyway, the closer I get to this girl, the older she becomes, until she turns into a middle-aged spinster librarian. Then I see that it's *me*. People keep coming up to her from every direction asking her for books. They are all going somewhere. In fact it isn't a library at all, it's more like a station. Everyone is in a hurry. They are all going somewhere except me. I'm trapped. One of the worst aspects of this dream is that from the very first time I dreamt it I've known, *within* the nightmare, so to speak, that it was one I've had before—an old, old nightmare of long ago. That gives it its special ageless, timeless, hopeless quality. When I awaken from it my space urge is upon me stronger than ever.

It was this space kick that made me leave Jim in the first place. It's this space kick that's going to turn me into the spinster librarian if I don't stop.

Oh God, there've been so many people since I came to Paris. Teddy and Larry and Claude and Jim. Bax and Wheero and dozens and dozens of casuals. I'm so tired. What happens when your curiosity just suddenly gives out? When the will and the energy snap and it all seems so once-over-again? What's going to happen to me five years from now, when I wake in the night (or can't sleep in the first place, like now), take a deep breath to start all over again, and find that I've no breath left? When I start running again and find I can't even put one foot in front of the other? Then, from outer space, that librarian who is going to be me, who *is* me, that dreaded librarian from outer space who is always waiting for me, always ready to pounce, is going to take over. And I'll be cooked. If I don't stop it.

Stop it!

I wish I could get away from here.

> Ah'll pack mah tru-hunk,
> A-and make mah getaway...

I got my allowance for June last week, so there's nothing to stop me.

# CHAPTER FOUR

July 1st.<br>Monday.

**D**IDN'T LEAVE LAST week-end after all. Decided it would be silly to run out on them with only one more day's shooting to complete. And I've got to hand it to them, they finished right on schedule. As a matter of fact now that it's over, I'm kind of sorry it is.

I met a wonderful old man with a donkey last week on the hills. I first noticed him because he looked so authentic fouleing around, and that's the hardest thing in the world to do. I mean most people look like exactly what they are, like people who've been hired to put on funny costumes and mill around a while. But this little old guy really had the knack. He somehow managed not to make his aimlessness pointless. Un vrai artist.

I noticed him the first take on Monday morning. He nodded to me as we passed each other on the hill and I suddenly found myself in another world. And what's more I knew what I was doing there. I had suddenly become a young maiden from the village below and I was going over the hills to visit my sick grandmother. (Little Red Riding-hood. Must have been the basket they gave me.) And I knew what he was doing there too. He was the Itinerant Tinker—whatever that means. Anyway, after the take we fell to talking, Tinker and I, and he told me he's been making a living for years now, he and his donkey, hiring themselves out to the various movie companies. He was so old and gentle. I hope he wasn't a great Comédie Française actor fallen upon old age.

I learned something from him, I hope. Lesson 1: No

matter what you do you've got to try to do it well. Otherwise it's unbearable. Those first weeks on the film wouldn't have been so bad if I'd only realized that.

I've been thinking. How many things have I ever done well in my life? Done *really* well? Done wholly with all my attention and concentration focused on the doing? None. Not school. Not college. Not Teddy. Not Jim. Not this.

Concentrate, Gorce.

(I have an attention-span of about two minutes long.)

Perhaps I ought to concentrate on Bax. He's really the most interesting person of us all now—or at any rate he's in the most interesting position. A month ago he found himself being dragged unwillingly into this movie deal and now apparently he's such hot-stuff, Hollywood's sent for him in a hurry. They want him there by the end of the month. He's going, too. And what's more, he's happy about it. It's merely a matter of accepting this new responsibility as calmly and seriously as he accepted the leadership of the Sea Scout troop or the Camp Fire group or the organizing of us in this villa. Shows great strength of character, I'm sure. And yet I go through the motions of kissing him a million miles away.

The film unit is folding now. Mac's job is over. The rest of the bullfighting sequences are going to be shot in Spain in the bullring and for that Wheero doesn't need any English.

Stefan surprised me by coming around to say goodbye to me—me personally—today. He's going back to Paris to co-ordinate things there. He gave me his card and told me to look him up. Said he might be able to help me get a job in the French Cinema. Said they showed more imagination in casting. Pinched me and left.

Larry and Missy are still vaguely fighting. Larry: Larry the Cipher. El Ciphero. What makes him tick? I still don't know. It's a hopeless passion, but I'd still take one Larry for a hundred anyone elses. He belongs to my club, I think. Les Compliqués.

No word from Jim and I guess I didn't expect any. I guess it's all for the best. I guess that's that.

Slept late, late, late this morning, and I'm going into

Biarritz this afternoon to get my hair done. Finally. I'm going to have it dyed silvery blonde, very pale, very subdued, because of my great sorrow. Then we are all going on the town tonight to celebrate the end of our movie careers—and the beginning of Bax's.

> July 1st-2nd. Somewhere between
> Monday and Tuesday. Late late late.

Our lives seem to be developing along the lines of Greek Tragedy—star-crossed and pursued by Furies. I'm not exaggerating. We ran into some old sparring partners tonight and it turned out to be a head-on collision. And here I am early in the morning again so charged up by all the clash-crashing I can't possibly get to sleep.

As a rule I'm rather fond of excitement. Raw, rollicking, riveting and toute cette sorte de crap, it has a way of forcing me out of myself and at the same time dragging me back in that I find truly exhilarating. On the whole I should say it's a fine thing; a stepping-up thing, a leading-to-action-at-last sort of thing. But is it an end in itself, I begin to wonder. I mean couldn't one have enough of it—or, to put it more plaintively—can't *it* have enough of me? I wish it would stop hovering over me like some privately commissioned thunderbolt.

When I recall the peace and harmony of the first part of the evening (a million miles away by now) it all seems such a shame. We were having such a good time. Old war-scarred veterans that we'd become by then, we had very nearly mastered the art of being together for over a certain length of time without slitting one another's throats. We were not only on to one another's foops and foibles, we were actually attempting to use this knowledge to smooth things over rather than hot them up, which was the usual game. Or—I don't know—maybe we were just in a good mood.

Anyway, in preparation for the celebration Missy had washed and ironed and even sewn a button on Larry's shirt. And Larry had let Missy take her time getting ready. He held her bag for her and smiled indulgently while she wandered back and forth around the room collecting the things she needed to put in it. He even went so far as to get down on his hands and knees to look for a stray handkerchief. He wrenched open the doors of the old Citroen for her and creaked them shut behind her. He helped her up and down stairs as gingerly as if she were a basket of eggs. We had, in short, returned to the loving couple of our Middle Period.

Bax, for his part, had at last shed his irritating is-this-really-such - a - good - idea - how - will - we - all - feel - in - the - morning-someone's-got-to-apply-the-financial-brakes common-sense attitude, and his attempts at frivolity were positively touching. Mac the Whack also came along, transformed beyond recognition by his three weeks of regular anxiety-free sponge-free meals, and was happily and lavishly throwing around his own not very hard-earned pelf. As for me, I was concentrating on Bax like a mad thing. I was determined to concentrate on him if it killed me. And he was being so foolishly, transparently grateful, it really was worth it. "Let him think you're leading him on," I told myself severely. "Lead him on. What's the difference? He's leaving soon anyway."

It was a wonderful warm summer's night. Presque parfaite. Everything in the sky that could be was out : Northern lights, Southern lights, milky ways, moons, planets, stars, shooting stars, whole galaxies of solar systems winking and twinkling eons away in their own heavens. Uncle Roger would have gone out of his mind.

As we drove off I remember looking back at the old villa with affection. We hadn't done so badly. We'd made friends of one another, made jokes of one another, had even—for better or worse—made things happen to one another. We were still young and gay and carefree. We had lived there all alone for two whole months without it burning down.

It was impossible to resist such a night. No one tried. Peace and harmony, as I said, prevailed throughout a ludicrously happy, ludicrously expensive meal at the Relais de Something near Hendaye. Then we went back to the Club de Caveau, where we'd first met Stefan and where, you might say, it all began. The little Englishman there remembered us kindly. Further celebration. Then we drove up to Béhobie to that other bar and I found I was so mellow I was even able to think about Wheero with hardly a twinge of bitterness.

Then we went up to that great suave hotel on top of Ascain (three star, crossed forks, crossed eyes, the works), and cavorted among the dead dummies.

Then we decided to drop into the Spanish flamenco boîte. The lights were down when we got there and the singing and dancing had begun. Undistracted by Wheero, Angela, and the whole hideous holocaust of that other night, I found myself really concentrating on the flamenco. The dancers were very young and supple and sensuous, and the singers, passionately declaiming what the young folk were up to, middleaged and fat and richly experienced. The contrast was delicious. Sexy beyond words—beyond *wahrds*, as Angela would say.

I was interested to discover I could be so roused by a floor show. I was beginning to think there must be something wrong with me. I mean I simply don't know what to do about a Nude Show, I just can't seem to behave naturally in front of them. The thing is, I don't get much of a charge out of them in the first place, so any act I put on is bound to be a phoney. But I still haven't discovered what you're supposed to do. I mean if you stare straight ahead with a bright smile pasted across your face you're being a prig, and if you look at it critically and say "They're really not so hot are they?" you're being jealous, and if you fling yourself into it and say "Oh, golly, doesn't *she* have a lovely body" someone looks at you very peculiarly and says "Hmm. You like *her* do you? That's *very* interesting," and if you just relax and look bored, you've committed the greatest crime of all; like looking bored at a bullfight, I imagine. So it was wonderful not to have to worry about whether I was acting sufficiently moved by the flamenco. I was sufficiently moved all right; stirred to the depths of my erotic soul.

The lights went up. We all sighed and smiled and ordered ourselves another round of chartreuse. And then, just as

218

everything was so absolutely apple-jack dandy, our old buddy-buddy the Contessa, that perennial glad rag doll, disentangled herself from the cackling crew at a nearby table and came over to us and sat down. A warm greeting to Larry, brief appraising glances at Bax and Mac, blank stares for Missy and myself, and she was off—jabbering away at Larry exactly as if we weren't there. Comme d'habitude. Like ole times.

"Does she write?" Mac whispered to me eagerly.

"Only on bathroom walls," I replied in a perfectly normal tone. "No," I corrected myself. "As a matter of fact she sculpts. Bathroom sculpture." I'd found a word for it, anyway.

"You are making a great mistake about that girl-friend of yours," the Contessa was saying tensely to Larry. She might have been talking about me. In fact I thought she was talking about me; I wouldn't put it past her. "One always enjoys making the acquaintance of any friend of yours, dear boy, but that girl is simply impossible. She is a Professional, no?"

"Don't be silly," snapped Larry with a vigour that made me want to cheer. "She's what they call a crazy mixed-up kid. There're millions of them. Haven't you met any before?" I still thought they might be talking about me. "What's the matter with her anyway?" he asked. "What did she do? I told her to look you up because she didn't know anyone in Paris and I thought you might help her." (Naïve, oh Larry, Larry, naïve.)

The Contessa shrugged. "Tout de même, je crois qu'elle se dope, n'est-ce pas?"

"Could be."

So it wasn't me. So who was it?

And here's where the Greek Tragedy part comes in. For my question was answered, and answered before I had time to put the button-hook on the question-mark, by the arrival of Lila, the old, old flame of Larry, on the arm of Teddy, the old, old flame de moi.

Larry, frozen with consternation, glared at them with the horrified fascination of one upon whom an entire troupe of furies has chosen to descend at once. It was frightening to watch; I was made afraid just looking at him. Nor was I at all purged by my feelings of pity and terror. I was as deeply embroiled in it as he was. I don't know quite what Lila is to Larry, but Teddy's been *my* main tormentor. I see him stalking me through the ages, always at hand with some fresh fiendish plot.

Lila was drunk—or, if the doping part was true, she was high. In any case she was in a very strange condition. A sly crooked smile kept sliding across her face as she slithered over to our table.

"Hello Larrybaby," she purred. "I think we can skip all that fancy-meeting-you-here crap and get down to business, don't you? Who's having who these days—that's what I want to know." There was a dead silence. "Let's see," she went on, "now don't tell me because I want to guess." She turned to the rest of us. "I'm intuitive, you see. It's one of my things." She looked at us for a moment. "Oh it's really too easy," she said, pointing her finger at Missy. "It's that one of course. The big blonde. The other one's a bit—umm—squirrelly," she added. That was me. She indicated Missy again. "That's the one all right, isn't it, Larry? Do you think she'll make a good model? Who knows, perhaps she is one already. Saves you trouble. Not me any more, though. I'm just not cut out for it. And I tried, Larrybaby, I really tried. You know what I think? I think I'm just cut out for you. Now what about *you*, darling," she said directly to Missy, sitting down and leaning forward intimately. "You can level with me, honey, after all, we're practically related. Come on now—are you a model?"

Missy was magnificent. Cool and unruffled, and in her iciest tones, she said "How dare you sit down at this table without being invited?" I'd never heard a Southern drawl come out so imperiously.

Lila looked at her with a pleased smile of someone who's been spoiling for a fight for a long time and has at last come up against something solid.

"Oh I've got an invitation all right. I've got a permanent invitation to Master Keevil's table, haven't I, Larry? Go on, tell her about it." Larry remained frozen. "O.K.," said Lila lightly, and rose. "I wouldn't dream of sitting down without being invited. I'll tell you what, I'll invite your Mr. Keevi to come and sit with *me*. You watch now, honey. He'll come too. You see if he doesn't. My, my, you've got a lot to learn," she flung over her shoulder.

We all sat there stupefied, as Larry stumbled to his feet like a sleep-walker and followed her.

Teddy was hissing in my ear "Quick, I must talk with you privately. It is of the utmost importance." Utterly dazed by it all, I let him steer me through the crowd to a corner table.

"Sally Jay," he began. "Please listen to what I am about to tell you. I don't know how far your affair with this Keevil has gone, but I do seriously believe you to be in very grave danger." He held up his hand to prevent me from interrupting. "I know what you're going to say—I know you have no reason to trust me, no reason at all. . ."

"What the hell's the idea of hounding me like this?" I said, finally recovering my voice. "You listen to *me*. Stay out of my way! I mean that. If you ever try to get near me again, I'll send for the police!"

"You hate me. Very well. You have every right to. That dinner-party I gave for you—the way I plotted and planned it—that was not a nice thing to do. I am not proud of it. But don't forget that my little ruse would not have succeeded if your friend Larry had not decided to prefer—for whatever his reasons—to go home with the Contessa instead of you. Part of my motive was to hurt you—you had hurt me and I wished to hit back. But only part. You may remember that from the first day I laid eyes on Keevil I put him down as an opportunist. I saw no reason why the likes of him should have you if I couldn't. So I wanted to open your eyes about him —disillusion you, if you will. Vindictive, maybe, but only if I succeeded. . ."

"Sure, Larry went off with the Contessa," I said wearily. "That proved only one thing. It proved he wasn't in love with me. Thanks for pointing it out. I'll never forgive you for it. And I'll never forgive you for doing it by sic-ing the sort of person the Contessa is on him."

"There is no point at present in going back over that,"

said Teddy quickly. "What I must try to warn you of as fast as possible is that he is not just an opportunist; he is a very dangerous man. He is a killer. It is he you should send the police for, not me, I assure you."

I looked at Teddy with revulsion and astonishment, wondering what I'd ever seen in him. And then suddenly I just laughed in his face.

"Do you mean to tell me you've come tooling all the way down from Paris dragging that hop-head Lila with you for the sole purpose of getting off a statement like that? A killer! I hope you remembered to bring his criminal record with you."

"I have brought it with me," said Teddy gravely. "Unfortunately I have brought this poor girl Lila with me. Excuse me if I express myself badly. It is because I cannot put it to you strongly enough. And let me make it quite clear that I never for a moment would have set foot down here if I'd known we were going to run into him. Quite the opposite. Her only hope is to get as far away from him as she can. As it happens he told her he was spending the summer in Germany. To state the case in the simplest terms: he ruined her. He was, I believe, the first man she'd ever known. The rest I imagine it was fairly easy for him. Do you know what she is now?" He paused. "She is a call-girl."

"So?" I felt myself trembling.

"Can't you understand? *She works for him.*"

I really felt sick. I wanted to strike him and I didn't have the strength to. I couldn't have touched him. Everything about him revolted me so; the hair on the back of his hands, his manicured finger-nails, the way he held his cigarette. I looked at his face and thought, I am looking at the face of evil.

"You are *hell*," I said, my voice shaking so badly I could hardly hear it. "Do you know I wouldn't believe you if you swore on a stack of Bibles?" Then I stopped talking. I was completely at sea. I couldn't find any words to tell him what I thought of him. Why is it that the most insulting things you can ever find to say in those circumstances are as

222

meaningless and unhurtful as you-dirty-lousy-double-crossing-son-of-a-bitch? I mean, have nine more meaningless unhurtful words ever been strung together? "You—you European!" I said finally. "You nasty, suspicious, vicious European. Stop ascribing your own vicious motives to everyone else. Anyone capable of playing the tricks you played on me is capable of anything, but I never dreamt you'd go so far. Why don't we take my case for a change? You were the first man I ever knew and you can hardly be said to have ruined me. I don't even remember you terribly well, if you want to know the truth. I wasn't very moved.

"I know what gets you about all this," I said—and suddenly I did. "I know what you can't stand. The only people you'll tolerate have to be stuffed into one of two pigeon-holes: they either have to have pots of their own money like the Contessa—you don't mind that at all, do you, as long as you have a hand in the spending of it—or they have to have good steady jobs like you. What you can't stand is the whole new young adventurous floating population with either just a little money or no money at all, no jobs, nothing, just a desire maybe to see the world awhile. Then all the jealousy and envy in your mournful little unfulfilled life rises up inside you and you have to invent all sorts of dark sinister motives for everyone. Larry's finances are shaky, so are Lila's. O.K. So are dozens of others I know, it's a perfectly normal occurrence in Europe today. But to you they have to become white-slavers and call-girls and God knows what. Pull yourself together, Larry's a director and a damn good one. Lila's a model and probably a damn lazy one. Some of the others are just bums. Who cares? Let them roam the earth if they want to. Nobody cares except you, who probably never had the guts to do the same thing yourself. It really makes me laugh. When I tried to explain you away to Larry once, I invented all sorts of cloak-and-dagger intrigue about you: rivalry at the Italian Embassy, burned papers, you about to be recalled, the works. But I certainly didn't kid myself for a minute that I wasn't making it all up."

"Sally Jay, you are so naïve."

"You're the naïve one! You've got so entangled in your cloak you keep stabbing yourself with your own dagger! Next you'll try to tell me about a gang of spies; big white-slave market operating around the world."

"That is not impossible."

"Don't you *know* what you really are?" I asked incredulously. "Can't you see it? You're a vain, vain man. An insanely jealous man. And you're getting to be an old one."

"Very well," said Teddy stiffly. "It is now impossible to continue this conversation."

"Oh no it isn't. There's one more thing," I went on. "Why don't we put your little theory to the test? You get Lila to come over here and tell me all about it. That shouldn't be too hard, since you're trying to save her from a fate worse than death, and Larry's a killer."

I forced myself to look around the room. Finally I spotted them. They looked anything but sinister. As a matter of fact Lila was talking her head off to Larry—probably giving him the story of her ruined life with Teddy. Larry looked exhausted and trapped and extremely bored. He caught my eye and winked wanly over at me. It was hardly the reaction of a guilty man.

"Go on. Go over there," I insisted to Teddy. "When you go around making accusations like that you've got to prove them."

Teddy went over to them. I hid my face in my hands and waited. Finally he came back.

"You win," he said. "Or rather he has won."

"You don't have much luck with your girls, do you?" I rose. "I mean that about the police. If I ever set eyes on you again I'm going to send for them."


Back at our table all was quiet. In fact it was empty, except for Bax. Missy had gone off in a huff, dragging Mac with her. Bax and I drove back to the villa alone.

On the way home I told him what Teddy had said. He was very quiet.

"Well, say something," I demanded irritably.

"I don't know what to say, Sally Jay."

I exploded. "You don't *believe* that junk, do you? What's got into everyone all of a sudden? All Larry ever does is to try to help people—in his own madly misguided way, granted —but he does try—and all he ever gets for it is a kick in the teeth."

"Yes, maybe."

"What do you mean, maybe?"

"I mean partly. . ."

"Do you or do you not owe your break in Hollywood *entirely* to Larry?" Bax nodded. "And you owe our villa to him and all of us coming down here. And you owe *me* coming down here too. I assure you I wouldn't have come if he hadn't begged me to."

Bax shook his head miserably.

"So what's eating you?"

"Sally Jay, I can't explain it. But you're very different from what I imagined you'd be."

"Sorry about that," I said coldly.

"No, it's just—I don't know. No, I don't know. Perhaps I'm not being fair."

I stopped concentrating on Bax.

So we got back to the villa. And Christ, all hell is breaking loose around here now. Missy sobbing downstairs in the living-room on Mac's shoulder, saying she won't stay another minute in the same house with a man who's allowed her to be insulted like that, and at the same time insisting that Mac stay on here with us to protect her from Larry, Bax pacing up and down in his room like a caged lion, me scribbling away trying to get worn out enough to drop off to sleep. . . Boy, oh boy, wait till Larry comes home. What's going to happen next?

# PART THREE

"Make voyages. Attempt them. That's all there is."
—Tennessee Williams (*Camino Real*)

# CHAPTER ONE

SOME DAYS AFTERWARDS—or maybe it was only two or three—I can't remember exactly any more—I got out of bed one morning and found myself all alone in the empty house. I put on my bathing-suit and went down to the untidy kitchen and made myself some coffee. Then I went out on the terrace and looked at the sky. It was a morning full of clouds; the sun shining brightly one moment and hiding under pearly greyness the next. It felt doom-ridden from the very beginning, out there among the ruins—very fin de siècle, fin du monde, fin de line. Bugs were climbing all over the roses, the chaotic breezes seemed wild and unfriendly, and the grass had burned brown. It was hard to believe that it was the beginning of July, not the end of summer. I thought : is summer only a state of mind? Is it always only two months long from whenever you start it? My arms would get no browner; my skin had reached saturation point, and the sun only succeeded now in bleaching them lighter—greyer. I shivered. I might have been something washed up against the River Styx. Or maybe I was waiting to be ferried across. I put on a sweater and went down to the sea.

I was thinking hard about Larry. I hadn't seen him since the night at the Spanish boîte, but I'd been thinking about him incessantly. After my final talk with Bax, my thoughts had grown more and more troubled and disturbed. It was very confusing to have to re-interpret all his past actions in the new light. I felt as if I'd been wandering through life like one of those comic-strip characters, while right, left and centre buckets of paint were falling off ladders, and cars were crashing into each other.

I very nearly jumped out of my skin when I saw Larry

lying there almost at my feet on the sands. His eyes were closed. They had deep shadows under them, and the pallor of his skin, on which his freckles stood out as if painted and the faint scar running up his forehead had turned into a livid gash, contrasted weirdly with his carroty shock of hair. He looked like a frightened clown. When he breathed I could see how near the skin his rib-cage was. In spite of everything I could have wept with pity.

He opened his eyes, now grey with fatigue, and smiled haggardly when he saw it was me.

"Lie down beside me," he said. I obeyed.

He took my hand. The electric current that always ran through it when he touched me started flowing again. I clamped down on it hard, producing a sensation as unpleasant as a short circuit, as deadly as the electric chair. Nevertheless I didn't pull away.

He sighed and stretched wearily. "They've all gone, haven't they? Every goddam one of them," he said.

"Yes, it's like 'Uncle Vanya' or something. How do you know?"

"I tiptoed around this morning and poked my head into all the rooms. No one but you. Where are they?"

"Missy and Mac took the morning train to Paris yesterday, and Bax the evening plane to London on his way to California. Where've you been?"

"I've been around. Around and around. I don't know, Gorce—all this rushing around, where does it get us? The rat race." He propped himself up on his elbows and looked at me. "You're still here though. You didn't run out on me like the rest. Why?"

*Because I've got to know the truth at last,* I thought. Only of course I didn't say it. I drew a few circles in the sand with my free hand and said, "Well, you can't really blame Missy for leaving, can you, when you didn't show up all this time?"

He shook his head. "Missy ran out. I suppose I expected it. She's a silly, selfish girl. But the point is you didn't. I knew I could count on you." He squeezed my hand tenderly (in a way it was quite easy to react favourably to Larry; it was a force of habit). "How come you're such a screwball, Gorce?"

"I don't know." I couldn't think what to say. "I was alone a lot as a child."

"Yeah. Maybe. I wonder how I got so screwed up? I don't seem to be able to reconcile art with life, that's my trouble." He fell back limply on the sands. "I've been lying here thinking of joining some kind of yogi monastery." I turned my head towards him. He was very near breaking down. His eyes were filled with tears. "I feel," he said, "I think I feel differently about you than other girls, you know that? Closer. We're more alike, I mean. You know what I mean? No. No, of course you don't."

"But I do, I do," I said fervently. "We are closer, I do understand you."

"You're sweet. I wish I had a little sister like you. Christ, how maudlin can you get!" He smiled bitterly. "Well, they've all gone, or have I already said that? The French, the English, the Americans, the Spaniards. Missy, Mac, Bax——"

Now was my chance. "I think we're well rid of them," I said, making my voice harsh. "Especially your friend Bax. You ought to know something, Larry: they all turned against you in the end. *Especially* your friend Bax."

"Yeah? What'd he say?"

"He actually tried to make me believe you told him I'd *sleep* with him down here! He said that was why he rented the villa in the first place. He said that was how you talked him into coming down." I snorted. "Of course I didn't believe him. It was so obvious from the beginning that he was jealous. He knew I preferred you to him."

Larry was too clever to deny it outright. He couldn't be sure just how much Bax had told me. "Now wait a minute, wait a minute," he said. "Let's not condemn Bax altogether. He's a nice kid. I like him. And maybe I did say a lot of things to him I oughtn't to. Man to man I may have intimated that you weren't exactly a prig. I mean I may have said I thought he had a chance or something like that. You know how guys go on. And he was good-looking and nuts about you." He stopped for a moment. "The trouble is I can't remember exactly what I did say. I forget. What's the use of remembering anything? If it was unpleasant it was unpleasant and if it was pleasant it's over." He was sinking low again; I could hardly hear the last part. "But there's one thing I want you to get clear, Gorce," he said, suddenly leaning over me, and for a moment, I swear, sincere. "Whatever I may have said to Bax about you I knew this : you don't have to sleep with *anyone* to get them to rent you a villa. You don't have to do anything. You just have to be. I've been around and I know who does and who doesn't. And Bax is no fool and he knew it as well as I do."

It was the nicest thing that anyone had ever said to me, especially coming from someone who, as he said, ought to know. It was awful. Suddenly I wanted to drop the whole thing; but I knew, of course, that I couldn't.

"Can you forgive me?" he asked.

"Of course I do," I smiled at him. "I know you so much better than the others. You like being In Charge, that's all; making things happen. Like Lila for instance. Teddy said the most awful things about you. Said you'd ruined her. . ."

"Now that is nonsense," he said vehemently. "That I do deny completely. . ."

"But of course," I said earnestly. "What Teddy didn't realize was that I'd actually overheard you and Lila last fall, when you were trying to make her pull herself together and start getting modelling jobs in Paris instead of coming down here—I mean if that's trying to ruin her——"

He looked at me strangely. "Where'd you hear this?"

I made a vague gesture. "Montparnasse, Saint-Germain, somewhere. It was late. I was with a lot of people, I can't remember."

"Yeah," he said wearily. "Yeah. I don't know why I try to help her at all. I feel sorry for her, I guess, that's it. But sometimes I'd like to kill her," he exclaimed passionately. "I really would. Jesus, I can't take this much longer—the drugging and drinking and all those stories she makes up about me——" Poor Larry, it was Art and Vice he was finding so hard to reconcile.

"Larry, darling," I murmured lovingly, now that he was really nervy (I still held his hand). "Larry, you remember after Opening Night when we went off to my hotel? There's something that's been troubling me about that night ever since. . ."

"Yeah?" Did he stiffen a little?

"Yes, it's been haunting me. I—I—never got around to asking you—you know, all that stuff about losing my passport and everything. . ."

"What's on your mind, Gorce?"

"Well, I don't know how to say it exactly. It's so embarrassing. It's just. . . What I mean is, well . . . why didn't you make love to me that night?"

He might have been able to control his stiffening, but he couldn't control his relief. His hand went limp in mine.

"Did it mean a lot to you?" he asked softly.

"More than anything in the world."

"I'm sorry, darling. It wasn't because I didn't want to, you know that. I must have had a million things on my mind. We can change all that if you like."

"I would," I said, "I would very much." Was he dumber than I thought or what?

"What are your plans for the rest of the summer?" he was asking me.

"I'll go back to Paris, I guess."

"Don't go. Stay with me. We've got the house for the rest of the season and the Citroen doesn't have to be sold till the end of summer."

"Golly, that sounds wonderful!" I said. "Let me think about it. Let's go swimming." I had to get away from him quickly before he read my mind.

The rest of the day was anguish. I still don't know how I lived through it—one minute emptying my mind to the point of blankness, and the next finding it reeling crazily about as old pieces of evidence fell freshly into place. Did he know I knew? How much did he know I knew? *What* did he know I knew? The worst of it was that part of me was still in love with him. Part of me refused to die; still hoped there was some simple, uncomplicated explanation that would clear up everything, like in movies. . .

I had to get away, that was all. But how? First I thought I'd confront him and then pack my bags. Then I thought no, better the other way around. Then I thought, forget the whole thing and just slip off. When? How? He never let me out of his sight. He was wooing me. We went to some terribly famous restaurant for dinner, the Auberge de Something-or-other, and I might just as well have been chewing on a mess of wet sponges.

He drove back to the villa with his arm around me. I had some crazy idea of expiating my block-headedness once and for all by 'going through with it'. It would teach me the lesson of my lifetime. And then I found I just couldn't.

"I'm so sleepy," I said, when we got into the living-room. "I'm so tired, I could drop."

He put his arm around me and helped me upstairs. He led me to my bedroom door. His lips brushed my forehead and at their warm soft touch I almost flung myself in his arms. He held me by the shoulders. "I'm tired too," he said. "We'll start out fresh in the morning." His green eyes looked into mine for the last time.

Later on, from my balcony window, as in a nightmare premonition, I stood and watched the grisly tableaux unfold: Lila in the moonlight, a breadknife gleaming in her hand; Larry quietly, *systematically* beating her up. When she was quite unconscious, he picked up her body and carried her off. I heard the engine of the Citroen start up.

I put on my dress and walked to the station. It took me three hours, but the man said I was in time for the morning train. Before I got on it I telephoned the villa.

"Where are you?" said Larry. "I've been going crazy with worry."

"I'm just getting on the train," I said. "I wanted to tell you that I know you stole my passport in my hotel room on Opening Night. I'm going to report it when I get back to Paris."

"I wouldn't do that," the voice replied. "It'll only get you in trouble, because I'll say you sold it to me."

# CHAPTER TWO

I ARRIVED IN PARIS late that night and went directly to my old hotel in Montparnasse and washed. Then I went over to the Select. Most of the Hard Core were away for the summer. There were only a few stragglers left over at the table. I knew them hardly at all, but I joined them anyway. We had a few drinks and started off on the rounds when I realized I just couldn't go on. It was a ride you could take only once. The streets and I looked at each other. "You *again*!" we jeered. They were too full of memories. Larry was right. What was the use of remembering? If it was unpleasant, it was unpleasant. If it was pleasant, it was over.

What it amounted to was that I, who had never been *anywhere* before, had suddenly been around once too often. I mean I'd felt like a *prostitute*, picking up those comparative strangers. Before, I would have eagerly sought them out for the pleasure and curiosity of meeting more and more people on my own hook. Now I had the sad little ulterior motive of trying to stave off my fear and loneliness.

What was going to happen to me, hanging around Paris like that? It was all such a terrible mess I didn't know where to begin.

It had taken me just exactly one year on my own hook to get myself in a really serious mess I couldn't get out of. Not that I didn't have it coming to me. I must have known all along (but without *really* knowing—like I do about so many things) what Larry was all about. But—tiddily pum, I'd never faced it and now I was going to have to pay for it. If I reported the passport as stolen—if I reported Larry as the thief—he was going to say I'd sold it to him. And it would be easy enough to make them believe that. After all, we'd been thick as thieves, to use the depressingly apt phrase, for quite some time. On the other hand, if I didn't report him, I was surely breaking some kind of law and worse than that, I was allowing him to continue along his merry way. And why the hell should he, when just *thinking* about some of the things he'd done made my bowels corrode with rage: that first day at the Café Dupont, for instance, when he started pumping me about my lost pearl necklace (for that was the *exact* moment of his beginning to take an interest in me, make no mistake), trying to find out if it was real, how I'd lost it, how much I minded, what I'd done about getting it back, etc; or my stupid phone call to him after I discovered the passport missing, blithely saying I suspected everyone but him because he'd found it for me at the Queer Club (*found* it—man, he was stealing it—and because I was such a cretin, all he had to do was give it back to me and steal it all over again later on). Why should I let him get away with such things? Simple. Because I had no choice.

Paris was boiling hot and all my summer clothes were in that bedroom overlooking the garden of our villa in St. Jean de Luz. I put on the torn print dress that I'd run away in and the same shoes that had walked three hours to the station, and went off to see Stefan the next evening.

"My dear child," he exclaimed, looking me up and down in astonishment at the doorway. "Such utter and abject poverty! You look poorer than anyone I've seen since I left Hungary."

"I had to leave St. Jean in a hurry," I mumbled. I wanted to burst into tears.

He sensed my distress. "Never mind, never mind," he said soothingly. "It's the same pretty little face. Come in." And he led me inside.

I saw a tall, dark, graceful erect young man seated on the sofa. He wore a pale grey suit, a pale pale yellow shirt, pale grey suede shoes and his tie of peacock-blue was part of a silk bathrobe-cord, at least that's what it looked like. A heady mixture, but somehow he brought it off. He looked gay and disarming. He looked like a dandy. He leapt up from the sofa when he saw me and we shook hands. He had long graceful hands and a warm impulsive smile.

"This is Maximilian Ramage," said Stefan. But I knew he was famous even before I'd heard his name. He had an aura about him.

"Not the photographer?"

"Yes. Why?"

"But you're so young! You're—you're just a boy," I heard myself saying, of all corny things. It was true though. I'd imagined him much much older.

"Well that's all right," he said gravely, still holding on to my hand. "You're just a girl."

"We're very lucky to have Max this evening," said Stefan. "He leaves for Ceylon in the morning. I've asked him to take some photographs of you. You'll need them for your work. Very important. Essential. Is that not so, Max? Well, what do you think? You will photograph her?"

"Definitely. Oh definitely." An English voice. I remembered reading somewhere that he was originally English. But he'd been everywhere.

"Gosh!" I was really overcome. I mean he's one of the world's top photographers.

"Fine," said Stefan. "Now that it's settled, let's have a little drink first. What'll it be?" But before I could open my mouth he said "No! Wait a minute. Let me mix you something. My own speciality." I looked over at the impressive array of bottles at the bar and nodded eagerly.

He turned his back to us and for a while worked swiftly and expertly, mixing an elaborate cocktail. My mouth was watering. Finally he handed it to me with a flourish. "Taste it," he said.

I tasted it. "It's delicious."

"Not too strong?"

"Perfect."

"Good." He turned back to the bar again and poured out

238

two more glasses. I looked over at Max, puzzled. "There's no liquor in it," I whispered.

Max was delighted. "Of course not," he said. "Once a Hungarian—Thank you, Stefan. Lovely drink."

Dear Stefan. He was so proud of himself. He didn't for a moment doubt he was getting away with it. What a wonderful evening it could have been if only it had happened a year before. B.P. Before Passport. Was I going to have to gauge everything that way for the rest of my life?

Max took hundreds and hundreds of pictures of me and afterwards we went out to dinner. We went to the Scheherazade or Monseigneurs, one of those expensive violin places. Stefan was expansive. Everyone knew him there.

"Champagne," he said. "First of all champagne." When the champagne came he took a sip of it. He was just about to accept it when he happened to catch my eye. "No," he said. "It's flat. Send it back."

The proprietor arrived. "What's all this, Gogo?"

"We don't like the champagne," said Stefan grandly.

The proprietor tasted it. "Don't be silly," he said, slapping his old friend on the back. "It's exquisite."

"Ah well." Stefan took it philosophically. "It's not like his old place in Vienna."

Max laughed. "Hungarians don't like each other, they *understand* each other."

"Don't be disrespectful," said Stefan crossly.

We looked at the menu. "Hah! Avocados," he said, brightening. "How I love them. Cheer up, my little avocado," he said to me, pinching my hand. "You know, these American girls are just like avocados. What do you think, am I right, Max? Who ever even heard of an avocado sixty years ago? Yes, that's what we're growing nowadays." His avocado arrived and he looked at it lovingly. "The Typical American girl," he said, addressing it. "A hard centre with the tender meat all wrapped up in a shiny casing." He began eating it. "How I love them," he murmured greedily. "So green—so eternally green." He winked at me.

"Stefan, please. . ."

"No, it's true. And I will tell you something really extraordinary, mes enfants. Do you know that you can take the stones of these luscious fruits, put them in water—just plain water, mind you—anywhere, any place in the world, and in three months up comes a sturdy little plant full of green leaves? That is their sturdy little souls bursting into bloom," he finished off, well satisfied with his analogy.

"Well, this one isn't going to burst into bloom," I said morosely, putting my nose in my drink. "What you've got here is a dead one."

"A what? A dud one?"

I took my face out of the glass. "No, dead. Dead. Oh, forget it."

Max raised his glass and smiled at me. "The dud avocado," he said, proposing the toast.

It was a party and I desperately wanted to be happy and I couldn't. So I drank and drank and drank and naturally I got very drunk. I behaved disgracefully. After the second course I tried balancing my glass on my little finger. Twice it fell off and I caught it just before it hit the carpet. Then my legs got pins and needles and fell asleep on me. I tried to stamp them back to life; a difficult and dangerous manoeuvre at best, under a table. Dessert had just arrived and in a magnificent tour de force I managed to overturn it on everything except my dress. Then my eyes went out of focus. The only way I could bring them back in again was by concentrating on my shoes, wiggling them about. Then my shoes fell off. I began singing quietly to myself "Plaster-board for hous-ing, ta tum ta tum Ta" to the tune of Fascinating Rhythm. Finally I got up and went to the Ladies Room. I looked at myself in the mirror and went out on to the street. I tried walking. Max was beside me.

He sobered me up at the Royal Saint-Germain with aspirin and slow spoonfuls of onion soup.

"There's a reason for all this," I kept saying to him over and over again. But I'd forgotten it.

"You're running away from some man, aren't you?" Max asked me gently.

Yes, that was it, I thought fuzzily. I was running away from Larry and when he caught up with me he was going to beat me up and if I'd squealed he was going to kill me.

"I can't tell you about it. I can't tell you about. . ."

"Never mind," said Max. "I think I understand. I'd better take you back to your hotel so you can get some sleep."

We got back to my hotel and the concierge said there was a message for me. I nearly fainted dead away. I had to read it three times before I could understand it. It was from Jim Breit. He'd heard I was back. Judy was in the hospital and wanted to see me. He'd pick me up at ten the next morning.

"You must think me the great neurotic of all time," I said to Max, not really caring at this point. "But I can't stay here tonight. You've got to find me another hotel." Boy, when you're really worried it's first things first. You don't let yourself get all bogged down with gentillesse and politesse and tout ça. One thing was clear, I wasn't going to spend another night at that hotel waiting for Larry to catch up with me.

You apparently don't need anything to get into a hotel in Paris except a passport. I was turned down five times. Eventually we found one so seedy it didn't even have a reception desk. That suited me fine. The more hidden the better.

"I'll be back in a month," said Max. "I'll send the photographs to be developed. Meanwhile, keep in touch with Stefan. I want to see you again. And—" he paused, embarrassed, "see here. I hope everything works out. But if you—if it's a matter of money—if you should need any—tell Stefan and I'll be glad to—that is, please don't have any silly feelings about borrowing from me."

My God, I thought dully as he left, he thinks I'm pregnant.

# CHAPTER THREE

JIM PICKED ME up at my old hotel the next morning. I'd slept hardly at all that night and was reeling under the blow of a bad hangover. Jim looked exactly the same as he always did and this shocked and annoyed me. How could he be so callous after all I'd been through?

It wasn't an easy meeting. I asked him how Judy was and he replied that I'd see for myself. We drove off in a strained silence. I made a few scattered remarks here and there that he didn't even bother to answer, and then I opened my mouth a couple of times and just closed it again. Nothing seemed like a good idea. He was probably being tricky about that awful letter I'd written to him in Florence, I decided. Well, the hell with that. I had more important things to worry about. I'd just remembered that Uncle Roger would be writing me about my new passport down at the villa.

I made Jim stop at American Express while I sent off two telegrams—one to the post office nearest our villa, telling them to re-route all my mail to American Express Paris, and one to Uncle Roger giving him the same address. I felt a little safer, hiding under the anonymity of American Express.

They were waiting for us at the hospital. "It's Miss Gorce, isn't it?" they asked. "We're expecting you." Swiftly they led me into an elevator which stopped at Judy's floor. I was already beginning to get uneasy. Flanked on either side by a doctor and a nurse, I was shown to Judy's room. I felt myself walking faster and faster until I was almost running down the corridor.

Outside the door the doctor stopped me. "She's very weak," he said. "Keep her calm. Be careful not to tire her out but don't frighten her either."

I opened the door. Even before I could see Judy, who was blocked from my view by a screen, I was seized with a slimy terror. I had expected to find myself in a hospital room, bare, enamelled, impersonal. I found myself instead in—I don't know—a shrine—or a condemned cell. There were paintings on the walls. Jim's paintings. Abstractions. There was a Mobile on the bureau. There was a bookcase and a chair that obviously didn't belong to the hospital, and other details. But it was the Abstractions particularly, the unnatural juxtaposition of Abstractions on a hospital wall, that somehow stabbed me with the same sharp irrational fear I'd once felt coming suddenly across two swallows swooping around loose *inside* a house. I was shaking with fear as I approached the screen.

Judy stuffed something under her pillow and turned. Jim hadn't changed but Judy had. Judy had changed almost beyond recognition. Her eyes were remote and withdrawn and gazed out from her wasted face at me, almost dreamily, without recognition. Finally she made an enormous effort and brought herself back. She leaned over and swallowed a pill. I felt the warm sunlight coming through the window. I forced myself to look steadily at the grotesque mortality of hair, eyebrows and teeth. I felt the earth turn.

"Judy darling, how are you?"

"I'm fine."

"You look fine."

"Oh, Sally Jay, what *fun*! They've found you. I was so afraid they wouldn't. You went to St. Jean, didn't you? How was it? I want to hear all about it." Her eyes, so dead a moment ago, were blazing feverishly. "Who'd you go down with?"

I told her.

"Larry! You don't mean Larry what's-his-name, that wonderful boy you were so crazy about who directed you in those plays?"

"Yes."

"How heavenly for you!"

"It was."

"Tell me all about it. What did you do?"

"Oh. . . Swam. Sunbathed. Went down to the beach. You know, what everybody else does."

"But what did you *see*? Who did you *meet*? What *happened*?"

"Judy, let's talk about you for a change. You're the one that's really had something happen to you. I mean—I mean—you're married."

Her eyes wandered to the Mobile on the bureau. She smiled peacefully. "Yes, isn't it strange," she said awesomely. "I got married. I never thought I would. I still can't believe it. It all happened so quickly, and then getting-sick again on top of it . . ." She broke off. "Please let's talk about you. *Please* tell me all about it."

I didn't know what to do. Keep her calm, they'd said. I was only exciting her by withholding information. And all the time it was such agony being there, and looking at her, and trying to behave naturally.

I told her about El Wheero and she smiled and said, "Poor Sally Jay, and then what happened?" and I told her about our being movie extras and she laughed a little, but she wasn't satisfied. I felt I was cheating. What did she want? A bedtime story? No, I was wrong. She wanted more than that. Judy was in danger and she knew it. She must have known it all her life, and that was why she was the way she was. My comings and goings were much more than bedtime stories to her. They were real. All the while she kept repeating "And then what happened?" what she really was saying was "Run for my life!"

Run for my life.

What made me think of that phrase? A loop in time took me back to my childhood. "Run for my life" . . . and then that nightmare again. It was all tied up somehow with that nightmare and that desk and that station . . . I had been given some task to perform. I mustn't fail. I pulled myself together : Sally Jay, cartoon-strip animal, about to embark on another series of adventures.

"Of course I've been saving the best for the last," I said.

"What is it? Oh, *what*?"

"The reason I'm back in Paris now."

"Tell me!"

"Well. One day in the South of France I was introduced to the photographer Max Ramage. *You* know who I mean. And the next thing I knew he'd taken lots and lots of pictures of me, because he said I was the Typical American Girl. Well, of course I was flattered to death, but I forgot all about it until a week ago, when I got an urgent wire from him telling me to come to Paris. It seems the pictures had come out terribly well and he'd sent them around to Paris-Match and Life Magazine and places like that, to see if they'd be interested in doing a spread about me on account of my being so typical and all that. And they said they certainly might be. So now it's all in the process of being arranged. I'm meeting with the various people next week."

"Oh no!"

"And then last night Max took me out to meet a terribly famous French film-producer."

"Gosh, weren't you scared?"

"Well, no. That's the funny part. As a matter of fact I was terribly cool and poised. And he was so impressed, he's going to commission someone to write a film script specially about me——"

"And maybe you can talk him into having Larry direct it."

"Yes, that's what I was hoping!"

"And then what happened?"

The nurse came in. "It's time for your rest now," she said gently, "you mustn't tire yourself out."

"Oh no, please. I've only just seen Sally Jay, *please*. Just another moment." She turned to me, pleading. "And then what happened?" she repeated.

The nurse shot me a warning look. A much more warning look, that stopped me dead in my tracks and took my breath away.

Judy leaned forward and grabbed my arm. She clung to me, both hands digging into my flesh. "And then what did you do? And then what?" she insisted.

"But that's all, Judy," I said shakily. "We just went to a couple of night-clubs and then I went home."

She was becoming hysterical. "And then what?" Her nails cut into my flesh. "And then what, what, *what*?"

The nurse stepped forward. "I'm afraid . . ." she began. Judy moaned and flung herself against me, upsetting the bed-clothes. I saw the handkerchief that she'd hidden under the pillow. It was covered in blood. I wanted to scream. She began coughing violently and I felt her relax her grip.

I held her in my arms. "Judy darling, please. That's all that's happened. Honestly I'll tell you more about it next time."

"Oh," she said. "Oh," with that heartbreaking dying fall, and she sank listlessly back into the pillow. No one was ever going to tell her enough.


I was sitting in the car with Jim. I'd stopped crying. "I've only made her worse, haven't I?" I said.

"I don't think so. In any case we couldn't have stopped her. She was determined to see you."

"Why didn't you tell me she was so sick before I got there? It's not fair."

"I'm sorry. They told me not to upset you before you came. They were afraid it might have a bad effect on her if you knew."

"But I don't know. What is it? How bad is she? You've got to tell me."

"It's a bronchial condition. She had a slight case of T.B. when she was fourteen and they made the mistake of col-lapsing her lung when it wasn't that bad, and it festered. It's been spreading poison through her system ever since. Then, too, she's taken so much aureomycin and penicillin in the past, they're afraid she's beginning to get drug-resistant. They're operating at the end of the week to remove her lung."

"Is she in much pain?"

He paused. There was a little muscle running along the side of his jaw and I noticed it twitching. It was the only indication of the strain he was under. "She's very brave," he said. "The only thing that frightens her . . . the only time she breaks down . . . is when she dreams of drowning. She's afraid of drowning in her own blood."

"Drowning in her own blood?"

"If her good lung should suddenly fill with blood she'd choke to death." His muscle twitched spasmodically.

"Jim, she'll be all right after the operation. I know she will."

"She'll be an invalid for life."

We drove along the Seine.

"You knew about her before you got married?" I asked him after a while.

"I've always known about her. Haven't you?"

"I suppose so, in a way. I guess I just never bothered to find out. I'm glad she has you. I know everything's going to be all right."

"I love her. It won't make any difference."

"And I'm glad you never answered my letter."

"What letter?"

"The one I wrote to you in Florence."

"I never received any letters from you in Florence. Why?"

I looked at him. He wasn't lying. Did I actually mail it? Did I stamp it? Did I address it properly? In the confused state of my emotions at the time a million things might have happened.

"Never mind, it wasn't important. All the same, I'm glad you never got it." He put me down in Montparnasse and I scribbled down my new address. "Will you leave a message at this hotel when I can see her again?"

"I'll get in touch with you after the operation."

"Good luck," I said, and walked quickly away.

# CHAPTER FOUR

I WALKED AROUND PARIS for four days, trying to decide whether to give myself up at the American Embassy or just lie back and wait for Larry to get me. For there wasn't a shadow of a doubt in my mind that he was in Paris by now, tracking me down. That was logic. I'd insured that by my smart-aleck phone-call to him at the railway station. The thing to decide was what scared me most—the American Embassy and what would happen when Larry counter-charged me with selling him the passport, or Larry himself and what would happen when he caught up with me. I walked and walked until my shoes gave out, and then I bought a pair of moccasins and went on walking. I stayed as far away from Montparnasse as possible, avoiding everyone I knew and eating in restaurants I didn't know. I sat in strange cafés. I went into practically every cinema I passed. I slept—or tried to—at my new hotel. The routine became fixed : Toss all night. Wait for the cinemas to open. Go in. Sleep in cinema. Lunch. Walk. Talk to myself. American Express (no word from Uncle Roger—obviously something was very wrong at that end). Another cinema. Back to the hotel. Go mad.

Every night great stinging welts would rise and burn all over my body, causing me to squirm and wriggle in an agony of itching. My nerves, I thought desperately, they can't take it much longer. I'm cracking. Then in my mind I would start off on the dreary trek to the Embassy. Fear and revenge would get me one third of the way. Moral principles another third. And then I'd get stuck. Either I'd imagine myself sent to jail as an accessory to the crime or I'd be shot for treason. Sometimes I would allow myself to believe I might be pardoned, and then the thought of *actually* betraying someone I *actually* knew would start me sliding back again. And all the time my skin was getting rawer and rawer from my scratching and my reasoning fuzzier and fuzzier from lack of sleep.

It's not real, I'd say over and over again. It *can't* be real. Judy lying in the hospital, probably dying. Larry pimping and thieving and beating up girls. Me in jail. How did it happen? We're all nice people.

And then the evening of the fourth day I knew—just like that—I knew quite calmly and without any fuss that I was going to the Embassy the next day. I was tired of waiting, that was all. I was bored. I made up my mind as I walked into the cinema. The film had already started. It was a good film and I gave it my undivided attention. When it was over I walked out and looked up at the marquee. "Le Jour Se Lève" was the title. "Amen to that," I said. "And now for a good night's sleep."

To my surprise the itching started up almost as soon as I got into bed, and more fiercely than ever before. Only this time, instead of tossing and turning and grinding and winding, I sat up quickly and turned on the lights. Bed bugs. The little bastards, slap-happy from their all-night blood-feasts, were at last too bloated to crawl back into the mattress fast enough.

I slept on the floor for the rest of the night. I slept until noon. Then I went into a great big comfortable restaurant and ordered an enormous lunch. My Last Meal. There was a worm crawling lazily around my salad.

God, how I hated Paris! Paris was one big flea-bag. Everything in Paris moved if you looked at it long enough. There were tiny bugs working their way into the baskets of ferns on the wall and a million flies buzzing around my table. In fact, all those shrewd, flashing glances, upon which the Parisian's reputation as a wit is almost entirely based, are motivated by nothing more than his weary, steady need to keep on the bug-hunt.

I lit a Gauloise to calm myself, and suddenly out of the

corner of my eye saw an ant inching towards me on the table. Down went my thumb and brutally I ground it into the table-cloth. Then, slowly lifting my finger, I saw that I had crushed the life out of a piece of cigarette tobacco.

I left the restaurant without finishing my coffee and went straight to the Embassy.

As I started to go through the gates I was stopped by a sentry. "Hey! Hey, Sally Jay, When'd you get back?"

I looked dumbly at the soldier who'd spoken to me. I peered under his helmet. "My God! Hugo McCarthy. Mac! I didn't even recognize you without the moustache. What in the world are you doing in that get-up? What's the gag?"

"No gag at all," he told me proudly. "I'm in training. I'm landing a big P.R.O. job at SHAPE in a couple of months. Assigned to guard-duty till then."

"You're *kidding*."

"I should hope not. Never more serious in my life. Say, Sally Jay, I'm glad I ran into you. Missy and I—hah—Missy and I are getting married soon. You'll have to come to the party. We found a peach of a flat right near here. Just around the corner. The Rue Boissy d'Anglas—d'you know it? It's not very big—just a room and a kitchen, but it's wonderfully furnished—cocktail bar and all that. Very snappy. Some big-shot Italian diplomat had it before, so you can imagine. Anyway, it'll suit us fine for a start."

"You and Missy!"

"Yeah. You know your pal Keevil gave her a pretty rough time, that bastard, but she's O.K. now. How is the old snake, by the way?"

"Oh fine, fine. I mean I guess. I haven't seen—but listen, *how* did this all *happen*? I mean. . ."

"Oh—oh," he said, suddenly stiffening to attention. "Brass hats. Run along, little girl. See you later."

So I ran along. And force of habit found me outside American Express. So I went in.

There was a letter from Uncle Roger. I held it in my hand awhile, breaking into one of the cold sweats that had formed such an integral part of my temperature in recent days, and then I tore it open and read it:

'Dear Sally Jay,

'That one generation cannot ever (*ever*) understand any other in spite of common ancestry and language and what have you is axiomatic. Your problems aren't ours in any sense and you will have to deal with them in different ways. I strongly support conventional maxims about youth standing on its own feet, sowing its own oats, and reaping its own whirlwind (if there is one thing my generation knew nothing about it was morai agriculture), and I believe you should be allowed to work things out with as little meddling from the outside as possible. But every so often an unlikely chain of events or a special curiosity about a rare specimen does draw me, does really draw me, towards trying to understand someone about whom I am by definition ignorant.

'In short, and in short words—how did you do it? How did such a cognizant young woman as yourself manage to get involved in what I cannot help (much as I hate so-called "value-judgments") calling a deeply unsavoury scandal, the details of which will no doubt erupt Etna-high and rock the Press back on what are aptly known as its heels? I dislike hortation, but I advise you to wonder, as calmly as possible, why it happened; for I am sure it need not have. Attribute this curiosity on my part, perhaps, to the Hydrogen bomb, which has revived my moribund affection for the fellow creatures with whom I share what remains of the pure air of this remarkable planet.

'And speaking of this, I must inform you of a great change that has taken place in my own special spheres of interest. For the approach of atomic destruction, coinciding with the approach of my own end, has quixotically returned me to earth after all my years of star-gazing. In brief, I have swapped the telescope for the microscope. And how fascinating is life down under there! I am embarking on a really splendid collection of insects. I have already a very fine ant community, a first-class bee-hive, and a most romantic corner of rare cobwebs which I call my Spidery. You must come and see it some day—by which time I hope to have expanded it considerably.

'But I mustn't wander too far afield—especially as it has just occurred to me (a sure sign of old age you will say) that this letter has been started back to front, and that it is possible, even likely, that you have not been made aware of certain recent events. I must enlighten you at once. I must indeed.

'Receiving your letter last month, I rang up Frank Carson in Washington and after a bit of delving he was able to inform me (rather humorously, I thought at the time) that your passport was perhaps the most famous passport lost last year. Your steady bombardment of letters to the Department was a source of considerable entertainment to the civil servants, not as devoid of wit as you apparently imagined, and Frank assured me the general feeling being that by then you had been sufficiently chastised for your carelessness, a new one was shortly to be issued.

'The next thing that happened was the arrival of Frank Carson on my doorstep in a state of considerable agitation —indeed, one almost matching my own, for I had just trained my microscope on a really interesting nymph of a cimex lectularius (dismissed so contemptuously by most entomologists as flat, ill-smelling, blood-sucking insects infesting beds—indeed my late friend C. F. Metcalf went so far as to call them "loathsome pests" in his otherwise excellent book, but I assure you, they are creatures of far more subtle and fascinating habits), and was watching it at work, when Frank burst in. He announced without preamble that your passport had been discovered, or rather accounted for, and then went on to relate the circumstances.

'It had been used to admit a somewhat reckless (perhaps I should say feckless) young French girl to these shores. She turned up at the Police Station late one night, at the end of her rope, begging to be returned to Paris. It was finally established that she had entered this country illegally. Upon arrival her passport was immediately removed from her by the vice-racketeers into whose hands she had been directed, and who thereby gained what they expected to be a permanent hold on her. Fortunately, however, the diabolical scheme back-fired. For the initial offer both to supply the passport and arrange the trip had been presented to the young lady in terms so disingenuous—to say the least—that, as a professional dancer of some ambition, she soon began to resent what she had been led to believe was merely a temporary side-line (i.e. being a prostitute) turning into a full-time career. Her back to the wall, she eventually took the only sensible way out and gave herself up to the police.

'The originator and executor of this scheme was a man named Larry Keefer, or Keeble (no doubt you can supply me with his exact name), and they were able through her evidence of dates and places and so forth, to identify the passport in question as yours. That was all the information Frank had at the moment, except that wheels were being put in motion for the arrest of the man in question. But as you may imagine, it left me with little stomach for returning to the study of my bedbug.

'Two days ago Frank came around with further news. Keefer had been apprehended in France in the company of a young woman driving northwards towards Paris. Questioned about your passport, he coolly explained that he had been instructed by you to pass it on to some mysterious persons and that, having no idea what the whole thing was about, had merely done so as a favour. Confronted with the French girl's statement, he began breaking down, but it was the girl in the car—his tootsie, or patsy, or whatever the current term is—that broke the case wide open. She had been under the impression until then that she was his sole employee, so to speak, and in a frenzy of jealous rage turned against him and began regaling the police with her own story. In the midst of these further revelations Keefer panicked. He started the car up and tried to make his getaway. The girl grabbed the wheel, wrenched it violently and smashed the car into the nearest ditch. They are both in hospital now, and he is suffering from severe injuries that will prevent him from standing trial for some time.

'When he came to, he made a statement of which I have the transcript. He had this to say about you—it's in the transcript, so I am quoting exactly. "I stole her passport. She had nothing to do with it. She didn't even know what was going on. Tell her I'm sorry. Tell her I meant what I said about her down at the beach that day. Maybe it will explain certain aspects of my behaviour Opening Night. I really liked her. Tell her next time to look where she's going."

'Well. He may have something there in that last sentence. What do you think? Meanwhile I should be most obliged if you would drop me a line explaining how someone who is not actually deaf, dumb, blind and feeble-minded could have gotten so ignorantly involved in all this.

'I note that our agreement has another few months to run. I look forward with interest to seeing you then.

'Your bewildered,

'Uncle Roger.

'P.S. Oh yes. I had almost forgotten. Your new passport will be ready for you at the American Embassy by the end of the week. Also I have enclosed a clipping of the French girl. Perhaps you can throw some light on that subject as well. R.'

I felt along the bottom of the envelope and drew out the news-clipping. I stared for a long while at the picture. It was Crazy Eyes' sister, the Mono-dancer. It really took me back.


I moved back to my old hotel.
I visited Judy. The operation had been successful, or as successful as it could be. She was weak but she was out of

danger. I told her I was going to Hollywood to sign a big contract. I promised to write.

I went to the Embassy and arranged for all the details of my passport—finger-printing, pictures and so forth. At the end of the week I plunked down the 3,000 francs for it and picked it up. Then I walked around Paris for the rest of the day and decided to get the hell out.

# CHAPTER FIVE

A WEEK LATER I arrived by plane in New York. I had told Judy I was going to Hollywood, and for some reason I now felt honour-bound to do so. In any case, I figured there'd be old Bax loping around the Reservation out there, and he could help me get started. So I went along to Grand Central Station and bought a train-ticket to California.

It wasn't until the train drew out with me in it that it occurred to me to wonder why I hadn't simply continued the journey by plane. I mean it was crazy, now that I thought about it, going to all the trouble and inconvenience of getting into town when all I had to do was just hop on the next plane out West. But I couldn't think clearly. The excitement and tension, the almost unbearable feeling of rushing head-long at my Destiny as we sped towards Chicago, prevented me from even attempting to analyse my strange behaviour; prevented me from trying to do anything except chase down the spooky sense of familiarity that the train ride was giving me. I kept telling myself that it was because I'd done this trip a million times before as a child, travelling back and forth from schools, visiting relatives and so forth. But it wasn't. And not until I got off at Chicago to change stations was everything at last made clear.

I wandered slowly through the La Salle Street Station, foudroyée in the middle of the terminal. It was my nightmare station; the station I'd dreamt of so many times with such fear and pain. And the recurrent desk, that desk whose elusive familiarity had worried me so—I knew just where to look for it. It was the Traveller's Aid Counter...

It was nearly ten years ago. I was almost thirteen, and I'd run away from a school back East and was heading out West to become a bullfighter. I'd sold most of my clothes and jewellery and hoarded a Christmas windfall from Uncle Roger to get together enough money to buy a coach-ticket to Albuquerque. I planned on hitching the rest of the way to Mexico. But somehow I'd forgotten entirely about food. By the time I hit Chicago my stomach was flat against my spine and gasping for breath. I saw the sign saying Traveller's Aid Society and decided I was in luck. I'd just go up to it and ask for a loan. The woman at the desk—actually she probably wasn't more than my age now, though she seemed older to my young eyes and wore her hair in a severe style that gave her a Librarian Look—disillusioned me about that immediately. She said they didn't dole out money like that, they were really only a reference organization and if I'd answer a few questions she'd be able to tell me which charity I might be eligible for. She was very kind. I liked her at once. I started answering her questions and the next thing I knew I'd blurted out the whole story. She listened attentively. She listened without making any 'listening' faces, but I felt she was on my side. It was the first time I'd felt that about any grown-up.

"Oh dear," she said sadly at the end, shaking her head. "I'm afraid it's a cut and dried case. You're a runaway. The worst kind. Under Age. Our rules are especially strict for under-age runaways. We simply hold on to them and wire the Traveller's Aid in the town they've run away from, and they provide the fare for the return and get it back later from the parents or guardians—but listen, don't go!" she called out to me suddenly as I started backing away. "I'd like to help you, I really would," she said. She leaned over the counter. "Why shouldn't you be a bullfighter if you want to be? I'm sick to death of standing here day after day sending people back to places they hate, places they've run away from. I just can't bear it any longer. I mean who are we to know what's what anyway? Look, here's a dollar. Go over to the soda fountain and have something to eat. I'll check the time-tables of the trains going West from Union Station and we'll figure out your next move when you get back."

When I returned she said, "Quick. Here's fifteen dollars, it's all I've got on me. Your train leaves in half an hour from Union Station and you've just got time to make it. I'll help you get a taxi. We've got a priority and they let us jump the line."

She left the booth and went over to pick up my bag. Then I saw what it was. She was lame. She had an ugly brace on her leg and she hobbled badly. I looked at it and looked away quickly. But not quickly enough.

"The blind leading the blind," she said casually, acknowledging the fact, as I followed the grotesquely hobbling figure out of the station.

"But I don't even know your name," I said suddenly, leaning forward in the taxi. "How shall I pay you back?"

"You don't have to pay me back," she answered. "Good luck to you. You're running for my life." She slammed the cab-door shut and, turning swiftly, hobbled away.

And that was why they didn't pick me up until Albuquerque.


I stood still in the middle of the station and made the porter put down my bags. So now I'd got to the bottom of it. I'd come the full circle and suddenly I lost my space urge. The dash to California seemed so utterly puerile now. Now called for something entirely different. Now called for something drastically *un*-running away. Now called for—what? Suddenly I had it. Now called for becoming a librarian! In that way I would be laying the ghost once and for all.

Yes. I would go back to New York (surely there were more libraries there than any other place in America) and, yes, I would actually *become* a librarian.

# CHAPTER SIX

Now here's the heavy irony. So I went back to New York to become a librarian. To actually *seek out* this thing I've been fleeing all my life. And (here it comes): a librarian is just not that easy to become. I'd taken my lamb by the hand to the slaughter and nobody even wanted it. Apparently there's a whole filing-system and annotating-system and stamping-system and God knows what you have to learn before you qualify. So I finally found a little out-of-the-way, off-the-beaten-track library downtown and they let me put the books away.

So I felt I was accomplishing something.

I wrote to my mother and father explaining what had become of my passport and all, and told them not to worry if they happened to see my name mentioned in a vice trial. I said I was studying to become a librarian (not strictly true) and that I had moved into an all-girls hotel (terribly true), and that I had turned over a new leaf of responsibility, etc., etc.

They took it stoically enough—my father rather more than my mother, no doubt because of his ecclesiastical training. And life went on. The one bright spot was my cousin John's letter assuring me that, come what may, blood, by God, was thicker than water and he was going to do everything in his goddam power to see that my name was kept out of *his* newspaper at all costs.

The months went by and I really tried. I never got into any trouble. I never went out with any men. I never did anything wrong.

Except one day I was up on a ladder putting away some rather heavy books on the top shelf (I don't know why they're so smug about their System : the heaviest books always turned out to belong on the top shelves), when I happened to drop a few and they happened to conk someone on the head. A man in a baize-green-coloured suit and a pale green shirt. He wore grey suède shoes.

It was Max Ramage, not that you could miss him.

He looked up to see what hit him.

"Well I'm damned. Miss Gorce—right in my own backyard. Come down at once. I've been looking all over for you!" he shouted up at me.

"All over *here*?" I was as stunned as if the books had hit me.

"All over the world. I just happened in here by chance. I'm going to Japan in a fortnight, so I thought I'd swot up a bit on it before I left. It's my local branch. What in heaven's name are you doing up there?"

But I was in much too much of a hurry to go into all that. There was something I had to straighten him out about immediately. Before another second flew by. I'd never been in such a hurry. I began scrambling down the ladder talking furiously the whole time.

"Listen, I've *got* to explain to you why I was in such a stew that night we met. I mean I *know* what you thought— only I didn't realize you thought it until you left and by then it was too late—and anyway it wouldn't have mattered because I still couldn't have told you what the trouble *really* was. I mean—what I mean is—*was*—that I *wasn't* pregnant. . . Honestly I . . ." And then my voice trailed off into a thin line of drivel.

He smiled up at me and stretched his long arms wide apart. "Come straight into my arms!" he said. Just like that. So I stepped right down into them. He hugged me tightly and I swayed a little and stumbled over one of the books and that made me come to. I pulled away, embarrassed, expecting to find the whole library in an uproar, but somehow nobody was taking any notice.

"There's something I've got to tell you too," he said. "Show you, rather." From the inside pocket of the green lining of his green jacket he drew out a handful of photographs and showed me one.

"Me," I said wonderingly. "It's me."

"What'd I tell you?" he said triumphantly. "You see, I have been looking all over for you. Why the devil didn't you keep in touch with Stefan? Never mind. Come on, we're wasting time." He took me by the arm and, stepping over the books, we left.

We went into a cocktail bar just off Fifth Avenue on Eighth Street. One of those suave, sexy bars, dead dark, with popcorn and air-conditioning and those divine cheese things.

"What'll you have?" he asked. "Champagne? Have anything. Money's no object. Look. Wads of it. Ceylon. Can't spend it fast enough. We photographers are the New Rich."

We had dry martinis; great wing-shaped glasses of perfumed fire, tangy as the early morning air.

"Now," he said. "I have to ask you three questions. How old are you? Are you in love? And what in God's name are you doing here?"

So I told him all about it. It was really a very long story. At the end he said "Good. Now ask me something. Anything."

"Where did you get that suit?" I asked him.

"This one? Nice, isn't it. Had a bitter struggle with my tailor over it. He refused to make it at first. Said the material was too soft. Said it would pick up things."

"It has," I said excitedly. "Look——"

"That's it!" he said suddenly. "That's the expression I remembered. Questing. You have the most questing profile in the whole world, Miss Gorce."

"No, but *look*," I insisted. "It *has* picked up something. It's picked up some popcorn." There was a popcorn ball balancing on his sleeve. It reminded me of the snails in St. Jean. "What's it made of?"

"Pool-table cloth," he told me, preening himself a little. "It's the only material that comes in this special colour. D'you like it?"

"I love it," I said, stringing a bracelet of popcorn around his sleeve. "I wonder what makes you dress like this."

"Brio. Panache. I believe in them." He waved his cigarette airily and I noticed he held it between the third and fourth fingers instead of the usual second and third. It looked wonderful.

Max's personality was beginning to emerge. Easy and flamboyant. Peacock. What a frenzy I must have been in not to have felt its impact before. Or had Stefan's even wilder flamboyance overshadowed it?

In any case, I had never been on such an intimate footing with a Famous Person before, and what surprised me most was how quickly, beneath the stark realities of the baize-green suit and the aura of fame, the *really* legendary figure was emerging; under that pale green shirt beat a truly original heart.

He talked about photography with passion. "I must be the only photographer in the world who ever began taking pictures *without* the aid of a camera." He said that even as a child picking up his pencil for the first time, the only sets of ground-configural patterns that presented themselves to him visually were geared to photography; he'd started right in *drawing* photographs. He said the only trouble was that his family absolutely forbade him a camera. Anything connected with films and the film world—and they lumped photography under that general heading—was mysteriously but strictly taboo. However, he'd somehow managed to get himself a camera and a dark-room, and in no time at all the walls of the Café Venezia, the centre of schoolboy Bohemia in Leeds, were covered with his weekly exhibitions. When he began to win prizes in the local newspapers, it all came out, of course, but by then it was too late for his family to do anything about it.

He had also, from a very early age, been in heated correspondence with the great Spanish photographer Bernardo Ruiz, and hearing one day that Ruiz was in London, he went to a store and bought himself a blood-coloured suit which, he felt, would cut the suitable sophisticated swath in London (and which fortunately he was able to get cheap, as it had been ordered and abandoned by a clarinettist whose outfit had gone broke), hopped on the next train and, photographs spilling in every direction, baited the Great Man in the lobby of his hotel. "I imagine," said Max, "it was the unexpectedness of my appearance as well as its bizarreness (I was very thin at the time) that disarmed Ruiz sufficiently to take me on. In any case, I travelled with him for two and a half years and he taught me everything he knew. And so," he finished, "I shook the dust of Yorkshire off my shoes for ever."

I had to laugh. "I can just see you then," I said.

He looked at me for a moment. "But can you see Leeds?"

I shook my head.

"It's not so funny," he said. "It was a narrow escape. I'll show you pictures of it sometime. The humdrum glum carried to its sub-human level. Sunday night in the Methodist church. You won't feel like laughing. You'll cry your eyes out."

He tried to flip a cigarette nonchalantly into his mouth like what's-his-name in the movies, but he missed. I didn't feel like laughing. A shadow had fallen across us, like suddenly coming upon a hunchback in a hopefully coloured tie or an unsuccessful actor with dyed bright hair in the middle of a sunny day.

"I feel like crying now," I said.

"Do you? *Do* you? Oh my darling!" He took my hand and kissed it. We looked at each other for a long, long time. "I know what," he said. "I'll give you two dollars if you can cry now. Two dollars if you can cry in one minute flat."

"Fifteen seconds," he said, looking at his watch fifteen seconds later. "Not bad."

"Now you," I said.

"Look at me." He had tears in his eyes already.

"What were you thinking?"

"I was thinking," I said, "that I'm happy. Now I'm happy. That's all." It didn't even occur to me to lie. "What were you thinking?"

"I was thinking: suppose I'd been right about her and she had been pregnant. Suppose she had died under the knife—or had got so desperate she killed herself." He was perfectly serious. "Sally Jay," he said earnestly, "promise me, *promise* me you'll never try to kill yourself."

"Oh I promise, I promise," I assured him, stretching lazily, feeling utterly euphoric. "The world is wide, wide, wide, and I am young, young, young, and we're all going to live forever!"

We were very hungry but we didn't want to leave, so we ate there. We had chicken sandwiches; boy, the chicken of the century. Dry, wry, and tender, the dryness sort of rubbing against your tongue on soft, bouncy white bread with slivers of juicy wet pickles. Then we had some very salty potato chips and some olives stuffed with pimentoes and some Indian nuts and some tiny pearl onions and some more popcorn. Then we washed the whole thing down with iced martinis and finished up with large cups of strong black coffee and cigarettes. One of my really great meals.

I don't know what time it was when we went into the bar, but it was dark when we came out. We went to a movie and he kissed me for the first time. We kissed right through it. Coming to life in a movie house on West Fourth Street is an apotheosis I'd have to leave to one of those mad seventeenth-century mystics like Herbert or Vaughan to do justice to. It's the *end*.

"Now let's kiss somewhere else," said Max.

I couldn't stop singing to myself in the taxi—that heavenly tune about taking a chance on love. It's terribly embarrassing and it's always happening to me: the words of a song will suddenly exactly echo my inner feelings and out they come. Like that awful time I kept filling in pauses of a hard-luck story someone was giving me with the Judy Garland song about the road getting rougher and lonelier and tougher. Couldn't stop myself. Could have died the way it just kept coming out.

I could have died now, but for another reason. It was all going much too fast. It was all wrong. I was falling back into all my awful old ways and all the awful old things were going to happen to me all awful over again. Stop the taxi! Take me home . . . I have to catch a train . . . I thought vaguely of saying. You'll worry about it later, I promised myself. You'll be sorry. Oh you will, you will.

Not that anyone could have guessed from the limp, humming form that remained in Max's arms that there was any kind of a battle raging around inside.

But it turned out that all he meant was a night club.

It was one of those casual ones. The kind where the musicians are playing as much to amuse themselves as anyone there and you're not expected to stop talking or drinking or anything else you've been doing while they're on. The music seeps through. They give you a good strong shot of bourbon and some soda and a glass swizzle-stick to poke in the holes of the ice cubes, and leave you alone. I kept writing 'Max' on the table with mine.

We danced and kissed through the jazz. It was cool and hot and blue. Midnight blue. Blue smoke. Blues.

After that we sat on quietly for a while. Max wore a look of bony concentration. He was thinking.

"Look here," he said finally. "Let's go back to my place, I want to talk to you. I'll tell you quite frankly right now that I very much want to sleep with you tonight, but if you turn me down it's not important. I'll ask you every day for the next five years and you can turn me down every day for the next five years—no, wait a minute—every day for the next *year*," he smilingly corrected himself. "You wouldn't be so cruel as to hold out longer than that, would you? You see I really do want you, Sally Jay. Come on, let's get the bill. As a matter of fact I live right down the street."

I'll bet you do, Buster, I thought, quickly collecting my wits. I felt cool as a cucumber. I crossed out the 'M' I'd started with my swizzle-stick. "But you're going to Japan in a couple of weeks, aren't you?" I pointed out quietly.

"My God!" He ran his hand through his hair. "Oh my God, of course I am. See what you do to me? I'd forgotten completely about it."

I'll bet you have, Buster, I thought. It was worse than disappointing; it was downright insulting. *As a matter of fact I live right down the street.* . . . Oh help. Take me out, coach.

"Tell me something," I asked him. "How long have you been in town this time?"

"A few days."

Oh really, it was too easy. Roving photographer, with a sailor's mentality and about a million light-years of sexual experience under his belt, blows into town on the lookout for a quick lay. Picks up girl whose picture (along with how many others?) coincidentally happens to be in his pocket, throws in a little soft soap and expects—and gets—her eating out of his hand in a few hours.

"What's the matter?" he asked. "Have I said something wrong? Tell me."

"It's nothing. I've just got to go to the john."

". . . If he'd just put it to me straight," I was muttering to myself all over the john, "if only he hadn't felt obliged to make such a song and dance about it, it wouldn't have been so bad. I mean, sure I was all ready to go right to his place with him after the movies, but that would have been a blow to my pride, not my intelligence. My intelligence. Ha!" Boy, I was learning fast. What did he care about all that? I was just a girl like any other girl, and that you-can-turn-me-down-every-day-for-the-next-five-years routine was a solid gold winner in any repertoire.

Two girls came into the washroom and started talking.

"You gonna let him take you home? He's an awful wolf, you know."

"Sure," shrugged the other. "I should say no to life?"

Yeh, yeh, I thought. Great, oh, great. Zop, zop, and all dot. De Village don't say no to life; jazz don't say no to life; but dis baby do. Right now. Cause it hurts too much. And I can't take it no more.

But when I came out and started back towards our table my heart lurched up around my throat and damn near choked me to death. I was so frightened I almost blacked out. Max had disappeared. Just disappeared. Vanished. I mean he just wasn't there. When I looked again I saw that there was somebody there—a man with sort of short dark hair and a bony face—and that he was sitting in approximately the same place that Max had been—but it wasn't Max. Logic insisted that of course it was: there was the fat man, who I remembered sitting next to me against the wall, now sitting next to the space I'd made between him and Max. But the ground-configural patterns of Max's face had shifted so violently that I didn't even recognize him. I mean I *did* recognize him but I couldn't accept the face as belonging to Max. It wasn't a face. really. It was kind of an unprotected skull full of dark shadows. The wounded skull of a young boy staring at me through troubled eyes. It was frightening.

Well, I thought, wrong again Gorce. You've gone and guessed wrong again. Now what?

"I'm sorry. I didn't recognize you for a moment," I said as I came up to the table. It was the wrong thing to say.

"How did you finally identify me, by my clothing?" he asked stonily.

"Oh no. No. It's just that I suppose I haven't got used to your face."

That was the wrong thing to say too.

"Well, at least you didn't wander off into the street like the last time in Paris. I suppose that's something. Or don't you remember? Come on. I'm taking you home."

We had reached a really gorgeous impasse.

We arrived outside my hotel in silence. Neither of us made a move to get out of the taxi.

"Aren't you going to invite me in for a nightcap?" he asked finally. "I won't bite."

"I can't!" I wailed. "It's a girls' hotel. No men allowed in the rooms."

"Oh yes, of course. Naturally. I'd forgotten that one."

"Couldn't we . . . have a nightcap at *your* place?" I asked desperately.

"If you like."

Grimly he gave the address to the taxi driver, but when the cab started up again he slumped back into the seat, flung one leg over the other, and, rubbing his ankle with his hand let out a sigh of relief. Out of the corner of his eye he caught me looking at him and he smiled sheepishly. We began to laugh.

"You own the whole house?" I asked, impressed, when we stopped outside the brownstone front on the little street of the jazz club.

"Yes, it's all mine. I bought it with my first billion," he said, letting us in. "I thought it would be a good idea. Roots and storage. Mainly storage, as it's turned out. I only live in a couple of rooms. Step over those boxes and come in."

We went into what I suppose you could call the living-room. It was very comfortable and cozy, with deep sofas and records piled everywhere, but it was a bit odd. There was a large gnarled petrified tree stump growing in the middle of the room with a tree seat running around it, and the bust of a Roman Emperor standing in a corner with a brown felt hat on. Halfway up one wall hung a delicately carved gilt chair.

He put on some records and sat down next to me. "We've been having some kind of misunderstanding," he said. "Would you mind telling me what it was all about?"

I told him I'd got sore because I thought he was handing me a line with all that five-year stuff. "I mean you didn't have to say that to get me to come here," I said. "I would have anyway."

"You mean you didn't believe me?"

"Oh, it doesn't matter——"

"Miss Gorce," he said rising. "You have the faith of a flea."

"Oh, please don't go away," I said miserably. "I want to believe you. I *do* believe you. Really. Please."

"Give me your lipstick." I handed it to him and he went over to the fireplace and drew a large heart in the mirror above it, with the initials M.R. and S.J.G. inside. Underneath he wrote in large letters 'I love Sally Jay.' "There, you have it in writing. Now do you believe me?"

"Oh yes!"

"Then come over here and kiss me." He was sitting down again.

"Hmmm—that's very interesting, I must say," he said a little while later.

"What is?"

"What you just did."

"What?"

"You just took off your ear-rings."

"I *did*?" I stared at them on the coffee-table, surprised. "Good Lord, I did it quite unconsciously."

He moved a little closer. "You know what that means, don't you," he murmured into my ear.

I said yes. I said I did.

"Where are you going to love me?" I asked him faintly.

"On a bed for a start," he said, helping me up.

"Oh good."

I sat up in the bed, naked under the sheets, and watched him get undressed. It was as if I'd never seen a man getting undressed before and come to think of it, I guess I hadn't. The others must have just kind of shed their clothes or peeled them off in a lump. I don't know. Anyway I'd never noticed. But Max undressed expertly. Methodically. And I'd never in my life seen anything as sensuous as the unhurried grace with which his knowing hands flew over his body, stripping it of its clothes. Fascinated, hardly daring to breathe, I watched him undo his tie in two clean sweeping movements— downwards to loosen it, sideways to slide it off—and then go on to his shirt, his slim fingers slipping each tiny button through its hole with one deft twist. He sat on the edge of the bed. He pulled off his shoes. He put his socks inside them, placing them neatly together at the foot of the bed. He rose and went over to a chest of drawers, his back to me, and carefully began emptying the contents of his trouser-pockets. I felt suddenly very warm. I sank back into the pillow over-whelmed by my own scent, the last few drops of eau de cologne I'd splashed on that morning. I heard the jazz from the club playing faintly down the street, and the thought that of all the people there that night I would be the only one to find out what Max actually kept in his trouser-pockets was unbearably thrilling. I sat up watching tensely: Keys. Money (silver in one pile, paper in another). A handkerchief. A baby screwdriver with a cork stuck through it. Two dead flash-bulbs. A pair of new shoelaces. A packet of new razor blades. Finally, catching sight of me through the dresser mirror, he slowly drew out—one from each pocket—my ear-rings, and smiling at me through the glass, arranged them, like fallen angels, one on each side, to encompass a space the exact width of my face. Then he took off his trousers.

I didn't dream it or invent it or imagine it. I couldn't have. There were things—two things in particular —that I just couldn't have made up. The jazz club blowing its lullaby through the night across the empty street, and the way he trembled when he came over to take me.

When I woke up this morning I found myself staring at rows and rows of books. My first thought was that I'd gone stark raving mad with my library obsession at the station in Chicago, and that I was now hallucinating in a looney bin. Max was sitting beside me in a dressing-gown.

"It's a library," I whispered.

"Yes, it's the library. Since I was always in here just before I went to sleep I decided last year to move my bed and things in as well. How are you?"

I stretched. "Wonderful!"

"Hungry?"

"Oh golly, yes." I suddenly remembered we hadn't eaten a thing since the chicken sandwiches yesterday.

"I'll see what I've got in the kitchen."

"Catch," he said, returning with two oranges. "I'm afraid that's all there is." We ate the oranges lying next to each other on the bed. I looked at his dressing-gown. "Plain blue," I said. "No leopard skin?"

He grinned. "It's a little too early in the morning, isn't it? Anyway, that's for Them. D'you know what I mean?"

I said I did.

We finished the oranges and he kissed me.

"I'm tired of living in sin with you," he said after a while. "Let's get married. Then I can take you to Japan with me."

I lay very quietly, not daring to say anything. I was afraid it was just cheap chatter. I was afraid he was kidding me. I mean why me? Why *me*?

"What's the matter? What is it?"

"This can't be happening to me," I said.

"Don't you like me?"

"I love you. If you hadn't existed I would have had to invent you."

"Don't you believe it. I invented myself. What's wrong? Please tell me, darling."

"It's too good. There must be a catch."

He sat up. "As a matter of fact, there is," he said seriously. He started to go on, but I stopped him. "Hand me my slip, will you?" I said. "I think I'll take this on my feet, if you don't mind." I put it on and began pacing around the room. "O.K. Spill it, old sport. It's the not knowing that kills me," I said gloomily.

He had that same troubled look I'd seen last night. "I'm illegitimate," he said.

I stopped dead in my tracks. "Oh, no! But how exciting! How perfect! How absolutely glamorous!"

"Well, thank you, Sally Jay." He didn't bother to hide his relief. "Yes, I suppose it is. I'm glad you think so, anyway. My family—that is, the aunts and uncles who brought me up —took a rather different view. They're on my mother's side. I took my mother's name."

"What was she like?"

"I don't know. She died soon after I was born. A rather wild young thing apparently, dashing off to the Continent for la vie de bohème as they called it in those days. Got mixed up with all those crazy godforsaken artists and actors and that lot. She was a lost soul to her family. A wicked wicked girl."

"And your father?" A look of uncertainty flickered across

his face. "Oh, I'm sorry," I said. "How stupid of me. Of course, you never knew who he was, did you?"

"But I do. The Aunts told me when they thought I was old enough. It was in the contract."

"Who was it?"

"Brace yourself," said Max.

I was standing at the back of a chair. I gripped it hard with my hands and then I leaned down over it. I don't know why. To keep the circulation flowing or something. "Who was it?" I repeated.

"Stefan."

"Yeow!" I nearly toppled over. I sat down weakly. "But why didn't you say so? Why didn't he? I just don't get it."

Max laughed. "Stefan admit to a grown-up son? In the presence of a pretty girl? You have a lot to learn about us Hungarians, baby," he said in Stefan's voice.

So now all I have to do is decide what sort of clothes to buy for Japan. They'll be all wrong anyway, I suppose. Perhaps I'll dye my hair black to get into the swing of things. Then we have to get married—the two years are almost up, so Uncle Roger shouldn't mind my contacting him to be best man. And then I have to go to Rockefeller Centre to get a new passport. An entirely new passport.

But isn't it the end, the very end?

I mean Japan for a honeymoon. It's so cool. It's so chic. It's so suave and so sleek and exotic. It's the end, it's the *end*. . .! It's the last word.

It's zymotic.